Acclaim from excited readers:

"Biker Bob soars into a journey we've all taken, becomes a soul we've all longed for. . .in a way we won't forget. You won't regret his incredible visit, and you won't easily let him go."
-Melody Wood Graphic Designer- (Yorba Linda, California)

"If you let life kick you around, if you can't find peace of mind, if you want to feel good about yourself, *Channeling Biker Bob* is a must read."
-Roy Varney -Police Lieutenant- (South San Francisco, California)

"Biker Bob is a fascinating man--a true manly man, bold & tough, yet at heart quite gentle."
-Margaret Chancellor, -Addictions Counselor- (Boulder, Colorado)

"*Channeling Biker Bob* takes you into the mind and soul of a real man."
-Greg Pickett, -International Lover- (Dallas, Texas)

"Riveting, captivating. A glimpse into what being a man is all about."
-Sanchez Prusso, -Local Drifter-. (San Jose, California)

"Biker Bob is my kind of man!"
-Ken Crockett -Operations Manager- (Shreveport, Louisiana)

"Biker Bob is the kind of man I've searched for all my life, One who's not afraid to show a gentle side. It's a 'Must Read'."
-Evelyn Jette retired -Ballroom Dance Instructor- (Connecticut)

"Nik Colyer takes us on a playful journey of love and lust, throwing us into a revelation of manhood and loyalty."
-Nate Key, -Shark Killer- (Orlando, Florida)

"Bursting with adventure and expectation, *Channeling Biker Bob* is simply good."
-Diedre Johnson, -Freelance Reporter- (Los Angeles, California)

"Finally, a book that gives ⁣‌⁣ ⁣‌⁣ makes a real man!"
-Becky Collier -⁣ ‌⁣ nia)

There is a moment in every man's life
when he must stand and be counted.
If at that moment he does not, he will be crushed
under the tyranny of his own impotence.

Atnov 4th century

Channeling Biker Bob

Heart of a Warrior

The first in a four part series by: Nik C. Colyer

Heart of a Warrior

Lover's Embrace

Magician's Spell

Wisdom of the King

Henrioulle Publishing Group
Nevada City, California

Henrioulle Publishing Group

Copyright © 2001 by **Nik C. Colyer**   -First Edition-

Publisher's Cataloging-in-publication
(Provided by Quality Books, Inc.)

Colyer, Nik C.
    Channeling Biker Bob : heart of a warrior, the first
in a four part series / by Nik C. Colyer. -- 1st ed.
    p. cm.
    LCCN 2001-087381
    ISBN 0-9708163-0-8

    1. Man-woman relationships--Fiction. 2. Men--Conduct
of life--fiction. I. Title.

PS3553.047855C43 2001   813'.6
                QB101-700241

Acknowledgments:
Thanks to my first editor **Nancy Morris**, who helped bring this story into focus and to my last editor **Bobbie Christmas** who refined my work into a polished novel.
Thanks also to Auburn Harley Davidson for the bike photo.

Cover by: Brook Design Group: www.brookdesign.com

Thanks to **Robert Bly**, **Michael Meade**, and many other less visible members of the men's movement who helped with my transition into manhood.
Printed in the United States of America.
10 9 8 7 6 5 4 3 2 1

To my wife Barbara.
Without her endless support
this novel could not have been possible.

To Dov Stein who believed in me.

To those generous souls who
helped bring this project to life.

To Gordon Clay, a man of vision.

Channeling Biker Bob

is available through your local bookstore or you can
purchase this book directly from
(free shipping in the U.S.A.)

Henrioulle Publishing Group

Nevada City, California 95959 (530)-265-3566
hpg@ncws.com

Quanity Pricing Available

Channeling Biker Bob
Heart of a Warrior

CONTENTS

Pg. 1   1 THE PROSPECT

Pg. 28   2 NEW BEGINNINGS

Pg. 78   3 TRIAL BY FIRE

Pg. 97   4 NICK BROWN

Pg. 108   5 HAWG HEAVEN

Pg. 126   6 A BRIGHT AND SHINNING STAR

Pg. 138   7 THE CIRCUS

Pg. 145   8 HELLO, BIKER BOB

Pg. 168   9 LETTERS

Pg. 174   10 WHAT ABOUT ME?

Pg. 183   11 EVERY DOG HAS HER DAY

Pg. 194   12 WHAT'S IN A YEAR?

Pg. 196   THE END

THE PROSPECT

"Come on damn it, we ain't got all night," yells a dark figure sitting on a throbbing apparition in the middle of my new lawn.

I pull on yesterday's Levis, a T-shirt and my gardening sneakers, step out my front door and cross the fragile grass.

Without saying a word, or glancing at the driver, I walk past the glaring headlight, swing my lanky left leg over the back wheel, and sit uncomfortably on a minuscule square of padded leather. The pulse of the idling engine tells me I'm sitting on a Harley-Davidson, my dream machine, my phantom.

After thirty-eight years of waiting, finally someone offers to take me for my first ride on a Harley. I don't care that he's a stranger and that I have no idea where we're going. This single ride has been a dream since I was a boy.

The second my foot leaves the ground, my buffalo-shouldered mystery driver revs his throbbing engine. His bike takes a long wheel-spinning arc across a lawn that I had so painstakingly planted only last month. While getting to the driveway, he maliciously guns his engine and digs his tire in my wife's flowerbed.

For a reason I don't understand, riding off into a hot predawn August morning with this total stranger feels right.

His bike lunges onto the roadway and leans into a deep left turn. Once the bike straightens out, I watch the burly stranger pull back on the left-hand lever. He guns his engine and snaps the clutch like a tightly strung bow. As the front wheel leaps off the ground and climbs high into the air, he lets loose a long, wolf-like howl into the sultry summer night. I'm thrown hard onto the support bar and feel a sharp stab halfway up my spine.

Not until we have traveled a few hundred feet down the deserted highway, with his engine thundering under us, does the slender front wheel gracefully settle back onto the pavement. This is my first taste of popping a wheelie while flying down the road on a Harley.

Wind whips at my stubble black hair, rips at my Sierra Club T-shirt and shrieks in my ears. I dare a look over his shoulders at the speedometer. Ninety-five miles an hour, and he's still pouring on the gas.

I lean back on the support bar and try to catch my breath. Just my luck, I get a ride on a Harley, and the driver is a lunatic.

He yells over the screaming wind, "Relax, Bob sent me."

Who is Bob?

He shouts, "grab me a brewski in the right saddlebag."

He's going almost a hundred miles an hour on a curvy country road, and he wants a beer? No way he'll get any alcohol from me.

He turns his head and yells, "Where the fuck is my beer?"

Although, I don't want to, I'm compelled to reach into the black leather bag and fish for the object of his desire. The bag is lined in plastic, with a six-pack of cans stowed in chipped ice. When I wrap my hand around a can, the frost feels refreshing. I pull the container out and yank the tab. A spray of foam blows in my face. Oh great, we get pulled over, and I'll smell like a brewery.

I see his long wiry hair blowing in the wind, and I realize that neither of us is wearing protective headgear. Excessive speed, consuming alcohol while operating a motor vehicle, no helmets, we're definitely getting pulled over; it's just a matter of time. Instead of taking a cool ride on a hot summer night, a quick jaunt on a Harley, a never-thought-possible-dream-of-a-lifetime, I'm sure to spend the rest of this night in jail. What will Renee say?

I hand his beer forward and catch a glimpse of the label. In thick black lettering, inside a brown shield, the words Harley-Davidson are printed across the can. Below the shield, I read: Heavy Beer.

Heavy Beer! The guy is a lost cause. He's rolling death on two wheels, waiting for a crash. What am I doing here?

He kicks his head back and finishes the entire can of beer in one long pull. With his head still lifted, I'm wondering how he sees the road at all. He expels into the night air a long guttural blast of a belch. When he throws the can over his shoulder, I hear tinny clangs on the pavement far behind.

Channeling Biker Bob

As a fully paid member of the Sierra Club, I grimace at the barbarian's casual act of profaning the environment. I vow to come back, find his can, then deposit it in a recycling bin.

He turns his head and yells, "You're here for Biker Bob to teach you about being a man. Forget about the beer can, Chance. Pay attention, because you got shit to learn."

I'm positive I never voiced even one syllable of my apprehension. How does he know what I'm thinking? How does he know my name?

He turns his attention back to the road, twists the hand throttle, and his bike, which I thought had reached top speed, leaps ahead as if we had been idling. We lean into a long sloping turn, flying past a familiar fifty-five miles per hour sign, a blur now, as his motorcycle leans deep toward the pavement.

"Oh-h-h, dar-r-r-n-nn," I scream, as we cut into the turn, drifting over the double yellow line into the oncoming lane. Sparks flash as his cycle leans over so far that the frame scrapes pavement. I'm a goner. I lean forward, both arms tightly gripped around his monstrous waist. As I tighten my grip, he erupts with a roaring burst of laughter, and another long wolfish howl. When we reach the far end of the turn, he shoots out onto the open and mercifully straight part of the highway, leading down the hill toward the State Capital, Sacramento. We're still alive, and it's a miracle.

In a sharp flick of his wrist, the engine decompresses. The bike slows hard and slams me against his thick backside. His downshift leaves a short skid. Still going fifty, I look back and see a puff of smoke roll off the rear tire as he shifts again. I spot an open gate a hundred feet ahead of us, when he makes a final downshift. In a measured lump-lump of an idling engine, he pulls off the highway onto a dirt trail where hundreds of motorcycle tracks wander off into a gray dawn.

"Where are we going?" I ask in a regular voice, now that his engine has stopped screaming. I'm delighted that my life has been spared, at least for now.

"It's party time," says the stranger. "Crack me another brewski, and get yourself one, too."

"No thanks," I say, "I don't drink. You wouldn't happen to have a nonalcoholic beer would you?"

He roars with that same wolf-like laughter and shakes his head, "You got a lot to learn, Stewey."

No one has called me Stewey since I was a kid. My nickname instantly brings up old forgotten memories. How does he know my childhood name?

The bike begins a long, slow journey along a dusty, rutted lane. My stomach flutters, but I have been feeling it tremble for the last forty-five minutes. His "It's party time," declaration leaves me suspicious that he will be partying at my expense.

I want to leap off his bike and sprint away into the gray fields. I want to be back home in safety. At the snail's pace he drives, I can jump, but I'm glued to my uncomfortable seat.

We roll over a rise and overlook a small semi-dark valley. The centerpiece of the basin sports a large open-pit fire. The blaze is surrounded by fifteen gleaming motorcycles, all Harleys. Twenty people dance and career around the huge blaze.

As my driver winds his way into the little valley, my anxiety rises. I'm not only certain that I will not fit into the party, but fear that I may the sacrificial lamb at a satanic biker feast.

He finishes his second beer and tosses the can along the trail. "Gimme another," he demands. "And don't you worry about where my fucking empties are going."

I'm on automatic pilot now and do as I'm told. I stretch my hand into his saddlebag as hooting and yelling reaches us from the meadow. I pop the top and hand the can over his shoulder.

After taking a long swallow, he broadcasts another jarring belch. A number of similar responses echo up.

What kind of crazy place is this? What am I doing here? Who are these rude, uncouth people?

As the engine lumps along in relative quiet, he turns his monstrous head and says, "You're here with us uncouth bastards to learn about being a man, Stewart Chance."

"How do you know what I'm thinking?" I ask.

He snickers. "Your real lesson begins when you meet Bob. Pay attention and stop thinking about them empty beer cans."

My driver rolls his bike into perfect position at the end of the line, turns off his engine, unfurls the kickstand, and dismounts his machine in one smooth movement. Not ready for such quick action, I'm left sitting on the back of a bike that unexpectedly drops toward the ground and comes to a jarring halt at a twenty-degree angle, jerking hard against the kickstand. I land face down in dry weeds with my long, gangly legs tangled in various protruding parts of the bike. He is already ten paces away, before I lift my head. The entire party gawks.

My hulking driver turns, looks at me, and shakes his head. With a sarcastic grin on his face, he says, "Don't think I ever saw anyone get off a bike like that before." The crowd bursts into laughter. When the noise calms, he says, "Would you stop fucking around and come over here. I want you to meet my buds."

I'm beyond embarrassment, beyond feeling like crawling into a hole, but with nothing else to do, I get up and try to stroll casually over to my driver. I notice for the first time that he stands a few inches

4

above me. He's more than six feet tall. The filthy black leather vest he wears can't fully cover his larger tattoos. The visible ones climb both his forearms. His thick, black hair thrusts straight out, a foot from his head. Only his ends begin to give way to gravity. His equally unruly beard, which hangs untrimmed to his chest, is made of the same coarse material.

"Well, come on over here," he demands.

I have stopped ten feet from the flame, a cushion from possible attack. As if his suggestion is a command and a chain pulls me, I leap three strides, stopping in front of him.

My ears buzz, my heart bursts and my throat constricts.

"This here's Stewart Chance, our new prospect."

How does he know my name?

"Prospect to what," I ask aloud. Looking at the crowd of half-drunk maniacs, I ask myself again, what am I doing here? Through the blaze, as smoke swings around to engulf me, I hear a number of chuffs.

My driver says, "you're first job will be to get more wood." He points to a pile ten yards beyond the bikes.

I have found my opportunity to get out of the spotlight, away from their glares. On my third step toward the pile, I slip in a hole and stumble, barely catching my balance.

"Kind of a gangly, sort of guy, ain't he?" I hear.

"Of all people," says another, "why's Bob chosen him?"

"You going to let him clean your scooter?" another asks.

"Hell no," my burly voiced driver says. "He'd probably scratch my paint, but I'm sure he can do a bunch of other shit."

A roar of laughter echoes off the hillside. When things get quiet, he says, "Bob just fucking told me to bring him here."

Around the blaze, they get quiet.

Even in my mind, I can't use the swear word he just spoke. As a young man, I decided not to cuss and not to be around those who do. That resolution has helped make me the spiritual, God-fearing man that I am today. I'm proud of my decision.

Why has this Bob person chosen me?

"Guess he'll be useful till Bob shows up," says another.

A female voice squeaks, "He's got sexy blue eyes."

At the woodpile, I'm relieved to have slipped away from that gang of thugs and misfits. Because I'm not interested in being a prospect, whatever that means, I'll find my own way home.

I walk away from the reveling bikers and, as if squeezed through a funnel, I shift from the wild scene in a meadow to lying beside my wife Renee in our quiet country home. Instead of being a slave to the biker gang, I'm in my bed, after all. I quietly soak in calmness and my wife's breathing. I heave a sigh of relief because I was only dreaming, after all.

Joyful tears well up in my eyes, thankful tears I express often, but only alone in the dark, or when Renee sleeps. I'm a man after all, and gushy expressions should be left to women.

As frightened as I was at the biker party, I'm also intrigued. The ride, now that I have made it out alive, was astounding. Although they designated me a prospect, a form of servant, I felt free and alive, merely from being present.

I look past Renee through our bedroom window at dawn.

Large red numerals in the clock on Renee's nightstand read 5:37, eight minutes before the alarm thrusts us into another day. Smaller numbers read: 09-17-00

I want to tell Renee about the weirdest dream I have ever had. I roll my body over spooning into her backside and put my lips to her ear. "Renee," I whisper.

I make physical contact with a body I have felt next to me every morning for eighteen years, a woman I have cherished every minute of our time. My secret tears well again. My maleness always stands at attention in mornings, but I hide that part of myself by turning slightly.

"Renee," I say, a little more insistent, shaking her slightly.

Her body stiffens. "What?"

"I just had a dream that was--"

"Let me sleep!"

I look over at her clock to double-check the time. "The alarm will go off in five minutes. I just want--"

"Let me sleep, you son of a bitch!" She rolls away from me and pulls the pillow over her head.

I have to tell you about my wife. Sometimes, and especially when she's a little grumpy, like now, she has been known to use profane language. I don't know what has gotten into her these last few years, but the fact is, a word or two will slip out. I have learned to adjust and take her mishaps in stride, but I wonder what happened to the sweet, angelic woman I married.

Rejection is familiar. The fact that she won't wake and listen to what may be the most exciting dream of my life is but a small sample of what I face daily. In less than two minutes, she will have to wake up, so I bide my time.

I rest my head on one arm, gazing out the window at a brightening day. A songbird warbles. A group of blue jays make their obnoxious squawking ruckus on the front porch. They must be getting into our cat food. All sounds are present, but my thoughts are on a wild ride through a canyon on that Harley.

The sound of her buzzing clock startles me out my reverie. Renee leaps out of bed, turns off the alarm, and sprints to the bathroom.

Channeling Biker Bob

I get a glimpse of her shapely, petite backside. Her long, black hair wisps around the corner as she closes the door.

It's okay, I'll wait until she's finished.

After ten minutes, she steps out with a towel tightly wrapped around her. She musters a sleepy smile in my general direction, turns, flips on her closet light, then disappears among her clothes.

If I don't take my shower now, one of our two kids will drain any remaining hot water.

By the time I have finished showering, Renee has gone downstairs. I towel myself off as I hear her ramble in the kitchen. Sound of dishes and glasses clanging, silverware clinking, makes me think that breakfast is being prepared. She's cooking breakfast for us like she used to?

This dream thing is bursting out of me, and I want to share my experience with her. With an impatient excitement, I dress and go downstairs to the kitchen. I want to talk to her before our kids show up and the breakfast nook turns to chaos.

"I've got to tell you about my dream," I say.

"I don't want to hear about your silly little dream right now. I've got too much to do before work." She butters her toast, sets the knife on the counter, turns and gets a glass of milk out of the refrigerator. She didn't make breakfast for us after all.

She is a busy corporate executive now; she doesn't have time to make breakfast for her family anymore.

With a plate of toast, a jar of jam, and a glass of milk, she sits across the table in total silence. After thinking long and hard of a way to broach my dream without getting her upset, I cautiously begin my tale. Not two sentences into my story, for no apparent reason, she slams her knife across the table, yells a string of obscenities at me, and storms out of the house. As usual, I'm left with the job of feeding our kids, getting them off to school, and cleaning the house before I go to work. I don't mind that much, because now it's my turn. She is a busy career woman, after all, and I must consider all those years that she was home as a housewife.

***

"I don't know, Katherine, if you weren't my therapist, I'd think you were on Stewart's side. That's why I see you without my husband. It's too confusing sorting my feelings with him around."

"I don't understand, I was such a nice person before I met Stewart. I was never bitchy, just sweet and loving. What has happened to me?"

"Sure, I'll tell you the story, but trust me, I'm not proud of it.

"When we got married, I promised to love, honor and obey Stewart. I swear, it wasn't a week before the obey part of our marriage went out the window. After our first year, not a fiber of my being would do what he wanted. At first, I found myself doing stupid things like not cleaning his white shirt collars, or putting too much starch in the wash, so that he itched at work. Once I even left a pen in his shirt. When the load came out, his clothes had little blue dots everywhere."

"We laugh now, but I was serious about undermining his every move. I realized too quickly that I wasn't able to obey Stewart in any literal sense."

"You're right. When I told him, I expected him to hit the roof. I wanted him to rant and rave. He should have stomped around our apartment, but he simply acquiesced. The amazing thing is, nothing has been said about that subject to this day, and what's it been, eighteen years?"

"Well yes, once my obey part went out the window, things went along pretty smoothly for three or four years. Our kids were born, I became a mom, and that, as they say, was that. Occasionally, we got into little skirmishes over sex, and namely the lack of sex. I swear, after the kids came along, hell, I didn't feel like having sex, so we did it as little as possible. I'm just not as turned on by Stewart any more."

"In the last few years, with our kids in their teens and me at work, the rest of those sacred vows have eroded."

"When did I first notice? Damn it, Katherine, haven't you been listening? I noticed the day I said my vows, like someone else had said them. I remember the exact moment.

"Two years ago, I found myself bitching to my girlfriend, Martha.

"I told her that I saw Stewart as a wimpy jerk, rather than the valiant man I had married. Martha wondered why it took that long. She said her husband changed a year into their marriage. She has seen him as a stupid slob ever since."

"You're right, it is sad. I asked her how she could love a man she didn't respect, and her answer struck me to my core. She said she hadn't loved Hank for the last eight years. Can you believe it? She stays with him out of convenience."

"Yes, I know, but I swear, I don't want to end up like Martha and Hank. Once respect is gone, I'm afraid so is love.

"I've been coming to see you for two years now, and though I've gotten in touch with many things, my love is slipping away. I can't bear sitting at the kitchen table with him; he is such a milquetoast wimp.

"With his constant whimpering about sex, sleeping with him gives me the creeps. I don't know how to get our love back, and I'm scared. I want to be turned on to him again, but I just can't find that old tingly place, anymore. Years ago, he was so sexy."

"I know what you mean, but the other day during break, I sat in a coffee shop minding my own business. That old familiar flutter rose in my stomach when a hunky guy who fixes computers walked in and sat at the table right across from me. I felt like a teenager. I couldn't speak, or think straight. I couldn't look at him without getting all shaky. When he noticed me, I almost pulled him into the back room and jumped him. Had he actually said something to me, I would have."

"No, you don't have to worry I didn't do anything, but I thought about it, and that part scares me. Stewart doesn't excite me anymore, and I'm not sure I even want to be excited by him."

***

Six long weeks have passed since I had that biker dream. Now that I have a little perspective, I'm convinced I had more than just a dream. I was only at that party for less than fifteen minutes, but the tension from being around a bunch of outlaws and their wildness was more than intriguing. I'm relieved not to be a slave to that weird biker gang, but I want more.

While arguing the kids to bed, I find myself longing for the roar of a harley engine. I think about the sound of wind whistling in my ears and the recklessness of that biker party. Being a prospect for their club might be worth experiencing their brand of excitement once more. Heck, being a biker servant can't be much worse than being a house slave around here.

When Renee works late, I try to stay awake until she gets home, but tonight I can't keep my eyes open. I finally go to bed. The moment I lay my head on the pillow, I fall asleep. The roaring engine of a Harley permeates my room as that same wild-haired stranger pulls up in front of the house. I'm scared and excited, while I quickly dress and go downstairs, then out the front door.

For an hour, we roar toward the party. The same turns, the same wild, spark-flying bank, on the same wide bend. He drives along the same dirt trail.

When he stops, I dismount when he does, but I catch my pant leg on the support bar and tumble onto the grass, again on my face.

He looks back at me and says, "It's a sissy bar, you dick. One of these times you'll figure out how to dismount a hawg."

On my third trip back from the woodpile, I sit alone on a log.

A skinny, goat-smelling guy, sits on the log next to me. He flashes a wide grin, unabashedly showing three missing front teeth. He proudly shows a gaping space between his remaining teeth. His smile is disconcerting. I try to glance away.

"Lost them a couple of years back," he boasts, "in a fight with the Gypsy Zeros from San Geronimo."

What?" I ask.

"My missing teeth." He points at his mouth and with a proud smile, show's that ghastly hole again.

Not knowing what to say and not wanting to focus on his mouth, I look directly into his ink-black eyes, and ask a question that has been haunting me for the last six weeks. I don't mean to ask, but the words spew out. "Why am I here?"

As soon as the words are out, he raises his arm. Thinking he'll backhand me, I automatically put my arms up in defense. He starts into a long peal of uncontrolled laughter.

A sexy female voice speaks from behind. "We came here to help you out, blue eyes."

I spin and see a petite blonde sitting across the lap of an outlaw. Her radiant smile is magnetic. Her hair hangs long over one slender shoulder. After that moment of visual ecstasy, I glance to her left, and come face to face with a scowl. He is a little younger than me, has distinctive carrot-colored hair and a neatly trimmed beard to match, but his face contorts.

Bellowing, he pushes the woman off his lap, scrambles to his feet, struts over and looks menacingly. "You got a lot to learn," he snaps. "For now, keep your eye's off my woman. Bob'll be here in a while, and he'll know what to do with you."

No sound of a rumbling motorcycle comes over any hill; no one strides across the open meadow, but without any warning, a new person appears in the circle of revelers. He steps so close to the blaze that his logger shirt looks like it might burst into flame. He walks past the circle of jeering bikers directly to me. Standing eye to eye, he seems much less threatening than Red.

He lifts his sinewed arm, and pulls back a few wild strands of blue-black hair, smoothing them into a ponytail that hangs to the middle of his back. A slight smile breaks that knife-edge face, showing uncounted wind-weathered creases. When he pulls at his slender, graying goatee, he studies me with a gleam in his golden eyes. He does not have a crazed maniac sneer, like the rest of this crowd, but a happy, glad-to-be-on-earth radiance. When he breaks into a smile, his remarkably large, pearly teeth make him immediately likable. "I'm Biker Bob," he says in a moderated tenor, holding his hand for me to shake.

My male instincts kick in and I jam my hand into open space for a hardy masculine shake. Instead, he brushes his fingertips across mine.

"You're Stewart Chance." He phrases it not a question.

I nod in what feels like a comical gesture.

"Come over here and take a load off. We got shit to talk about." He points at a log out beyond the revelers. I follow in a daze and sit.

Channeling Biker Bob

"Why am I here?" I repeat my question. This time I don't feel like I'm going to get punched for asking. Bob seems different, more stable than the rest.

"Well, in a way, you asked us here," he says.

"What do you mean? I don't remember asking you anything. I've never met you until tonight."

"Remember the New Year's party last December?"

"Sure, but what does that have to do with me being in the middle of this. . . Hey, how do you know about New Year's?"

The bikers resume their loud displays, crude remarks and physical abuse of one another. Bob and I are swallowed by the darkness, while the carousing unfolds in front of us.

"Remember how your wife nagged you into helping her clean your house for the party," he whispers, "then left to go to the grocery, and didn't return all day?

"Remember how you cleaned the house, mowed the back lawn and fielded all the calls? You knew she invited her favorite people and left your friends off her list."

"Sure I remember, but what's your point?"

"My question is, how did you feel?"

"What do you mean?"

"She bailed and left you with the dirty work, when it wasn't even your party."

I'm speechless. This is the first time anyone has put into words what happens between Renee and me. Our real truth has been spoken for the first time. The soul-wrenching truth has not been spoken by the good Dr. Farrell, Renee's therapist, nor by Sally Herfner, my ex-therapist, but instead, by a middle-aged biker guy. How can he get it so right, when the professionals couldn't?

"I guess it felt all right," I say in a feeble attempt to protect myself. "I didn't mind too much."

"Okay," says Bob with a patient smile. "How about in February, when you went on your two-week vacation to Cancun? Who came up with that idea?"

"Well, Renee, I guess."

"Who made travel arrangements? Who carried the bags, and packed them into the cab, then schlepped them to the plane?"

"Umm, I did, I guess, but how do you know all that?"

"You might say you've acquired a temporary group of unique guardian angels. Like many nice guys, you are hopeless.

"I want to ask one more question," he says, toothy smile widening, "then I'll shut up and let you think."

I get a feeling this one will be a doozy.

"How often do you and Renee have sex, and who chooses when, where, and how?"

I look at a star thistle growing at my feet.

"Oh yeah, I forgot," he adds. "Why in the fuck are you seeing her therapist?"

***

"Once he said that, I woke up," I say, sitting in Renee's therapist's office. I'm being careful not to repeat any questionable language. I have been recounting my two dreams about Bob and his gang of cutthroats. This is the visit Renee talked me into a week ago, just three days after my second dream. I have not wanted to return, especially after Bob's poignant questions, but Renee said my help would be supportive to her healing.

"What kind of dream did I have?" I ask the good Dr. Farrell, "Because it didn't feel like a dream. It was like real life."

She has not begun to approach my question. She answers me with a question of her own.

I answer, "Well, no, we don't have sex too often. Once every month or so, I think."

She is a therapist. Maybe she searches for hidden answers.

"Well, no." I hear my whimpery voice. Every time the subject of sex with Renee comes up, I turn a little whiny.

"Her rejection doesn't bother me anymore, but I remember years ago when she couldn't get enough. You know, I miss that.

"I understand she's going through a great deal in her therapy and needs as much support as possible, but Biker Bob has raised interesting questions, don't you think."

"Yes, of course I'll continue supporting her healing. What about my healing? What does he mean when he says I'm hopeless?"

What do you mean you don't know? I want to scream. I'm paying you a fortune, and you don't know? I want to get up and storm out of her office, but I sit in quiet contemplation.

She gives a nervous glance over my shoulder at a hidden clock and reminds me that my hour is up.

I walk in a daze. A twinkling of anger boils, and I'm directing my rage at Dr. Farrell. I have never been angry with her, or any woman before.

"Why do I feel so angry at her?" I mutter to myself as I walk along the street. "She's just trying to help."

How I get to my car, I don't remember. I open the door, and slam my open hand on the roof. Had it been any other car than my '56 Chevy, I would have left a dent. My hand stings all the way home.

Channeling Biker Bob

Out on the highway, I drive five miles an hour over the speed limit. Driving fast is inconsistent with my nature, but law abiding is low on my priorities today.

When I get home, my thirteen-year-old Melvin, arms folded across his chest, face enraged, is waiting at the door. "Sheila went into my. . ."

The rest of what Mel says, though he is almost screaming, doesn't penetrate. I can't get out of my mind what Biker Bob said. What did he mean when he said I'm hopeless? I walk around in a daze, continuing to think about that word, 'hopeless' until I begin cooking dinner.

Why is this happening to me? I've had a steady job with Tridine for twelve years. I am a man with two incredible kids and a wonderful wife. Until six weeks ago, I believed I had led a blessed life. Well, not everything is perfect, but almost everything. The biker has planted a fungus in my thoughts, and it's growing.

Renee gets home late, and I'm in bed asleep. Our bed tugs and shakes as she slips under the single sheet. By September, things have usually cooled off, but a stifling heat continues.

A short seven hours later on my way to work, I roll down my window, and for the first time all summer, cooler air has a promise of autumn, my favorite time of year.

I usually find interesting sights during my ride down the freeway. Today, I only think about what that biker said. I see nothing except a center divider and the hair on my knuckles.

At the entrance to the vast parking lot, in automatic repetition, I unclip my badge from the open ashtray and flash my plastic sheaf to a guard. Just as automatically, I clip the badge to my white shirt pocket.

I read 7:53 on my watch and breathe in one last inhalation of fresh air, then reluctantly join the multitudes in the sealed environment of the computer factory. The air inside is a steady 68 degrees, with a slight tinge of ozone.

Last year's promotion moved me out of a cubicle and into a real office. Having a door to close is worth any extra work.

I walk three flights of stairs for exercise, march to the far end of a congested hall, slip through my door, sit at my desk and open the computer. Normally I go right to work, but today I stare at my screen thinking about Biker Bob. What does he mean when he says I'm hopeless?

I'm not sure how long I look at my screen, but obviously long enough to get the attention of my finicky little boss, Sheldon Wheeler.

Other than Wheeler and his Gestapo tactics, I like my job. Normally, I keep grinding away at my computer, mostly to keep ahead of Sheldon, but today I can't stop thinking about that biker.

My door bursts open and Wheeler stands at his full height of five-six. His arms are crossed over his expensive, meticulously tailored suit.

Nik C. Colyer

He steps inside with a disgusted look on his face. He never has to say anything; we all know what a visit from Sheldon Wheeler means.

My immediate response is to reach out and pick up the first of a hundred documents. I never look up, nor am I expected to. I begin in earnest, the long process of entering yesterday's data. Thirty seconds later he turns and walks away, leaving my door open. When Sheldon Wheeler shows up and does not close your door, everyone knows that he expects the door to remain open for the rest of the day. Never mind that outside noise is distracting; we're expected to catch up and give a good showing, or our door will remain open the next day, and next, until we do. His open door policy is also a message to the staff that we are being reprimanded. Embarrassment alone is enough to keep everyone, working hard. When I reach for a twelfth document, in the space allotted for a name, I thoughtlessly type, 'Hopeless'.

As soon as I realize what I've typed, I delete and reenter Bullard Construction. Three more invoices go through without a problem, and the word appears again, 'Hopeless'.

How does this word keep leaping out at me?

As quickly as I type that renegade word, I delete and continue. As usual, my concentration goes numb after a third or fourth entry. On the fifteenth invoice, I realize, in place of names of each company, I have again typed the word 'Hopeless'.

I'm in the middle of repairing all fifteen mistakes when Sheldon Wheeler appears in my doorway again.

"What's your problem?" he demands in his annoying squeak.

"I don't know, Sir," I reply in my usual groveling manner. I'm ready to confess all, when, without standing or walking toward Wheeler, I'm instantly transported fifteen feet across my room. As the door slams louder than I have ever heard a door close, I look for Wheeler, but he is no longer in my office. A sudden change from sitting in front of my computer to standing at my closed door leaves me dizzy. I stumble back and lean on my desk in utter confusion. Whatever I said to cause Wheeler to slam the door like that must have been a doozy.

***

I sit for twenty minutes picking at dinner, before I get the courage to talk about Stewart Chance. "Something strange happened with one of my workers in the office today," I say to my portly wife, who just happens to be Vice President of Tridine's Sacramento office. She reads her morning stock reports. Her five-year string of promotions, while I remain buried in accounting, sticks in my craw, but I never mention a word. I never say much of anything anymore. A more accurate statement might be that she never says much to me. Resentment is a festering wound in our family, but neither of us speaks of it.

The odd occurrence with Stewart Chance upset my fragile digestion. I've been chewing Tums and drinking Maalox all afternoon. I want to handle this situation on my own, but I could use a suggestion or two. I didn't dare tell my supervisor for fear of being reprimanded. My corporate brown-nosing wife Hilda, is the only person to turn to.

Because she doesn't answer, I repeat my opening lines. "A strange thing happened this morning." When she still doesn't answer, I continue. "While monitoring my workers, I came across Stewart Chance's blank computer screen." I pause, hoping she will look up, if just for a second. When she doesn't, I go on. "I say it's strange, because Chance is normally a conscientious employee and always does his work in a timely manner. He's no one special mind you, but I seldom have to go to his office, much less leave his door open."

"You still scolding your employees with your police-state tactics," she says from behind her paper.

I know where we will go if I answer that loaded question, so I ignore her and continue. "The strange part happened a short time later when I scanned him again. Several of his invoices had the word 'Hopeless' in place of our customer's name."

She drops the top edge of the paper and glares over her reading glasses, but says nothing. When she drops her gaze back to the paper, I continue. "I returned to his office to get him back on track, but as soon as I walked in, he jumped up, with a murderous expression on his face, then growled, and I quote, 'Get a life, Wheeler and get the fuck out of my office.' He almost shoved me out of his office and slammed the door in my face."

When she drops the top of the paper again and gazes at me over those tortuous shell glasses, I notice her short, jet-black hair for the first time. Wasn't it blond yesterday?

I crack a hint of a smile, because I finally have her attention. "His over-reaction startled me. All I could do was stand in front of his closed door, afraid to turn around and face a hundred staring people."

Without saying a word, her gaze drops back to the newspaper.

"I want to retaliate," I say in a last ditch effort to regain her attention, "but I can't think of a thing to do."

She snaps the top of the paper back up and dips her head, probably spotting a story near the bottom. "You're going to have to deal with him," she says.

I patiently fork my mashed potatoes until she rustles the paper again. You got any ideas?"

Hilda is already engrossed in the next article and doesn't come back to our conversation for another three-minutes.

When she rustles the paper again, I slip in a question. "Well, what do you think?"

She looks up as she folds the paper back, then says, "What do I think about what?"

"Do you have any ideas?"

"About what?" She has already spied another article, and gets ready to lose herself.

"Stewart Chance and his slamming-the-door routine."

"I'd walk in Monday morning and promote him."

***

I spend Saturday morning catching up on Renee's long list of home repairs. The day is hot and sultry, too hot to move around under the sun. By mid afternoon, I sit on our porch swing a moment and find myself depleted. After repeated attempts to get back to work, I give in and recline on the uncomfortable swing.

In an instant, I'm back on that Harley, the wind blowing past my ears. The growl of the engine exhilarates me.

This time we're riding during midday and my driver, I keep meaning to get his name, turns right, instead of a usual left at the junction. His bike roars uphill on an old two-lane. He slams each gear with a pop of his clutch and a squeal of the back tire. Without being asked, I reach into his never-empty saddlebag and pull out a cold 'Heavy Beer'. I open the can and hand it forward.

"Looking good!" he yells back, then chugs its contents in three gulps, throwing the empty over our heads. I know it's a dream, and I don't worry about the cans. I don't worry about his speed, either. I lean back on the sissy bar watching as we roll past trees and houses, smelling hot air. Smoke wafts by. Cool water-laden air hits my face as we pass over a bridge. We pass a skunk flattened on the road. Ignoring our roaring motorcycle, three crows peck at the carcass. Later I breathe a sweet smell of pine and remember a high-country lake my family used to camp near. Although I can't recall its name, I remember the canoe and how we used to paddle into the placid lake to just sit. We threw in a line, mostly as an excuse to stay.

In my reverie, I barely notice the bike has turned left. We roll fast along old broken pavement. Jarring me back to attention, the bike hits the first of many ruts. I cushion my ride by leaning forward, putting weight on my legs.

My driver pulls up to the same group of bikers. I'm prepared to dismount in an orderly fashion. He steps off and away as his bike leans onto the kickstand. I put my left foot down. My dismount looks like a success, like I'm actually going to pull this one off. At the last possible second, my shoestring catches, and I find myself, once again, flopping embarrassingly onto the grass.

"It's a reason we wear boots, you dink, so we don't trip over laces." My driver joins the group's guffaws and jeers.

I untangle myself, stand, and brush off.

"Bob's over there," says one of my tormentors, pointing at a large tent-shaped canopy. Through the glare of the sun, I see someone sitting in the shade. Obediently, I walk past the revelers and to the tent.

"Why do you hang out with these darn people?" I ask when I enter the open structure.

Bob's smile shakes off my question. "You got a number of jobs to do here, Chance. One of those jobs is to learn how to dismount a Harley." He motions me to sit in an aluminum lounge chair beside him. I sit facing the group of partying bikers, relieved that they have gone back to their cavorting.

"Why are you with them?" I ask in a quiet tone. "I mean, you're different. You could choose any group, why them?"

"Many years ago I searched out a place I could belong. I hung out with many different kinds of people. You might say I tested the tepid waters of our country and sadly most men either fall seriously short of being masculine or are dangerously predatory. I wanted people with more individualist natures, more willing to stretch the limits."

"These guys stretch limits?"

"Not exactly. Artists are true individualists, but they're shy and reclusive. To get a group of artists together in a room is a bitch. To get them to agree on anything takes an act of Congress. I admire the artistic nature, but no one is around to hang out with."

"I've never been around artists."

"These guys don't look like much, but they know exactly who belongs where in their community. Although they are usually exaggerating their roles, they have a deep sense of masculinity."

"Masculinity?" I ask.

Most men in America lack their maleness. Here, men are men, women are women, and that's just how it is."

"I can't believe you're saying this," I whisper to avoid being overheard. "They are overblown machos. They drink, swear, probably use drugs, and have no sense of anything other than a can of beer and their bikes, probably in that order."

"In certain ways you're right, but they do have a sense of masculine honor, at least more than most."

I sit silent for a moment watching the party. A loud burst of laughter breaks a relative silence, as two men jostle. The others cheer them on.

"Honor," I say. "I don't even know what that word means."

"Webster's dictionary says, 'Esteem paid to worth,' but even Webster's doesn't know how to adequately describe honor."

I scrunch my face, a question posed.

"Describing honor is difficult," Bob says. "I think it means doing the right thing. We have a culture paying homage to God through different religions, but no one really honors God. If they did, our world would be a much different place."

"I honor God."

"Imagine how much better a world we would have if the group advocating right-to-life spent as much effort honoring children already living as they do saving the unborn."

"What's that got to do with honoring God?"

"How does our culture honor this place we live, yet continue to rape every resource earth has? Honor goes to a god all right, but their real god is money and greed." Bob smiles and looks out over the partying group. "I choose to hang out with these guys because they may carry the only honor left. Yeah, they have a twisted and drunken honor, but at least they're consistent. I much prefer people who understand honor. Hang around, because they have something to teach you about being a man."

"Being a man," I say. "I don't see a man among them! I see a bunch of overfed, over-indulgent little boys dressed in tough-guy garb."

Bob's smile widens. "Oh yes, you noticed. I wouldn't say it too loud, though, most of them will take offense."

I forgot that we are sitting less than five yards from the noisy party, which gets quiet. Every person glares at me. I redden in embarrassment. I shrink into my seat and look around for escape.

Their intense stares leave no doubt that they heard me, no doubt that they are thinking about what to do with me. My driver steps forward in a menacing manner. If I am to be torn apart and cooked over the campfire, he could section me single-handedly.

"I. . . Well. . .I. . . I didn't. . ." My mouth works, but I can't speak.

As a whole, the group moves toward me as my frightened bladder decides to let go. My leg soaks slightly before I clamp back down, but I'm too late to stop the flow completely.

Although I'm sure no one sees, they all stop their advance, look at one another and howl. In the next moment, they are hanging off one another, barely able to stand. A minute later, they are back around the fire. I hear an overabundance of comments about scaring the piss out of me. Each time a comment is added, their laughter rises.

I stand, turn and step out onto the meadow to finish relieving myself. Jeers and taunts follow me, continuing until I'm back at my chair.

"Good move," he whispers.

"What do you mean?"

Channeling Biker Bob

"The peeing your pants thing was distracting enough to allow them to make a joke of you and saved you from being hurt."

"How did they know?"

"We know because we are a part of your dream."

"Oh great, I got to pee my pants to fend off this pack?"

"Whatever works. You have to understand, honor also has a dark side. Not allowing insults to go unnoticed is an important part of their code. They could deal with the rules in more healthy ways, but their honor exists. It's something most men in our nice-guy culture can't understand."

"You mean to say you advocate ripping someone apart, because he insults you?"

"I don't, but letting insults pass and not taking a stand applies to many things. Punching someone out because he's insulted you has a place somewhere back in the caveman era, but something must be said for standing up for yourself and not letting others, like your little toad of a boss, walk all over you."

"Oh that."

"Not letting women walk all over you is also worthy."

I'm silent, knowing I've tried to please Renee too much these last years. Bob's commentary strikes deep.

"A man can't allow certain things, and those are the very things a woman will do to him or for him. I'm not saying women do it on purpose; they aren't bad people. It's in their nature to want to fill emotional voids."

I think about Renee, and realize that he's right.

"If a man has a bunch of holes in his character, a nurturing female will want to fill in his gaps to make their unit complete. If she's forced to fill in, she'll eventually resent him. More often than not, guess where her resentment surfaces."

I shrug.

"Sex!"

He's getting too close. I'm sure he knows what's going on between Renee and me. "How does what you say apply to day-to-day stuff?"

"A woman's first line of defense is her pussy," he says, completely ignoring my attempt to change the subject. "If a man wants to gauge his relationship, all he has to do is look to the woman. Women are wonderfully sensitive creatures. Our job is to be aware of what they are doing, then be ready for whatever comes up. Being in our warrior, ready to discuss or argue with them with honor and fairness, is not easy."

"Geez Bob, how do I do that?"

"Learn to listen." He stops for a moment, takes a sip of his beer and looks over the wild gathering. "These guys are just beginning to

19

follow their women. They still act like Neanderthals when they're together, but the ones who are married, or have long-term relationships,
have home lives that are shifting. The two sexes are getting honest,
maybe for the first time in centuries."

He looks over as I open a bottle of water and I hide myself in a long
swallow. I'm hoping he'll look away before I finish, but his gaze remains
steady. Finally, I have no choice except to lower my bottle. I can't look
at him. Instead, I stare at the party.

"You got a long way to go in your relationship," he says. "Don't de-
spair, you can do it."

I look over at him. "My relationship with Renee is just fine. I'll thank
you to--"

"If your relationship is so fucking fine, if the two of you are doing so
hunky-god-damn-dory, when you get home, look for places where
you give yourself away."

"What do you mean?"

"Places where you override yourself to make a situation go away or
smooth out. Places where you would rather take an emotional beating
than confront a situation."

"I still don't know what you mean."

"Sure you do, you just don't want to."

"Give me an example."

"I suppose you love doing dishes every night."

"I like doing dishes."

"Oh, sure. You like doing dishes like I enjoy taking a dump. Both
things need doing, and we feel so good once they are over, but the
two aren't much different; they're both shit work.

"See how you feel when you give yourself away like that."

He's nailed me, so I do a little back peddling.

"I know how it feels, I just don't know what to do."

"Don't do anything to change your situation right now, Stewart, just
mark the times where you give it up. Get a little note pad and write
them down."

I hear gravel crunching and realize that the bikes and meadow are
gone. I open my eyes as Renee and the kids come rolling down our
driveway. I jump up and run in the house to splash water on my face.
Bob's voice echoes in my mind. I realize immediately that I wasn't
ready to get up, but I didn't want get caught sleeping in mid-afternoon.

"Oh gosh," I say to myself, "I haven't been awake five seconds, and
already I've begun my list."

By the time everyone is in the house, I have slipped out in the yard
trying to look busy. I start my list by jotting down the first few situations
where I gave myself away. Each time I write one, I get more depressed.

Channeling Biker Bob

Each time my situation seems more hopeless, I vow to make changes. I have my page filled by bedtime.

I'm desperate, because I don't know what to do. As I'm falling asleep, Bob's words return. "Don't do anything, just be aware."

Tomorrow is Monday. I'll be glad to go to work and put my little experiment behind me. A full page of situations where I gave myself away is hard to take.

Monday morning's household repetition fills another half sheet of paper. I'm in my car and driving down the hill, relieved to not think about my family.

In my office, I open the screen and gladly begin my mind-numbing morning entries. Who cares at this point? Anything is better than counting ways I fall short.

I'm completely engrossed in my work and don't look up until my door opens. Because no one knocked, I know who it is. I glance at the clock on my computer screen: 10:47. My door swings hard and bangs a chair.

I'm sitting at my desk one moment, and the next second I'm standing behind my slamming door, an exact duplication of Friday's experience. Did Wheeler have a determined look?

As before, I lean on my desk to get my bearings. Once my dizziness subsides, I step two paces and open the door a crack to peek out. The entire office is silent. Every person is staring. I close the door and go back to work. I don't know what is going on, and I'm not sure I want to find out.

During lunch, Bill Franklin sits his pudgy frame at my table. Something has changed. His stupid green eyes look different. When he speaks, though he tries to whisper, his baritone voice rolls across the hall. "Wow, you pulled a doozy this morning."

"What?"

"Telling Wheeler off like that and slamming your door in his face. Hey, all I got to say is you got balls. What do you think is going to happen?"

I want to say, I don't know what he's talking about. I want to ask where he got such a story, but I keep quiet.

We eat in silence until Franklin starts in again, "I wish I had guts enough to tell Wheeler off like you did. I mean, just once I'd like to give the sleazy little bastard the old one-two."

Oh, sweet Jesus, what have I done? I'm a goner if I've said even a tenth of what that exaggerating Franklin tells me. I keep a straight face the rest of my meal. I try to hold my own.

***

"That guy slammed his door in my face again," I say to Hilda while eating my morning oatmeal. "I went in to his office and he jumped out of his seat like he would murder me. He yelled for everyone to hear, 'Get out of here you dick, I've got work to do.' I didn't know what to say, he looked so dangerous."

Hilda looks up over her morning paper, and for the first time since I remember, a small, but noticeable smile breaks her jowled stone face. "What did he say next?"

"I don't remember. He didn't have much more to say, but I got confused, and backed out of the room. I swear he would have taken a swing at me, if I hadn't. As soon as I retreated, he slammed his door in my face."

Beyond that hint of a smile, Hilda's expression doesn't change, but for a second, she looks interested in what I'm saying.

"I wanted to open the door and fire that son-of-a-gun right on the spot. I wasn't sure if I could, simply for slamming a door."

"I don't think so," she says, and returns to her paper.

"Well, what should I do? I can't tolerate mutiny on my floor. You remember what happened to Williams in Marketing. Things got so bad that he had a nervous breakdown. If I remember correctly, it happened as a result of one person like Chance."

"Unless he isn't doing his work, you can't fire him." she says, without raising her eyes from the paper. "His union is too strong."

"That's what I thought." I absently toy with my gruel.

I must find a way to get rid of Chance. If I transfer him, I'll have to promote him. I'm not about to upgrade that jerk to get rid of him.

Sitting at the kitchen table, with my vice president of a wife reading stock quotes, I see wisdom of a promotion theory. Twenty minutes whisks by before I understand the genius of my idea.

I'll promote him to some hellhole far away from anything. He'll be so miserable, he'll beg for his old job back. Maybe a place like Tonapaw, Nevada; or Farmington, Colorado.

I take a first mouthful of my breakfast. Now that I have a satisfactory answer to the Stewart Chance dilemma, maybe I won't have to constantly be sucking on the Tums in my coat pocket.

Life is getting better. All my little ducks are falling in position. I have purpose. When I get to the office, my job is to search out the worst location available in lower level management, the next step of promotion for Stewart Chance.

"Whatever I need to do," I say aloud, "will be worth it."

Hilda isn't listening.

I hurry to the office, then bury myself in my computer. My first choice is somewhere like Saudi Arabia or the North Pole, but after a morning of concentrated searching, I find a perfect position for our Mr. Stewart Chance.

"Yes, Barstow, California, will do fine," I say aloud. I've driven through Barstow to see Mom in Vegas. A remote Tridine outpost sits just north of Barstow; Chance will be miserable.

***

"Stewart," Franklin tries to whisper when he sits at the cafeteria table across from me. "Have you seen Wheeler?"

Lucky it's Friday, because I can't stand this idiot another day.

"No," I say, feigning interest.

"I don't know what's going on, but I've never seen him so happy. You'd think Wheeler would be in the dumper after the reaming you gave him Monday."

Here is the business of me giving my boss a hard time again. I wish people in this office would stop staring at me, stop talking to me like I was an idiot.

"If you ask me," Franklin says. "I think he's got some kind of revenge planned. You know how spiteful the little sleaze gets. Remember last summer when Kitrick almost punched him out."

When the subject turns to Franklin's favorite pastime, gossip, my consciousness goes to sleep. I hate listening to his boring inner-office stories. My face is set in an attentive expression; my eyes look at him, but I wonder what kind of horrible revenge Wheeler is cooking up.

Besides my fearful concern of Wheeler, one thought keeps coming back to me. As much as I try to shut the experience out, I remember the exhilarating feeling of that Harley ride. I keep thinking about the wind in my hair, and a roaring engine.

One thought that keeps coming to me is how I would feel in the driver's seat of one of those monstrous machines. What if I turned the throttle and the engine responded to my wishes, my direction, and my speed? How would it be to ride alone on a hawg, flying down a long open highway, turn the throttle and go anywhere, as fast as I want? The dream seems unattainable.

I'm a family man with responsibilities. It would be foolish to jeopardize my life for a childish thrill. Heck, I'm thirty-eight years old. Going off on a Harley is not exactly adult behavior.

My workday ends and I walk to my car, but I can't get the wind out of my thoughts. A rumble of that deep-throated machine rings in my ears. I smell leather and oil, rubber and gasoline, envision a gleam of steel and chrome.

I'm so engrossed in my fantasy, I almost miss checking my gas gauge. Before pulling onto the freeway for home, I swing into a station and find myself fourth in line to get gas. My thoughts wander beyond my windshield, far beyond stoplights, over the mountains toward blue skies and open desert. A rude honking brings me back, but just long enough to pull forward. Second in line, I drift off, but my attention catches an unfamiliar neon sign. I blink and look again. Slowly I become aware of the noisy station, the hum of evening traffic, honking horns, squealing brakes. I've come to this same gas station for five years, but I've never seen that sign. Red neon glares from across the street, stretching full length on the roof of the one-story building. It's at least seventy-five feet long and six or seven feet high. The thick letter 'E' in the first word catches my attention. Obviously ready to burn out, the letter blinks. I read the sign aloud:

"HARLEY-DAVIDSON MOTORCYCLES"

During the whole procedure of pumping gas and paying, I ogle the sign. When finished, I pull my car forward and park next to the pay phone. I get out and make my way across the busy four-lane boulevard. I don't remember the last time I've crossed in the middle of a street, a clear sign that this is not a normal situation.

I look through a large plate glass window at a line of thirty Harleys. Without giving a second thought to what I'm doing, I step through glass doors and look at the sparkling bikes.

The last time I stepped into a Harley shop, I lived in New Mexico. As I turned twenty, my dream was to own a Harley.

The instant I step inside the door, a familiar smell brings back a flood of memories. A bent old man: Hill Baker, no Hal, Hal Barker, owned the place of my youth. He put me to work helping around the shop. He knew I liked bikes. I wanted to own one, but at the time, fifteen hundred dollars for a used Harley was a great deal of money. I squirreled every dollar away and spent every waking hour thinking about owning a powder-blue Harley. I have a single flash of memory; I waxed the tank of a blue Sportster and thoughtfully counted how many paychecks I would need to add to the 437 dollars in my account. In 1982, that was a ton of money.

Any hopes of getting a motorcycle got squelched when Renee became pregnant. I found myself a better job in the sugar mill. My days with old Hal Barker ended in an instant.

I walk around in bright lights, gandering at a completely different breeds of motorcycle. Full-dressed highway-patrol machines have sleek, mostly black, paint jobs. One bike looks like the same model James Dean rode in, "Rebel Without a Cause". I look at bikes with extended front ends and squat front ends, full dress front ends, springer front ends, every front end imaginable. Many bikes have leather or plastic saddlebags. Some have fat front wheels, while others sport large, slender wheels like the bike I rode on in my dream. So many varieties sit on his showroom floor that it's hard to take everything in.

"Hey how you doing," a high-pitched voice echoes in the room.

I spin and see a pimply-faced youngster wiping his hands on a blue shop towel. He can't be more than fifteen.

"Looking for a bike?"

"No," I say. "Just walking down memory lane."

He comes out from behind the counter and walks to the far end of the room. "Over here is the coolest one we have."

From a side view of him, I notice that same longing stance I had at his age. I walk over and look at an antique, cherry red, Indian motorcycle. It has an in-line four-cylinder engine. The machine is clean, well polished, and looks like it belongs in a museum, not in a showroom.

"You get to ride this one much?" I ask.

"Not on your life. My dad would just as soon kill anyone who even sits on this bike."

"Your dad's motorcycle is nice."

"I've grown up around bikes, and this one takes all the prizes."

We talk for ten minutes until he tells me he's closing.

I walk back out to normalcy, leaving the Harleys and my motorcycle memories behind.

I drive home in a daze. Snarling Friday traffic is a dream. I follow brake lights, the only thing I can concentrate on. I nearly miss my turn.

Ten minutes later, gravel crunches under my tires as I pull into my driveway. I turn off the engine and sit in the coolness of my air-conditioned Chevy for five silent minutes. I'm sure that once in the house, I'll have two teenagers who will want me to intervene in their bickering.

Reluctantly, I get out of my car and head for the front door. I step on the porch as my son Mel sprints out onto the fragile front lawn slamming the heavy door inward against the wall. I'm positive the handle has pierced wallboard, but it doesn't bother me. Sheila, following close behind, screams unintelligible obscenities. When she sees me, mid-sentence, she changes to a barrage of "darns," and "I hate you."

Mel sprints across the lawn. When Sheila realizes that he'll outrun her, she stops and, as usual, turns to me. "Daddy he. . ."

Her demand for restitution does not stop, but I hear nothing. With a blank gaze, I step into my house, close the door behind me, and walk through the entry hall. Before I get to the kitchen, I turn and look back through glass crisscross patterns of the door. Sheila's gawking slack-jaw makes me smile. It feels good not to intervene in their squabbling.

In the kitchen, I open the refrigerator.

While I'm chewing on a glue tasting sandwich, my daughter walks in with a worried look.

"Are you okay, dad?"

"I'm okay, tired today is all."

"I don't know, you're acting kind of weird."

I take another bite while sifting through mail with one finger. The fifth envelope is from Tridine. I recognize it's light gray exterior as food catches in my throat. I try to swallow while I pick up the letter and read my name through a plastic window. I recognize the shape, a special size, slightly under legal. I recognize the placement of the window, different from any other piece of Tridine correspondence. I have seen similar letters that look so innocent and benign. I have seen this type of letter in people's boxes at work. I have seen the downcast looks of people who receive them. After seeing a fellow workers with one of these letters, they disappear. Economic relocation is Tridine's term. We call it getting fired, and usually Tridine finds a way to do it with little notice. I still don't know how my union puts up with it.

Wheeler has been much too happy all week. I knew he had something planned. Now, I'm sure his surprise lies inside this gray envelope. I sit in front of the letter, then wash down the languishing wad of bread by drinking milk directly from its container.

"Daddy, are you sure you're okay?" Sheila asks. "You look like you saw a ghost."

I can't respond.

She grabs a glass out of the cupboard and fill it with water. "Here, drink this, Dad. The coolness might help you feel better."

Realizing I still haven't said a word to my daughter, I try to speak. I only further embarrass myself with an unintelligible, squawky sound.

I drink the water as my heart plays jump rope in my chest. My lungs allow only a cupful of air to go in or out. Sheila walks me over to the sofa and helps me lie down.

I'm lying on the couch, Sheila hovering over me like a mother hen, the gray unopened letter of death lying on my chest, when Renee walks in.

"Dad's not well," whispers Sheila, following my wife upstairs.

Five minutes later they return. I hear rambling, jars clinking, and soon, no surprise, Renee and Sheila return with two spoonfuls of a nasty concoction.

I'm being force fed a second spoon of the gelatinous goo, when Renee spots the letter and plucks it off my chest. My condition allows me only a weak grab with one hand as she tears at the envelope.

I watch her eyes scan a half page of type. As she gets to the laid off part of my letter, I look for a grimace. Curiously, she has no expression until she finishes the letter, then a most incongruent sneer crosses her face. "You bastard, you knew all along, but you're too much of a coward to tell me." She slams the letter back onto my chest and storms up the stairs. From her curious response, I'm forced to read it.

NEW BEGINNINGS

Tridine Industries Inc.

September 25, 2000

Mr. Stewart Chance
Accounting
5726 Oak Park Drive
Diamond Springs, California 94543

Dear Mr. Stewart Chance:
    With much consideration on this matter, our office has come to the conclusion that your performance these last two years has warranted the following action.
    We feel your talents would be better utilized in our corporation in a management position.
    This letter is to inform you that Tridine Corporation will move you and your family to your new position as managing director of the accounting department, with a pay scale at the M-1 level.
    As of the above date, you are hereby relieved of all duties in our Sacramento office. You will be allowed one month, with full

pay, to relocate to our office in Barstow, California. The contents of your desk will be shipped to you. Thank you for your services.

> Sheldon H. Wheeler
> Manager of Accounting
> Department 3-A
> Sacramento Office

***

M-1 level means my pay scale jumps from barely scraping by twenty-nine thousand a year to over fifty-two.

"Oh, my gosh," I say. "Oh my!"

I'm back on my feet and walking around rereading the letter. I go upstairs to our room and find Renee fuming as she sits on her mother's rocker staring out the window.

"Do you know what this promotion means? It means--"

She spins around and glares at me. "I know what it means. You're going to have to move to the armpit of America, goddamn Barstow, California, and I'm not going!"

I reread the letter and still don't fully comprehend the location of my new position until I see the word Barstow. Thinking fast on my feet, I say, "With a substantial pay raise, you won't have to work any longer. I can easily--"

"You can easily what, support our family? I have got news for you, buddy, I like my job, and I'm also up for promotion. I won't give up my job to go to Barstow. Your last promotion forced me to leave Seattle and move into this damn inferno five years ago. I've finally adjusted to the heat and found a job I like. Don't think you're just going to pull up stakes again. You're going to have to go without me. You'll catch me in fucking Barstow late in the next century, and not a minute before."

She's in a rage now, because I hear cussing again. I had better get out of here soon or she'll start throwing things. Do I turn and leave? Instead, I try to reason with her. I praise the attributes of Barstow, which doesn't give me much to work with. She throws the first shoe. I watch her spike heel rotating through the air toward me and duck just in time. Behind me, I hear a thunk against the wall, but don't hear any clunking of the shoe as it falls to the hardwood floor. I turn and see her heel has pierced the wallboard, a second hole in our beautiful house in one afternoon. My list of honey-do repairs has just grown, especially if we're going to have to sell our house. I retreat downstairs.

***

29

"Doc, to tell you the truth, I came in to see you because Renee is a very persuasive woman. She said it would help in her healing, but I don't see how."

"Yes, I am confused. If I take this new position my income will double, but I'll be forced to move away from my family."

"No, Renee has already said she won't move with me. She won't budge. If I take the job, I'll be going alone."

"Being alone in a strange town? Oh, I don't think that will be much of a problem. My concern is that all that extra money I'll be making will disappear supporting two households. I'll be in a new town, without my family, and netting the same money. It seems a little ridiculous, don't you think?"

"Yes, I did consider turning down the promotion. I called Monday, but my boss gave me two choices; take the job or quit. I've been with Tridine too long to quit. In this economy, any kind of job is hard to find, much less a good paying one. I'm afraid I'm stuck between the ol' rock and a hard place."

"Yes, I tried to talk to Renee, but she is so angry that I can't get her to talk on any subject, much less the subject of uprooting our family and moving to Barstow. Heck, the move thing is not even my fault. If I had a choice, I would stay right here in Sacramento. To continue paying bills, I'm going to have to move."

I leave Doctor Farrell's office feeling once more like she doesn't understand. One plus to leaving town is I'm not going to see Renee's shrink ever again. Even at the best of times, I never feel like she's much help. Now, when I really need some help, she drops the ball by leaning on her boring therapy methods.

"How can I be angry with such a nice woman," I mutter, as I walk along the congested street. As usual, I talk myself out of anger by the time I get to my car.

***

I'm riding down a dark, deserted highway. A slight nip in the autumn air whistles through my hair. A motorcycle rumbles beneath my uncomfortable little square leather pad. Each small bump jars my body, making my teeth clank. My driver opens the throttle as we begin up a long hill. I still haven't learned his name. We're climbing into the mountains again. With a suddenness that pulls me out of my thoughts, we pass another bike parked on the roadside. I look back and see the bike pulling out, then rapidly catching up. It might be the police.

My driver yells back to me for another beer. I protest, but he lets out a bellowing laugh. "Get me the fucking beer, Prospect, and let me worry about the cops."

Channeling Biker Bob

Fishing into his familiar saddlebag, I drag out a beer, snap it open, and hand the can forward.

As the second bike closes in, its single headlight glows on the back of my driver's head. I hear the two engines harmonize. I expect red and blue flashing lights, but the bike pulls up. I turn and see it has pulled to our right, five yards behind, as we go through a turn.

Once back onto straight road, my driver hugs the yellow centerline, and the second machine pulls beside us. When the bike is parallel, I look over and see Bob's big toothy grin.

I'm in another biker dream.

Bob sits low in his saddle, reaching high to grip Ape Hanger handlebars. They are connected to the longest extended front end in existence. His front wheel might be as much as six feet ahead of the bike. Chrome spokes of a skinny twenty-one-inch front wheel glisten in our headlight.

Our two engines synchronize, as the drone of throbbing machines play a melodic rhythm. Bob's thick black ponytail, wrapped tightly for riding, whips in the wind.

I sense more headlights coming from behind. I turn and count six more bikes pulling in and forming a tight group. It's like I'm sitting atop a single, multi-engine organism. Being with a group of bikes, floating up that long hill together, is more than exhilarating. I lean back on the sissy bar and my senses are alive. I smell dry autumn air, a scant scent of leaf mold. I'm feeling the chill of the predawn, seeing the stars above, and most of all hearing the sound of eight rumbling Harley engines. I may be in a dream, but it feels so real.

No one gives any signal, but as a unit, our entire procession pulls off the highway and into the huge parking lot of a gas station. I would be hard pressed to buy gas from such a rundown establishment. The filthy burger joint next door is a grease pit, if I've ever seen one.

On the far end of the parking lot, a squat wooden building hides under a large oak tree. The dilapidated wooden slat doors are closed. Above the doors, a single light shines on a small, but well executed yellow sign with red letters: Cycletherapy.

Bikes jostle for position in front of the small building, then park. They try to out do one another with revving engines. Bob parks his long machine at a key position in front of the door. As my driver finds his position, I remind myself to ask his name.

I concentrate on getting off his bike gracefully. As usual, his dismount is as smooth as silk. I'm ready and slide my leg over the back fender just as smoothly. I keep my attention on the foot peg as I swing my leg over. For the first time, I succeed in a dismount. As I step over to Bob, jeering and cheers come from the other bikers. Although when they ridicule they sound the same, I know they are congratulating me.

31

Bob's grin widens as he announces over the din, "I think we got ourselves a prospect." Another melee ensues as my driver steps over and slams my back, knocking the wind out of me.

The fifth bike carries red-beard with the striking blonde. He pulls up, dismounts, reaches into his pocket, and removes a single key. He struts over and unlocks the rickety double front door. As he walks in, the blackness swallows him. A moment later, the shop illuminates. Fourteen people follow, and someone closes the door. Five Harleys sit in a line, not on steel motorcycle stands like in most motorcycle shops, but each rests on its own two-foot wide, ten inch tall, grease stained section of a tree. Each machine is at different level of completion.

The powder-blue bike, first in line from the door, looks almost ready to drive. Except for its color, the bike looks similar to the James Dean model I saw in the Harley shop two days ago. It's a fully loaded version, with fat front and back tires, a squat front end with lots of chrome, including both fully chromed spoke wheels. The dark leather fatboy seat and matching saddlebags are freshly oiled. Everything looks like original equipment. Longhorn steer-shaped handlebars, with leather tassels hanging from the ends, are the clincher. I step back and look at the bike. If I've ever seen a Harley to drool over, this is the one.

A canary yellow bike, next in line, sports a long, narrow, freshly chromed springer front end. Other than a missing front wheel and a number of engine parts, the bike looks nearly complete. The one sitting on the next stump has a fresh fire-engine-red tank, a matching bobbed fender, and a custom frame. The Sportster style tank has wild hand-painted yellow and orange flames. Six boxes of parts sit under the bike on crumbling concrete. Many bigger parts, narrow glide front end, wheels, seat, hang from the wall behind the bike.

The two closest to the back wall are obvious parts bikes. They are weather worn, with ancient spider webs stringing off handlebars. So many parts are missing from those two machines that their days are obviously numbered.

I give a momentary glance at the other bikes, but my focus is on the blue one.

"What do you think?" asks my driver.

"Hey, what's your name, anyway?" I ask.

Bob steps up as my burly driver with the perpetual beer in his hand opens his mouth to answer.

"Bitchin, ain't it," Bob says.

"Blue is my favorite color," I say. "Who's shop is this?"

"Hey, Nick," Bob yells over the party noise.

The red-beard walks over and Bob introduces us. His movie-star teeth gleam when he smiles. He slowly swings a grease stained mechanics paw in front of me, nipping my outstretched fingertips. Because they all acknowledge one another this way, I assume it's a secret biker greeting.

"Good job," I say. "Especially this one."

His grin widens. "We thought you'd like it. Bob's having me build this bike for you."

I blanch and look over at Bob, back at Nick, and over to Beer, a secret name for my driver.

I'm dreaming and anything can happen in a dream. He bellows in a half-drunken salute, "I like the name, Beer."

I ignore Beer's sloppy drunkenness. While stroking leather tassels hanging from the handlebars, I ask Bob, "how did you know I would like this kind of bike?"

"Remember kid, we are in your dream. Being a dream, we all know, because we're a figment of your imagination."

My glow fades, when I realize I'll never be able to ride this bike in the real world.

"That's not exactly the case," Bob says, reading my thoughts again. "We all pitched in to have the scooter built for you. Your bike is in the real world, but you're going to have to find Nick."

"Find Nick?"

"As you see, he's almost finished. Your job is to find him."

"You mean you're not going to tell where his shop is?"

"Shit, Chance, don't think we're holding out on you. We don't know ourselves. Remember, we're in a dream. Most of the time I don't even know where we are. I only know we're here and having a hell-of-a good time. Nick's shop is somewhere out in the desert southwest."

"You want me to traipse around the desert searching for Harley shops to find my dream bike?"

Bob flashes me his toothy grin.

"What am I supposed to do for money? When I was a kid, Harleys were not cheap. I'm sure these days prices for a machine like this are outrageous."

"Nine thousand," Nick chimes in.

"Nine thousand!" I exclaim. "How am I suppose to come up with that kind of money?"

Bob's smile widens. His big teeth are more obvious. "Why do you think I got you the promotion?"

"Huh?"

"I got you out of that dead-end job in Sacramento and into the desert where you can ride your heart out."

"How do you claim you got me the promotion, and who's to say that I'll take the job? I may quit to stay with my family."

"Stop fucking around, Chance, and take the job."

"Renee has dug her heels in, and she won't budge."

"Take the job Chance. You can always go home on weekends and see your loving wife and ever-pleasant kids."

"What kind of remark is that?"

"Look Stewart, the things that are in play here you can't imagine. Take the job and stop whining. You haven't got a chance in hell, if you don't." He steps over and places one hand on my shoulder in a fatherly gesture. "Trust me, in the long run, you won't be sorry. Take the promotion, then go out and find your bike."

***

One second I'm in the cycle shop with a bunch of loud, half-drunk bikers, and the next I open my eyes in the reddening sky of dawn, lying in my quiet bed next to Renee.

***

"I swear, Stewart's promotion is getting to me, Katherine. It pisses me off that he is such a weenie. He'd rather quit his job and start over than take the promotion and go to Barstow without me. I'm so sick of him hanging around."

"You're right, I'm angry even when I say his name. I love him, I guess, but he has grown into such a mouse, I can't stand being around him. A big part of me would just as soon see him go off and take his big promotion. At least he wouldn't be moping around with his lost puppy-dog looks. Sometimes the way he acts sickens me."

"Okay, I'll tell you about the early part of our relationship again, but I'm getting tired of rehashing all of that crap."

"Yes, more stuff comes up every time I retell the story, but it's getting a little old."

"What's it been, nineteen years since we first met. He was so much more self-assured, like he knew what he wanted. He was saving his money to buy a motorcycle. Back then all he wanted was that goddamn motorcycle. His dream was kind of simple and cute, so I went along until I got pregnant. With a child coming, I wouldn't allow him to even think of such silly things as motorcycles. He quit his stupid job at the Harley shop and got a real job at the sugar mill out on the edge of town. When little Bobbie was born, he was working steady.

"We didn't know at the time, but Bobbie had a rare tumor. After a long bout with illness and many trips to the hospital, a year later little Bobbie died, and that, as they say, was that. I cried every day for months. Stewart was very sweet. In many ways, now that I look back, his support kept us together. Anyway, I was a mess, and Stewart was so strong. Back then, I wanted sex more than he. How things change over the years. . ."

"I know what you mean. When times are hard, men are worth having around. They are so solid and consistent. "When Sheila came along, I worried I might lose her, too. Stewart stayed with me, the rock of Gibraltar, helping Sheila and me through the first year or two."

"I don't know what happened, Katherine. I remember a time when he was strong and self-assured. Lately I won't even look at him; he is such a spineless puke."

"Sex, you ask? Sex these days is nonexistent. I have to wait until he is not home, to please myself. I can't stand the thought of having Mr. Milquetoast lying on top of me. I hope he takes that job in Barstow."

"Yes, I guess you're right. I am angry, but I don't know where to put my anger. I've been such a bitch, I don't know why he even sticks around. When he is too sickeningly nice, I get even more pissed."

"Are you serious, an hour is gone already?"

"Oh, I don't know. I'm not sure I want to see you with Stewart. I don't think I would be able to talk with him around. He stifles me."

"No, not in the way you think. He's much too mousy to oppress me. His presence just hampers me from saying what I feel. I wouldn't want both of us to come in, not right now, anyway."

"Okay, if he decides to take the job, I'll come in with him before he leaves, but only once."

***

Is this what they call midlife crisis, I think as I get out of bed and go to the shower. Hot water pummels my sleepy body as steam clears my mind. I have a real taste for that motorcycle. Can it be a passing fancy, or is it more like a longing, more of what I wanted to do all along, but never got the opportunity? While dressing, I think about the blue Harley with the leather saddlebags. I think about chrome wheels, short front forks and chrome engine parts. I imagine the rumbling sound of the engine.

I dress for work as our kids make their own rumblings downstairs. I want to revel in the sounds of my Shelia and Mel getting ready for school. Most every morning I find solace in their adolescent noises. I find peace knowing they are my family. I'm secure when they are around. They are my island of sanity.

That blue Harley keeps invading my thoughts. I long to feel the leather and chrome under me.

I shuffle downstairs in a haze and sit at the table. Mel pesters Sheila, and she looks at me to intervene. I have barely heard any squabbling because the two-wheeled wonder consumes my attention. I eat my eggs and drink a glass of orange juice without even knowing what I'm doing. The kids are off to school, and I'm automatically preparing for another week at work, when I realize I don't have work to go to. I am so consumed with Biker Bob, I wouldn't be much good, anyway.

Renee runs downstairs and grabs the toasted bagel I prepare for her almost every morning. She bolts out the door without even an excuse, anymore, about why she can't stop and give me a kiss. Today I don't mind. My thoughts are on one thing, and its color is as blue as a desert sky.

Noon comes and goes before I come up from the depths of my thoughts. One o'clock passes before I even begin to get antsy. I consider doing chores, but the appeal is negligible.

Finally, after hours of aimless milling, I jump in my car. I'm not surprised when the long, red neon Harley-Davidson sign comes into view. I stop across the street where I parked two nights ago.

The young kid must be in school, because an older guy comes out from the back, wiping grease from his hands. "You looking for a bike?" he asks.

He acts a little put out, I assume from having to leave his work to wait on another looky-loo.

By the time he walks the length of the room, I have already scanned his entire stock. The burgundy bike in the corner has similar attributes to last night's blue. I casually point. "How much is that one?"

Marginally more interested, he begins his sales ritual. He spews forth a long list of specifications and accessories. He tells a story about the bike. At the end of his pitch, he hasn't said the price, so I ask again.

"Twelve thousand, five."

"Can I get a similar one in powder blue?"

"Sure," he says. "I'll order one for you today." He begins to liven up, more interested in a possible sale.

"It will cost more for a special order, and you'll have to wait a year for delivery, but we'll get whatever you want."

"A year?"

"Ya, ain't it a bitch? You also have to put a massive deposit down to place an order. Harley-Davidson orders are backed up that far in the future."

He brightens. "We could take this one apart for you and repaint. The whole process will take under a month."

Against the disappointment of having to wait a full year, he'll have the bike repainted in only a month? I know the setup; He is holding a carrot out in front of me. I nearly say yes anyway. I mean, I'm close to saying yes, when I remember Bob telling me that the blue one waits in Nick's desert shop.

Channeling Biker Bob

I don't know why the bike has become important, but it feels like an itch I can't scratch.

"Can I sit on this one for a minute?" I ask.

"Sure."

The wide stance of the handlebars feels great. He helps me lift the bike off the kickstand and into a balance position. This is the first time I have ever sat in the driver's seat. I've come home. It's a dream long forgotten. I have not allowed myself to consider such things for years.

For a few moments, I imagine myself flying down a road under a bright desert sky. I lean the massive machine back on the stand, give him a lame excuse, and walk out of his shop.

My journey home is dreamlike. I keep trying to put my longing back where it has lived for so many years, but I'm not successful.

As I approach my house, something happens as unexpected as going all the way to Sacramento to sit on that burgundy bike. I don't know why, but I don't turn into my driveway. Like I have no control, my old Chevy goes right by our house heading south. Two miles later, I stop at Peterson's corner and turn right onto highway four. I know where I'm going. I know what's happening, but I'm not sure why. I'm headed for the desert to look for that blue Harley.

When I get gas in Stockton, I call home and leave a broken, disjointed message.

"Renee, um. . .I'm. . .well. . .going to the desert. I don't know why, exactly, but I'll be gone for a while. I don't know how long, but I'll call you in a few days. Oh, yes, I'll have a look at my new job, too."

You know how it is, once you leave a message on someone's machine, you immediately want to erase it. I almost call back and apologize, but I leave well enough alone and get on the road.

After stopping in Bakersfield for a deli sandwich and a cold drink, I take Highway 58 and come to the base of the foothills.

Halfway up the hill, I pull off on a side road and stop to eat my sandwich. Away from the freeway the landscape is pristine, with no human improvements to muck up my view. I revel in a silent country setting for an hour before I continue.

Back on the freeway, I step on the gas and fly over the Tehachapi pass, finding myself in the town of Mojave before dark.

Exhausted from driving, I book myself a room along the main highway and spend a night overlooking the never-ending traffic. I'm so tired that I drop off to sleep without any trouble.

During the night, I dream of the blue Harley, a regular dream, without Bob or his biker buddies. I envision the bike in a small shop with a low flat roof. I can't get a clear picture, but the building looks like the walls are constructed out of stacked car batteries. I awake and write down my dream.

In the morning, I awake early and realize I have neither a change of clothes, a toothbrush or a razor. I pull on yesterday's clothes and walk down the street for breakfast.

The establishment is filled with truckers and working people eating breakfast, or sipping an early morning cup of coffee. The food has a typical greasy, nondescript flavor, but I eat, thinking of the coming day. I read a local paper from cover to cover. I haven't had time for a newspaper in years.

At nine, I leave the restaurant, get in my car, and drive across town to a small department store. I buy three sport shirts and two pairs of Levi's, adding two packs of underwear and socks to round off the next few days' needs. Buying clothes as I need them adds to the excitement of my adventure.

I go back to my motel and shower. By eleven, I'm back on the road traveling east through a scruffy desert.

Kramer Junction is a little outpost thirty miles from nowhere at the crossing of Highways 395 and 58.

On the far side of Kramer's, the terrain takes on more of a desert quality. Scrub and a small number of cacti thicken as I continue east.

I glance at my map while poking along an arrow straight highway. I pass a sign that reads; Barstow, thirty-one miles.

In no hurry, I stop periodically to take hikes into the desert.

By three-thirty, I've booked a room off the beaten track in a quiet little corner of town by an old unused highway.

I look in the directory, first for Harley shops, of which I find one, and for then Tridine's phone number.

Passing through a number of switchboard operators and secretaries, I finally reach my contact person, William Layton. He is the man I'm bumping up the ladder.

I can't figure out a reason, but he sets up an interview and a tour for the next morning. Not wanting to make a bad impression, I agree. After hanging up the phone, I jump in my car and drive across town with an expectation of finding Nick Brown and his little Harley shop at the East end of the old bridge. Much to my disappointment, I walk into a small bike shop and find an older gentleman. He has never heard of Nick Brown or Cycletherapy. I thought this would be easy, but the quest for my Grail might be harder than imagined.

I decide that a systematic approach will be needed. I spend my next two hours searching through phone books, but not finding Cycletherapy. I find thirteen N. Browns in a radius of three hundred miles.

By late evening, after calling all thirteen Browns, I come up with a big fat zero.

Back at my room, I call Renee.

"Where have you been?" she demands.

Channeling Biker Bob

"I set up an interview with Tridine in the morning."

"I've been worried sick about your sudden disappearance. You can't take off without telling us."

I don't want to try to explain myself, but I hear a demand for an explanation tagged on the end of her sentence. I make a couple of false starts, which sound more like lame excuses. I finally give up trying to explain and wait for Renee's response. Will she rail at me for shirking my responsibilities? I'm sure she has a lot to say, but twenty seconds goes by with a silent line. I must be in real trouble. I don't remember Renee ever leaving this much time between any sentences in our eighteen years of being married. When she does say something, I expect either screaming and a slamming of the phone, or her patient, I'm-going-to-help-you-through-this-one-Stewart voice. I prefer the former, but she astounds me by asking, "How long will you be gone?" I sense her controlled rage. I'm seconds from a slammed receiver. What the heck, I respond. "I don't know. I guess I need to decide if I'm going to take the position or not."

The phone has not slammed yet, so I give an excuse about my motel room door being left open. As quickly as possible, before she has a chance, I say good-bye and hang up. I stand in the dark phone booth realizing I have nothing to say, except excuses. She has nothing to say to me, except to berate me for not doing the things she wants.

I walk, for how long I don't know. I think about us having nothing left to say to one another. Thoughts of trying desperately to make conversation with Renee, and failing, haunts me long after I shower and climb into bed. Hours later, when I do fall asleep, I find myself on a street of a small town without my pants. My dream is a familiar version of a recurring dream I've had for years. The only difference between this dream and all my others is I still look for Nick Brown's Harley shop. It's hidden among a long row of Harley shops. In fact, Harley shops are all the little town has to offer, but I can't find the right one.

Toward the end of my dream, Bob rides past on his long machine. I yell to him, but he doesn't hear. I find myself sprinting to catch him as he turns into an auto parts parking lot. I sprint a hundred yards to the lot. I have a list of questions for Bob, but he disappears, and the parking lot has no other exits. I think he must have jumped a curb and ridden along a hidden dirt path. I walk the parameter of the lot searching for tire tracks. I'm so busy inspecting the ground, I nearly miss an old one-car garage sitting twenty or thirty yards below the paved lot. Although it looks like every other tattered shanty structure on that barren dirt drive, one thing is different. A crushed corner, with broken and chipped stucco, allows a view of the inner structure. In place of wood studs and a concrete foundation, someone has stacked old car batteries atop one another to make the walls. The weight of the roof has apparently crushed the batteries and broken the stucco.

An inner knowing tells me this is the building where I'm going to find Nick Brown and my sky blue Harley. I bound down a steep slope and walk around to the front of the building. A hand-painted, yellow sign with red lettering hangs over the weathered double wooden doors. I read a single word: Cycletherapy.

A large truck rumbles past my motel startling me awake. Except the memory of the old battery building and red-lettered sign, everything in the dream quickly fades.

I still don't know what town the little building is in. I look, and my watch reads five-thirty. I know I'm not getting any more sleep, so I get up, take a shower, dress, and go out into the dawn of a sleepy section of town. Walking down a lane, I turn onto the main boulevard and stroll over to the first of a long row of restaurants. The battery building haunts me.

***

I sit in the plush, mauve reception room of William Layton and scan a Forbes magazine. Why I'm meeting with him, I have no idea.

The secretary, a slender blonde in her early twenties, continues to glance my way. During my ten-minute wait, six staff members parade through the outer office, obviously to have a look at me. With all the whispering, I feel like a celebrity.

Interminable time passes, and Layton finally opens his frosted glass door. He lumbers his pudgy body into the room. "Well, Mr. Choice, good to meet you."

I stand and grasp a flabby hand. I look into washed-out green eyes that dart around, apparently unable to focus on any one thing for more then a second.

"My name is Stewart Chance."

"Yes it is, and why don't you come into my office, Mr. Choice."

I look at the secretary, instinctively knowing what I'm about to submit myself to. I want to pull my hand away from that sweaty doughboy paw and run screaming from the building. As I dutifully follow, she gives me a genuine look of sympathy. The man will spend an hour trying to suck every ounce of energy I have. The next interminable sixty-minutes will be filled with his exploits, maybe hunting trips, women he's known, or movie stars he has met. It will certainly be designed to inflate his flaccid ego. I'll have to endure it, and I hope to be strong enough to eventually extricate myself from his clutches. There is no reason for me to be here, except as a victim of his diatribe.

Channeling Riker Rob

I follow him through his door and hear the latch close like a prison gate. The steel lock clicks, but sounds like a clank. I'm trapped.

My brain goes dead in five minutes. Halfway through the interview, my eyes glaze over. I'm losing consciousness. Out of a dense verbal fog, something wonderful happens; his phone rings. During the five minutes he talks, I stand and step over to a row of tall tinted glass windows. I look out on a high bluff. The building overlooks a wide expanse of virgin desert. Ancient saguaro cacti dot the hillside. Desert scrub and jimson weed fills in the soil between the giant cactus trees. Not one other building can be seen in the entire expanse. Not one man-made object blocks my view. I draw solace, knowing that, if I chose, this could be my view.

The thought gives me enough energy to get through the next twenty-three minutes.

I come out of his inner office feeling pale and drawn. I glance at the secretary, and she gives me a I-am-glad-you-survived smile. Layton incessantly talks as he ushers me through. I have not heard a word since that wonderfully interrupting phone call. I look at his shifty green eyes and shake his, puffy hand. Once his interminable handshake ends, I get the heck out of his office as quickly as possible.

Layton is still yammering as I close the door of his outer office and make a quick dash down the hall toward freedom. I still hear his finger-nails-on-chalkboard voice until the elevator door closes. In a moment, I'm back in the lobby. Walking across terra cotta tiles, I hear a deep voice call, "Mr. Chance."

Oh God, not another. I look for the closest route of escape.

I want to run, but I'm getting an inkling lately of my need to please everyone, so I can't run. If I'm going to work here, I had better not make a fool of myself before I begin this job. I turn and see a huge man striding across the lobby, a yard with each step. His wide face breaks into a grin. He slows as he gets to me and puts out a gigantic hand. If he uses only a tenth of his ability to grip in a manly handshake, my hand will be pulverized. Unable to refuse his offer, I wince as I reach to shake. To my surprise, he doesn't crush my bones. I'm relieved when I pull back and still have a hand.

"I'm Steve Sinder," he says. "Acting head engineer in production." He stammers with his job title.

His goofy grin widens. "Congratulations on surviving a whole hour with Layton. Many a man has gone into that office, but none have lasted a whole hour."

I get his drift and crack a cautious smile.

"We had a bet on how long you'd last. I won fifty bucks. I guessed one hour, three minutes, and seventeen seconds. Because I won, I'll buy lunch?"

"How long did I last?"

"One hour, two minutes and fifty seconds. Sylvia kept time."

"Who's Sylvia?"

"The blonde in the outer office."

I see that he is serious, and say, "She had a strange smile when I came out. Now everything fits."

"Well, I won, and I'm buying lunch," he says in his baritone, you-can't-refuse-if-you-want-to voice.

I can't get a handle on the colossal, over-exuberant young man. He can't be thirty. At least he has a sense of humor. Consistent with my inability to turn anyone down, I agree to lunch, certain the next hour will be more interesting than the last.

Between explaining company operations, he throws in hilarious jokes and anecdotes about people at Tridine.

Halfway through the hour, a serious expression comes over him, and he looks me straight in the eye. "We'll be more than happy to welcome you aboard our little ship out here in the desert," he says. "I'm glad to see you're an okay Joe. Besides, we would do anything to get rid of that slug Layton."

"He acted a little odd." I'm being generous.

"My only regret is Layton will be bumped up the ladder, spreading his ineptness in an even wider circle inside the company. With his political connections, I wouldn't be surprised if he makes President of Tridine some day."

There is a lightness about him. His laughter and joking is contagious, and I find myself having a good time. Before I left Sacramento I couldn't decide about the job. If a man this vibrant works here and is happy with his work, I should have no problem adjusting. Of course, the most important reason for taking my new position is my secret quest for the sky-blue Harley and extra money to buy it.

Driving back to my motel, I think of Steve Sinclair, Sindlar, Sindler, I can't remember his name. I also think of my new job, but mostly I think of Nick Brown and his Cycletherapy sign hanging from that mythical building of old car batteries.

During the evening, I fill out a questionnaire, the only thing of value Layton gave me during the grueling hour. I sign the bottom of the document, agreeing to take my new position.

After an hour of waiting for an open line, I finally ring through. "Renee," I say,. "I'm taking the job."

A long silence intensifies until she says, "I'm not coming!"

"I know." I try to sound resolute. Inside, I jump for joy. I'm being selfish, but I want my desert experience without the family.

"I'll come home on weekends and holidays."

The line goes silent until she breaks the awkward moment. "You needn't, you son of a bitch. You leave me here with our kids and this falling-apart house while you go traipsing off to who knows where."

I hear a familiar pitch in her voice.

She begins another salvo of insults and accusations. Will she lose her composure? As expected, in less than a minute, she blows up, starts screaming something unintelligible, and hangs up.

I walk back to my room wondering what the heck is going on. The other day, she was coaxing me into taking the job, almost insisting that I move to the desert without her.

Only last week, she told me Dr. Farrell thought the promotion might be the best thing.

Why she is bent out of shape now, I don't know.

In the morning, I head out of town going south. Trying to take a systematic approach, I decide to cover larger, more populated towns first. By noon, I have cruised Victorville, Apple Valley, Hesperia, and many smaller villages. I stop at gas stations and grocery stores. I've talked to everyone I come across without a hint of Cycletherapy or Nick Brown.

I sit in a roadside restaurant, studying a map, trying to find the path of least resistance, when a big ah-ha hits me. I'm going about this all wrong. Gas stations and county offices are not going to know. Nick is a renegade biker. I'm going to have to search out biker bars and poolroom hangouts. I need to ask people who would have use of a good motorcycle mechanic, the bikers themselves. The minute I decide to change my strategy, a group of seven road-weathered Harley riders pull up to the restaurant. They line their bikes in a neat row in front of the building. A minute later, the group sits at a large round table in a corner across from me. I wait until they have ordered, take a couple of deep breaths, and walk over.

"Can I ask a question?"

They are startled into silence, which makes me even more nervous. Is this the first time a straight person has asked a question?

I get so nervous I fall back into an old habit of stuttering. "I, I ju, ju, just want to ask--"

"Spit it out," says a goateed little guy across the table, next to a striking brunette. "Ain't none of us going to bite."

I try for a friendly smile, take a deep breath, and close my eyes to concentrate. "Any of you heard of Nick Brown, or Cycletherapy?"

The small guy adjusts his chrome-studded leather vest, but I see the brunette out of the corner of my vision, and what a vision she is.

A voice from my right demands, "Who's asking?"

I shift my gaze away from the small guy and his stunning girlfriend and settle on a buffalo-shouldered fellow with a dark beard. The first thing noticeable is his black gloves with each fingertip removed, but the most conspicuous feature is a silver spike atop each knuckle. I glance at his gloves, back at his hairy face and coal-black eyes, then at a thick gold hoop hanging from one ear.

"Wa, wa, well," oh gosh, here I go stuttering again. "Ma, ma, my name is St, Stewart Chance."

"No dink, what business do you have with Nick Brown?"

Oh, now I get his reluctance. He's protecting his source.

"I'm n, n, not the cops or anything--"

"We know," says Buffalo, as the others snicker.

"B-ba-Biker Bob told me Nick is building a Harley for me." I close my eyes for a second. I don't mean to tell them I'm chasing around the country looking for an illusive motorcycle shop called Cycletherapy, because I had some stupid dream.

When I open my eyes, the whole group is staring at me.

"You know Biker Bob?" asks Buffalo, awe in his voice.

"Well, kind of like," I say.

"Six years ago I met Bob," says the little guy.

I'm glad to shift my gaze back to him to get another peek at the milk-skinned brunette. "You met Biker Bob?" I ask. My flush of embarrassment dissipates, replaced with goose flesh.

"Well, kind of like," the little guy says. "I worked in a boutique on Venice Beach, when Bob came to me one night in a dream."

I'm so startled that I lose my balance. I'm standing in front of an empty chair, so I grab the back to steady myself. Without thinking, I spin the chair around and sit. "Me too," I say, and watch everyone shift attention to me.

"Me too," says a knife-faced guy with a graying handlebar moustache. He is sitting next to the little guy. He takes a deep breath, flashes a pinched grin and says, "I busted my butt in a shoe factory sweatshop nine years ago. My boss was an asshole from Palos Verdes. He thought his every move should have been recorded for posterity. He had been riding me for months. He tried every way he knew to get me to quit, so he wouldn't have to pay unemployment. One day I blanked out. When I came back, I found him on the floor with a bloody nose. I never hit anyone before, and I didn't even know I'd done it. The funny thing is, at the time I thought I'd get fired or sued. Maybe I would even go to jail, but nothing happened. Well, not exactly nothing. The guy never said another word, but within a week, he promoted me. Without Bob around I would have been arrested.

"Bob started visiting me in my dreams. Eventually he had a bike built for me, but I had to find Nick Brown first." He looks over at me. "Probably what you're going through right now."

"I guess it is."

Channeling Biker Bob

He continues, "I eventually found his little building outside of Tucson. Cycletherapy was the name of the shop, and Nick Brown built that bike for me." He points out the plate glass window at the line of bikes. "The cherry-red one."

Everyone murmurs agreement.

"What happened to your job?" asks Buffalo Shoulders.

"Hell, I chucked that piece of shit job soon as I got the bike paid for," he says.

Everyone laughs.

The waitress serves an armful of platters. "You going to eat with these guys?" she asks.

I realize I'm sitting at a table with seven of the roughest characters I've ever seen. I jump up in complete embarrassment. "Oh, w, w, well no, I, I--"

"Ah, sit down an join us," says Buffalo. "Anyone's met Bob is a friend a mine."

Everyone agrees, and I cautiously sit back in my seat.

The waitress scurries away and returns with her second load before I get settled.

"Tell us your story, Stewart Chance," says Brunette in a deep, sexy voice that makes me blush.

While I'm eating my cardboard tasting sandwich, I tell my story.

When I finish, Buffalo says, "When you find your scooter, come ride with us." He fishes into his vest pocket and pulls out a solid shiny black business card with five words printed on its face. I expect a logo like, Hell's Angels, or Gypsy Jokers, or Vegas Renegades. The card simply reads, all in gold leaf, block letters, ONE PERCENT OF ONE PERCENT. My gaze rests on his name and a phone number. This mountain of a man is called Twiggy.

"One percent?" I ask, but I don't mention my other curiosity.

"One percent of the population rides motorcycles," the little guy strokes his goatee, "and one percent of them is like us."

He gets six murmurs of agreement.

"What does that mean?" I ask.

"The second one percent means bikers who are learning how to be more human," Twiggy says. "For me, it's doing the emotional inner work Bob set out for me to do."

Emotional work? Am I talking to outlaw bikers, or therapists?

As I slide the card in my pocket, I want to change the subject. I'm not sure what they mean by emotional inner work, but I'm also not inclined to discuss the matter either.

I ask my first question again. "Does that mean that Nick Brown is in Tucson?"

"Last I saw," says Twiggy, "but that was nine years ago. Who knows where he is now."

"I saw him three years ago," says the little guy. "He moved his shop outside of Vegas."

"Well, at least I now know where I'm going," I say. "Las Vegas is a big place. Finding a bike builder who refuses to advertise will not be easy."

"Hey, nobody said it would be easy," says Twiggy.

I take a few quick bites of my sandwich, stand and say apologetically, "I got to go."

Twiggy lets out a horse laugh. "I did the same thing for more than a year. Whenever I found a solid lead, I'd be off on another chase. Well, you better get out of here, Chance. When you find your bike, come ride with us."

***

I detest Vegas, but if I have to, well, what the heck.

I get gas and pull out onto the highway, traveling north, excited to finally have a direction.

The rest of the day I spend rolling across open spaces, passing trucks and watching a slowly shifting horizon. Long after dark, I pull over a rise and see the distant glow of Las Vegas. Within a half-hour, the garish lights fill my windshield with a glow as bright as daylight. Driving along one of the most famous and ostentatious strips in America, I sense Nick Brown is no longer in town. I slowly follow traffic past ten miles of casinos, pawnshops, and restaurants. On the north end of town, I find a small motel off the main road and get a room.

I am so exhausted that I stumble up the stairs, flop on the bed without removing my clothes, and immediately fall asleep.

Long before the sun rises, a couple in the next room starts moaning and banging their bed against my wall. As I come fully awake, I hear panting filter through my opposite paper-thin wall. Stereo lovemaking. I hope both men are premature ejaculators. Unfortunately the noise continues.

A half hour of ungodly noise, and I go out to my car to get my last change of clothes. While digging in my trunk, I hear a clicking of high heels from behind me. When the clicks get close, I stop what I'm doing, rise, and turn around to look at the most beautiful, scarlet miniskirted, red high-heeled, long blond-haired woman I have ever seen.

"Hi," she says in a husky voice. "You Stewart Chance?"

In the semi dark, I can't see her every detail, but instantly, butterflies flutter up. "Do I know you?" I say.

She smiles, parting her crimson lips. She reaches over with her bright red fingernails and takes the package of T-shirts, my folded

46

Channeling Biker Bob

Levi's and fresh socks in one hand. She reaches out and gently takes my hand in her other. "Close the trunk," she says. "Bob sent me."

I don't remember a thing. We're standing at the rear of the car one second, and the next, we're back in my motel room. I feign weak protest while being undressed by that strange, exotic creature. I watch her gently bend over to pull off my shirt, rubbing her soft hands on my skin as she does. Each time she removes an article of my clothing, she walks over and slowly bends over to place the article on the floor. The first time she does, I watch a dangerously short mini-skirt hike up her silk thighs. When her dress gets high enough to expose her sex, "Oh my God, she has no underwear."

***

The full light of day bursts around tattered curtains. I awake with car horns, traffic, and a thundering jet. I've had another visitation from the biker group, but all I remember is a long-legged blonde with her red micro-skirt. With such a pleasant memory to draw from, I happily prepare myself to face Vegas. Other than two embarrassing experiences in high school, I have never carnally known another woman but Renee.

For the first time in days, the powder-blue Harley is not primary in my thoughts. Neither are Bob and his group taking that much room in my brain. It was a dream, but it's a shame that kind of sex can't happen in real life. I wish Renee could take lessons from the blonde.

After I shower and shave, I get into my car and drive downtown to the Sahara for its breakfast special.

I wonder what the blonde meant when she said, "Bob sent me." How did she know my name? Things are never normal, where Bob is concerned. That was the best dream I ever had.

With my newspaper up to block out other people in the restaurant and my breakfast getting cold, a tingle of delight climbs from my toes and rests somewhere in my groin. Renee has not been interested in sex for years. She always has an excuse. When she does, sex is more like a duty to her than pleasure. I always end up feeling diminished. This woman wanted me. She wanted me to take her. It was an equal coupling.

I'm wondering what happened with Renee and me, and what I must do to get her to want me again.

I'm deep in thought and hardly notice as my waiter comes and goes. People in the restaurant do the same.

The rest of the day, I roam Vegas, asking questions of the local Harley shops and at known biker hangouts. In the late afternoon, I pull up to a stoplight next to a canary-yellow machine with red flames. I yell over the thump of his engine, "You heard of Nick Brown?"

"Sure," he shouts. "Everybody's heard of Nick Brown." The light turns green, and he roars off. I'm weaving in and out of traffic to catch him as he cuts a straight line on the center divider. Finally, he's stopped at another light, but I'm stuck five cars behind him. I get out of my car and run forward to his bike.

"Hey, pull over, so we can talk about Brown. I've been looking for him and--" The light turns green, and I'm left standing in front of a honking business-green Ford, the driver waves me out of the way. I step aside just in time to keep my foot from getting run over. He flips his middle finger at me while passing.

Five cars rush past, and I'm faced with a barrage of honking horns behind my parked car. I run back and open my door as a large long-shoreman-type gets out of his car. My shift lever drops onto drive, and I gun the engine, pulling a small strip of rubber as I leave the big guy in my exhaust.

I'm sure the biker wants nothing to do with me. Because I have lost him in traffic, I continue casually driving east. But then, I catch a fleck of yellow and chrome in a huge Costco parking lot. When I shift my head, the driver is straddling his machine.

I pull up, park my car, and quickly walk over.

"You said you know Nick Brown?"

"Sure, doesn't everyone?"

"Apparently not. I have been searching all day and come up with a big fat zero. Where is his shop?"

"Don't know. I just see him around, you know, out puttin'."

"Puttin'?"

"You know, out riding around."

"Well, where does he hang out? Maybe I'll catch him there."

"I saw him in Waley's, over on Tenth." With one smooth, even stroke, he jumps in the air and kicks his starter pedal. Before the pedal is down, the bike roars into action, and he drives off.

I roll out into traffic and find a gas station to check a map. Forty-five minutes across town, and I drive up to the front of a squarish, turquoise building sitting in the back of a broken asphalt parking lot. A fluttering neon Waley's sign and three Harleys sitting in a line out front, are the only indicators that the bar is open. Carefully circumventing numerous weed-infested potholes, I park next to the building. When I get out, I gaze at a last vestige of daylight behind distant western hills. A last look at the reddening sky for courage, I take deep breaths to calm my shaky nerves and walk in through the paint-chipped door.

The hinges squeal as I push inward. Although the music inside blasts the Doors, 'L.A. Woman', every head turns and gives me an unfriendly glare, a common biker greeting I'm getting used to. Two men are in the back corner shooting a game of pool. I try my best at a young Marlon Brando swagger, as I step across an empty room and find a stool at the bar. The bartender is a thickset man with wide hairy tattooed shoulders. He dries a beer mug with massive hands. His only incongruent feature, much as he tries to look tough, is his extremely smooth, uncommonly friendly, baby face. I'm sure no one mentions that fact to him.

He steps up. "What'll you have?" he asks in a deep voice. A suspicious glare crosses his face.

Every person's gaze is boring through the back of my head. I want to order a nonalcoholic beer or a Coke, but I'll be laughed right out of the building. If I'm going to get any information out of this group, I'll have to fit in. "Bourbon up," I say, not knowing exactly what 'up' means. I heard the term somewhere, maybe an old Bogart flick.

Tension in the room lessens, while Baby Face pours a shot glass to the brim. I have not had much experience with down-the-hatch, kind of drinking, but I have seen it done many times in the movies. Lifting my glass, I down half the liquid in one fast, I'm-a-man's-man, Jimmy Cagney gulp.

Jesus criminy, it is too late to spit it back. My eyes water. I gulp and feel my entire esophagus freezes. My stomach tries to retch before it is too late. I must concentrate on keeping the burning fluid down.

The Doors song ends as the liquid fights for supremacy in my stomach. Beads of sweat break out on my temples.

As I take my first gasp of air, Baby Face frowns, "You okay?"

I mouth words, but my larynx emits only a croak.

Oh sure, now I'm making a good impression. I try, and don't succeed, for a second inhale of cooling air.

Somewhere off in the distance, I hear Derek and the Dominoes, 'Layla' on the jukebox. What, is this oldies night? I'm relieved when the room fills with sound so I can gasp without being heard. I try for a third breath, and it comes easier, then a fourth, and a fifth. My stomach loses the battle and reluctantly submits to its victor. I look up with tears filling my eyes. I'm thankful to see Baby Face has lost interest in me. He turns to continue his chores. When he returns with a grin, he sets a glass of water in front of me. I gladly drain half the glass. The coolness relieves my burning innards, and I finish without thinking.

A warmth spreads from my solar plexus, leaving me a little fluffy when the bourbon reaches my head. The feeling is good, though, and after such a rough start, I could carry the world on my shoulders. My euphoria spreads as 'Layla' ends. I'm a god, a satyr, a man among men. I'm able say or do anything. I spin on my stool and say into the room, in a louder voice than I intend, "Anyone know Nick Brown?"

I hear whirring as the jukebox removes Derek and the Dominoes and picks another selection. Baby Face clinks glasses to my right. Over a pin-drop silent room, I hear my own heart beating nervously in my chest. As I open my mouth to repeat my question, Johnny Cash blasts into the room with his old standard, 'A Boy Name Sue'. I don't think I've heard this song since I was a kid. The music is so loud I'm sure I won't be heard, so I turn back to the bar. I'll wait until the song ends.

Out of nervousness and without thinking, I pick up my glass and take another small belt. My body is better prepared as the sip goes down without a ripple.

By the time I finish my bourbon, my entire body is numb. After Johnny Cash, I decide to give my question one more try. "Anyone know where I'll find Nick Brown?" I say with a decided slur. No one turns to look. I voice my request again. "Does anyone--"

The jukebox blares Dan Hicks & His Hot Licks, 'Where's the Money?' I turn back feeling a sense of failure.

I find myself on my feet moving shakily across the room toward the front door. As I step outside, a cool evening air feels good on my numb face. Night has a different feeling.

I sway to my car when I hear a female voice behind me. "Why are you looking for Nicky Brown?"

I turn a little too fast and stumble then fall to the asphalt. My head spins; my eyes blur. I'm being lifted to my car.

"You okay?" she asks. Her voice has a familiar huskiness, I try to place.

I say, "I'm sorry, I don't drink much, and the alcohol went straight to my head." My head clears as I look up and get lost in her eyes, then I realize who she is.

"You're the blonde from last night."

My vision is far from clear, my mind is scrambled, but in her blanch, I feel a pea-soup tension.

"I don't know what you are talking about," she says.

Like a fool, I persist. "You're the woman in my dreams. We were at the hotel last night."

She steps back and puts her hand to her mouth. She is ready to turn and run back into the bar. I try to think fast to keep her from leaving, but I can't come up with a thing. A single word comes forth. A mousy, "sorry," emits from my numb mouth, and I immediately regret saying anything. That single word seems to leak though, because she stops eight or ten feet from me.

Her facial features, though chiseled like the woman in my dream, have a different look, a softer, quieter expression of womanhood. She looks thirty. Her hair is strawberry instead of blond, and she is not quite as leggy as in my dream.

"Sorry, I thought you were someone else."

Channeling Biker Bob

She relaxes more, but still maintains her distance. "You're searching for Nicky Brown?"

"Do you know where he is?"

"Well, yes and no. Last I saw, he drove out of town in a moving van going west on Interstate fifteen, without even saying good-bye."

"Where did he go?"

"To Palm Springs, I heard, but knowing Nicky, he could have landed anywhere."

From her forlorn expression, I think our Mr. Brown took a big chunk of her heart when he left. Not wanting to pry, I stick strictly to business. "When did you last see him?"

"I don't know, maybe a year ago."

I don't know why I say the next sentence to her, nor do I expect her to understand, but I blurt, "Bob sent me to look for Nick."

She lightens. "You know Biker Bob?"

"Bob knows me. I've been sent to find Nick and his bike shop."

"Oh," she says. Her expression darkens. "You must be one of Bob's prospects."

"Did Nick leave you?"

She says nothing, but vitality drains from her face. I understand everything in one glance. How much he hurt her with his disappearance, I will probably never know.

"When you find Nicky, tell him hello from Melinda, will you."

I need more information. Maybe she will lead me closer to my grail. "I'm Stewart. . .Stewart Chance."

She holds out her slim little hand, grips mine with an overly confident tightness, and says, "Melinda Chambers."

When I touch her hand, compelling memories of last night crop back up. I fear that a familiar tingling sensation in my groin may color what I say next. I need more answers, and though Melinda had not seen him for more than a year, she is the closest person to Nick. I need more time, but I can't think of a word to say. I stand in silence, hoping she will not walk away.

"Biker Bob told me to come here tonight," she says, breaking the spell. A distinct sheepish quality invades her voice. Her darkness lightens as soon as she changes the subject. "I thought Nicky would be here, but maybe I'm supposed to meet you."

"Bob's suggestions are always mysterious," I say.

With her fist closed, thumb up, she points over her shoulder to a coffee shop. The dingy neon sign says Big Bob's Eats. A twenty-foot tall plastic chef, holding a burger, stands on the front lawn.

"Let's go over and get a cup of coffee," she says. "Maybe we have things to talk about."

51

Without a word, I follow her across the boulevard and to the grease-pit cafe.

When we approach the front door, a rotund man steps out of the double doors and waddles past. He gives us a sad smile, leans close to Melinda and whispers. I think he knows her and is making a snide comment about me. Without breaking his lumbering stride, he walks past us and out to his car. Melinda stops and turns to watch him.

"What did he say?"

"He said 'Bob.'"

"Bob?"

"His one word confirms that we're on the right track."

"Right track? I ask. What do you mean?"

We step inside the drab building as she says, "For no reason at all, a complete stranger walks past me and says one word. That word has been on my mind since last night. Don't you think it's a little strange?"

"Well, I guess."

"I don't know what any of this means, but we're supposed to be in this restaurant."

A gaunt, wrinkled woman seats us.

As we slide into an avocado colored corner booth, I notice an aging biker sitting at the counter seven seats away. His back is to us. A faded leather patch spreads across his dirty Levi jacket. Thick, hairy arms burst out of ripped-off-at-the-shoulder sleeves. The inscription on the patch is hardly legible, the jacket is that filthy. After staring for a minute, I make out: Vegas Voodoo's.

He nurses a steaming cup of coffee, and maybe, from the way he leans over his cup, a hangover. As he sets his cup back on the counter, I notice a faded tattoo individually lettered across all four knuckles of his right hand. The word love is forever tattooed on his hand?

Miss Chambers orders me a coffee and fries.

I stare at the black tangled hair of the biker and remind myself not to get him riled. I'm definitely not going to ask why he wanted the tattoo "love".

"Bob came to me last night in my dream," Melinda says, pulling me from my distracted gaze. "He said to wait at Waley's. The last few years I've followed Bob's suggestions."

"Why?" I ask, between sips of java. I pick up a plastic bottle of catsup and squirt a puddle on the plate of fries.

"Heaven sakes, Stewart, why are you following Bob?"

"Good point. I can't give you one good reason."

"Three years ago, I quit a great job in Philadelphia and a good relationship, just to follow Bob, but I can't tell you why."

"What are we doing in here?"

"I don't know yet. Let's wait and see what happens."

Channeling Biker Bob

I grab another limp french fry and dip it in catsup.

"Nicky and I had a thing going until last year. I thought we had something special, but I guess he didn't see it the same way.

"I have to find him and finish what we started, or find out why he left, or at least slap him across his face a couple of times for leaving the way he did. It was unconscionable."

Her face drops; her gaze follows into her lap. Her voice gets quiet. "I want to know if Bob told him to leave, or if it was something I did." Her eyes glass up.

Heck, I never know what to do when a woman cries. I fall back on my old standard and do nothing.

When she regains her composure, she says, "Bob obviously sent you to me, or me to you, that much I know for sure. Are you going to continue your search for Nicky?"

I motion yes while popping another french fry in my mouth.

"In my dream last night, Bob also said. . . Well, I wonder. . .I mean, could I tag along until you find Nicky?"

I jump back as if a snake has bitten me. My cup topples, spilling my coffee. The watery brew races across the table toward Melinda. I grab for my napkin and cover the sprinting spill, stopping it a few inches short of dumping in her lap. I cautiously sit, right my cup and glance around the restaurant. All ten or twelve people are gawking.

"I don't know," I whisper. "I have never had a woman ask to tag along before."

She holds up her right hand. "I swear I won't be any trouble."

"I'm sure you won't, but will my wife like it?"

The biker swivels out of his seat and walks toward the checkout counter. As he passes, pulling out his folding money, a fifty-dollar bill slips from his fingers and floats to the floor under my feet. Without thinking, I reach out and touch his wrist, noticing his left hand also has a tattoo. It says, h a t e. My still-blurry mind takes that split second to make the connection: l o v e on his right hand, h a t e on his left.

"Hey buddy, you drop--"

He spins and glares. "What's your problem?"

I'm trying to slide my foot around to hook the loose fifty while keeping my attention on him. If I don't produce his money, I'm sure he's going to swing on me.

"You dropped some money."

My foot contacts the bill, and I slide it out into the aisle. Lightning fast, I reach down, snag the money, then lift it up to his clenched fist.

"You dropped this."

A big smile comes across his face as he plucks the bill from my fingertips. He whispers, "Bob sent you, didn't he?"

"Well, no, Bob didn't send me. You dropped your money, and I'm returning it."

Disappointment crosses his face. His smile drops. "Oh," he says, and turns toward the checkout.

Without thinking, and I've been doing many things without thinking lately, I say, "but, I know Bob."

He turns back, "He did send you, I knew it!" Before I get another word out, he sits next to Melinda. "Okay, what do you have?"

"I don't have anything. I only retrieved your money."

Melinda, obviously more used to this kind of disjointed conversation, says, "Bob sent me, too. Maybe there's something you're supposed to give us."

He looks confused. "I don't think so. Bob came to me last night and told me to wait here."

We talk for a minute before we realize that he knows where Nick's shop is; at least he thinks he knows.

"I rode with him to the Calaveras Frog Jumps in Angels Camp, last spring. He and I kind of hung together till he hooked up with a little brunette. That was the last I saw of him."

Melinda flushes with the mention of the brunette.

"Where is his shop?" I ask.

"Well, hell, last I seen he was in a little garage made out of car batteries in Barstow."

"Car batteries in Barstow," I say. "I knew the building would be made of car batteries, but I searched in Barstow, and I couldn't find even a hint of Nick Brown."

"I don't know where he is now, but six months ago I stopped in his shop on a dusty little side street off the main drag in Barstow. He had started on a powder blue hawg for some joker. Doesn't happen he's building that bike for you?"

I flush. "He should be almost done by now."

"Shit, man, Bob commissioned Nick to build that bike?"

"How did you know?"

"I didn't know, but I know one thing, when Bob has Nick build a bike, the thing becomes a magical machine. I mean, all kind of mysterious stuff comes along with one of Bob's bikes."

"All kinds of things? What do you mean?"

"Different things for each guy, but when Bob has a bike built, shit happens. I rode with a guy one time and Nick had built his bike using Bob's specs. Man, that guy could do no wrong. He and I rode with one another for a month, and the weirdest things happened to him. I mean, don't get me wrong, they were weird things, but never bad. Like the guy had a guardian angel riding on his shoulder. One time we rode, and he. . ." The biker launches into a story that brings him to tears. It's

Channeling Biker Bob

frightening to see a full-grown man torn-up over a story about Harley riding. His story goes on for three minutes, before he stands.

"I got to go. I'm sure you're the reason I waited. Now that my job's over, I got a wife and two kids at home. She was pretty pissed when I left. I'm sure she'll be burning by the time I get back. Hey, good luck."

He daintily shakes Melinda's hand, reaches out and brushes my fingertips, turns, and moves quickly toward the door.

I look at Melinda. "Well, I guess I'm going back to Barstow."

She looks embarrassed. "Take me with you?"

"I don't know. I have a wife at home, and traveling with another woman might not be too good for my relationship."

"Heaven sakes, I won't be any trouble. I'll pay for a separate room."

I never had a woman ask before. Her request is so incongruent with my normal life that I say yes, and we leave the restaurant. We drive to her motel, where she fills two suitcases. While she goes to the office, I see a phone booth at the end of her little court. I must be feeling guilty, because, though it's almost eleven, I make a call to Renee.

On the fifth ring, her sleepy voice comes over the line. "Hello."

"Renee."

"Stewart?" Her voice turns to razor blades. "Stewart Chance, where the hell have you been? We've all been going crazy."

I realize my mistake by calling her. Instead of hanging up like I want, I answer her question. "I'm in Vegas."

"Las Vegas! What the hell are you doing in Las Vegas?"

Oh yes, I sense the tension. Her bitchy barbs leap through the line. I want to hang the phone up, but I continue. "I can't explain much, Renee, but I'm searching for someone." Every word I say digs a deeper hole, but do I quit? "I'm searching for Nick Brown. You remember we talked about him."

I hear a gasp, a deep sigh, a clicking of her tongue, and finally, "Nick Brown. You mean that biker from your dreams?"

Is she beginning to understand my situation? I'm ready to sigh with relief.

She says, "Stewart Chance! What do you think you're doing? Get in your car right now and get your butt back home."

A long string of loud, single-sentence demands comes over the line. I have no chance to explain. I can't even get one word in. I'm holding the phone away from my ear, when Melinda comes from behind me. "I'm ready, Stewart," she squeals with excitement.

Oh shoot. The line goes dead. I put the receiver back to my ear expecting, truly hoping the line has actually gone dead.

"Is that a woman calling your name?" Renee says. Her dagger is poised at my jugular. Since my policy has always been to tell my wife the absolute truth, I want to say yes, Honey, but it's not what you think.

55

I just met her, and we will be traveling together for a while. We will have different rooms and separate everything. I'm won't sleep with her, I assure you. Instead, stuttering, "I... I... I..." is all I get out before the phone, this time, thank the heavens above, thank God, thank all the saints, goes dead. I listen closely to see if Renee is sitting on the other end holding her breath, gathering enough energy to let me have it big time. When a dial tone returns, I draw in a deep breath and feel the relief of being able to hang up the receiver.

"I'll have heck to pay when I get home," I say. "For now, no one understands what I'm going through."

"I understand," Melinda says.

By midnight, we're rolling across the desert. Through my rear view mirror, the lights of Vegas fade. Melinda naps against the door with her bare feet on the bench seat of my old '56.

***

"I swear, Katherine, last week Stewart took off and left me with the kids, our falling-apart house, and all the bills. He left a message on the answering machine, and that is the last we have heard from him. I can't believe he's so goddamned irresponsible and devil-may-care. What does he think he's doing?

"I looked all over the house. He hadn't taken anything except the clothes on his back and his beat-up old car."

"Well, yes, I guess I'm okay with him taking off and all, but he has only called me twice and what's it been eight days. Until last night, I worried about him, but the son of a bitch was in Las Vegas, and I heard a woman's voice in the background."

"What do you mean? Of course I'm sure a woman is with him. The idiot bitch called his name over the phone and something about being ready. I have a mind to go to Vegas and find him. If I didn't carry all of the responsibility for our family, I would."

"Damn you, Katherine, I thought you were on my side. Yes, I've been asking him to do something on his own for a long time. I want him to stand up and be a man, but I didn't want him to run off with some. . .some bimbo. He has responsibilities, if you know what I mean. What right does he have running off to Vegas? What right does he have going off without me?"

***

Late into the night, somewhere deep in the desert, I pull a mile off the main highway. In a quiet cul-de-sac, I maneuver my car onto level ground, stretch out Melinda's sleek legs so that she'll rest more com-

56

fortably, and climb in the back to fall asleep. Far off in the distance, I hear a faint whine of big trucks roaring up the long grade.

I think of this adventure. I think of Bob. I'm especially thinking of the lovely redhead lying prone on my front seat. After a long while, I find myself dozing. As quickly as I fall asleep, I'm riding on the back of Bob's ridiculously long Harley, leaning against his sissy bar. We are riding fast over an open expanse of desert, a warm wind whipping in my ears. His headlight is off, leaving only stars and a crescent moon to light our way. In the vastness of the desert, there is plenty of natural light to illuminate the road.

Bob's long, black, tightly bound ponytail whips around. He turns his head, his big-toothed grin is easy to see in moonlight.

"How's my prospect doing with his task?" he yells.

"Everything is okay. Melinda and I have a direct line on Nick. We are going back to Barstow to see if the lead works out."

"Glad to see you hooked up with that woman. You'll do well to continue your journey with her."

I have a bunch of questions, but I don't want to spoil the moment. I sit on the back of his machine as we roll off the miles. Eventually, I see something at the bottom of what might be a fifty-mile wide valley. In the center of the massive bowl a single light flickers, the only sign of life in the entire expanse, and we're heading directly for it.

We take a delicious, wind-whipping, twenty more minutes to approach the flicker. The wind caresses me. The sound of his thumping twin cylinders roaring into the night air lulls me. A strong smell of desert sage sharpens my senses. I'm alive!

As we approach, I already have guessed that the light is another huge fire, and probably one for me to stoke. When Bob lets off the gas and allows his engine to slow, I've already seen a line of Harleys. Twenty people wildly moving around the blaze. Are they dancing? I have never heard of bikers dancing as a group. The closer we get, the more I'm sure who they are. Big clunky guys, little skinny ones; everyone dances around the blaze.

Not until Bob shifts into third gear do I realize the fire blazes in the middle of the asphalt. As we pull up, familiar faces look our way.

Bob shifts to neutral, kills his engine, and coasts the last hundred yards to a stop.

This time there is a difference in the party. The same people are here: Beer, Bucky, Tazz, Max, Shorty, and others, but they act different. As we dismount, their dancing stops. We walk over to a solemn circle of men. I want to ask where the women are, but things start to happen, and I don't have time. The circle opens for us. Bob reaches out and grabs my hand. I want to pull away. What is this holding hands thing? I have not held another man's hand since I was small. The more

I try to pull away, the tighter Bob holds. Shorty, on the left of me, grabs my other hand. I look around and see every man has linked hands to complete the circle. I look over at Bob.

He speaks in an odd singsong manner. "I begin this circle standing north, and honoring the direction of north that brings us frozen winds of winter and snow. North, the element earth, rules growth and nature, fear and silence, the fields and mountains. North's colors are blue and black. I honor north."

When Bob finishes, Tazz, a lean man in his late forties with a big scar across his right jaw, steps forward and speaks. He does so in a similar Buddhist-temple kind of voice. Although he has gone to seed a little in midlife, he still stands strong and buff. He is a quarter of the way around the circle to the left and takes over, honoring the direction of east. He takes a few minutes to describe the attributes of east, but when he finishes, I find myself fully informed on his perspective of that compass direction.

The next direction is south, and to my complete surprise, my driver, Beer, with his enormous gut, usually a can of suds in his hand and a slur to his voice, stands in a south position. He begins a completely sober, entirely out of character, eloquent speech about what south has to offer.

A lanky black man speaks about the western position. His voice has a slight quaver, starting and stopping often, like he is not sure what to say, but he does a good job.

When he finishes, Bob takes over and opens the circle of men. He acknowledges each man by name. He honors his father and grandfather, his grandfather's father and further on down the Biker Bob lineage into a distant past.

Once the honoring of the ancestors is complete, we all break our sweaty hand locks, and everyone sits directly on the asphalt in a circle. This is my chance for escape, but something about this group of unlikely men sitting in reverence is intriguing. I expect this kind of activity of a Sierra Club gathering-sitting around a fire, doing silly rituals-but of renegade bikers misfits? These guys make a circle of men genuine.

Bob produces a carrot-sized clear quartz crystal, its points terminating on both ends. He hands the stone to the man on his right, and it goes around to Max, a lean, hard man, bald as a billiard ball. His normal intensity is fierce, but tonight his eyes have the softness of a monk.

When he begins to talk, I'm astounded.

"Donna and I are having big trouble." He goes on to explain a rocky place he and his wife are in. He not only explains the facts, but also how he feels about his situation. I have a hard time imagining any biker guy talking about his feelings. Even more unimaginable, toward the end of revealing his personal family life, he breaks down. The tough, potentially violent man, lapses into deep sobs. He proudly holds his head up, crying like a baby, obviously allowing everyone to see tears streaming down his face. After five minutes, he calms, sniffles, says he is finished, and hands the crystal on. The stone moves past three men until Bucky stops its progress.

He stands, handling the crystal like a stiletto. He steps forward and turns toward Bob. "I maimed a man last week, and I'm feeling pretty shitty about it," he says. "I place my remorse at your doorstep. If it wasn't for you guys, I wouldn't feel bad about my actions." His voice is terrifyingly intense, like he will jump over and attack Bob with the crystal. Bob has cracked an even bigger grin than normal. His smile is infectious, and smirks break free on many faces. I look back at Bucky expecting anger, but a goofy grin also spreads across his face. Bucky is the one man in the group I have never seen smile, but he smiles with the rest of us tonight.

He tells his story about a man he put in the hospital, not in a boasting manner, but more in a somber, contemplative confession.

When he sits, I am relieved. The most dangerous man has already done his thing and thankfully, nothing happened.

The crystal continues around three times in the next hour. Everyone has told his story except me. The crystal comes to me, and nervously, with a shakiness to my voice, I tell a story about meeting Bob and searching for Nick Brown. Unlike many renditions, mine is a safe story, one I'm comfortable telling. A snack in a banquet of men's issues.

After I finish, a round of discussion ensues. Although there is a lot of exasperation about women and their rage, Bob has been vigilant to not let us fall prey to women bashing.

After the subject plays out, Bob gets up and paces circles around the dying fire. "It might not look or feel like it while your woman is screaming at you, but part of what she's demanding is for you to stand up to her anger. The nice guy manipulates his woman by refusing to witness her rage."

Oh no, he's talking about me again.

"A woman wants a man to be able to stand up to her without turning to stone. One job of the warrior is to face a women, without taking her anger on, belittling her, or allow the situation to become violent."

"But what about our rage?" says Tazz, who sits across from me.

Bob stops pacing and looks at him. "Even if he never lifts a finger to hurt her, a man's rage is too frightening for most women. Many women feel abused by even a raised voice, much less what us men really feel inside. That's where men's gatherings come in. Men can witness each others anger without flinching. Bring your rage here, don't take it home."

"That seems so unfair," says Tazz. "They get to dump on us, but we must hold it in."

"Not hold it in, bring it here.

"At some point, she will be ready to witness your fury, but it's a slow careful process of introducing your anger to her in stages. She needs to get used to each level of your wrath, and to talk about it often with you, before you can go to the next step."

"So what you're saying is we need to be able to listen to women rant and rage," says Bucky, "but keep our mouth shut."

"The truth is that many woman are afraid to get angry. We often only see their anger when they have held it in so long that the only way it can be released is through a pressure valve called rage. Once she has lost control, she feels guilty. If we give her the room to feel her true power, before she needs to resort to rage, our relationship will be stronger because she will feel heard. Many women simply need to be heard, especially by their men."

"But how do we do that?" Bucky asks.

"Our warriors can prepare to do ritual battle with our women without shaming, hurting or running away. A woman may start out by blaming you, but if you can give her room to talk it through without responding or taking offence, often in twenty minutes, she will come to an entirely different conclusion on her own. If you allow yourself to become defensive, then the two of you must deal with both issues for hours, days or more.

"It's not easy, but then relationship is not for the feint of heart."

This evening has left me in awe. I have a new perspective on what I thought was a gang of cutthroats and renegades.

***

I awake inside my Chevy. The color of the desert sky shifts from black to a deep plum. My hour in the circle didn't feel like a dream, but so authentic that my mind has a hard time adjusting.

I sit up, rub my sleepy eyes, and quietly open the back door. Sliding my legs out, I walk ten paces away from the car to relieve myself. The memory of Bob and his buddies hangs heavily on my thoughts. I feel strangely close to the men, like I've finally come home. I'm no longer alone. I have support in my floundering with Renee. Although I shared little about myself, the stories I heard confirm my not-so-unique situation in dealing with life. I'm secure knowing other men have similar problems.

I'm peeing into a shallow gully, overlooking a long bowl-shaped valley, when I notice a single flickering light, far off in the bottom of the expanse. It's Bob and his pals. I look around for landmarks. There is the valley, the two-lane highway, definitely the same desert with the same crescent moon, now low in a dawn sky.

I jump back into my car. When I start the engine and pull onto the pavement, Melinda awakes, looks around, then snuggles back into my jacket she's using as a pillow.

I push my accelerator to the floor, and the old engine roars down toward the fading light.

Dawn develops into a morning sky. The stars fade back into obscurity, and the moon becomes a pale sliver on the horizon, before I'm able to get close enough to confirm that it is a fire at all. By the time I pull up to the spot where last night's circle took place, little is left but a large indention in the asphalt and a pile of ashy embers.

Melinda has not stirred during my rush for the bottom of the valley. She continues to slumber as I pull the car to a stop several yards from the pit. I get out and quietly close my door. When I step around the front of my car, tire tracks and telltale Harley oil puddles dot the pavement. I walk to the pit. This is my first direct contact with Bob and his group outside of my dreams. The bikes are gone and Bob is gone, but there is the real proof.

I stand long enough for the sun to peek over the rim of the valley. I feel the heat from dying coals knowing that we stood here only minutes ago.

I pull out of my trance when Melinda rolls down her window. "Where are we?"

I look over and see tangled strawberry hair encircling her sleepy face. I give her a longing smile. "I don't know."

I want to tell her of my experience, but know that she would have had to be present to make it significant for her.

She gets out of the car, looks at the embers still giving off a single finger of smoke and says, "Bob was here?"

"Yes he was."

"How come I wasn't invited? I'm usually at his gatherings."

"I have never seen you?"

"I'm the blonde in black leather and spiked heels."

A chill runs up my spine. "Last nights meeting was men only."

"Oh."

"Which one are you?" she asks, after a moment of silence.

"What do you mean?"

"Which player are you in Bob's dream world of bikers?"

"I don't know. I have only been to three of Bob's gatherings. Until now, I have never considered it as anything more than an odd dream. You have been to Bob's parties?"

"Many times," she says.

"Since I left Philly, Bob has given me three suggestions, all of which I have followed. His last recommendation led me to the bar where I found you. So far, things don't look too promising, but I'm willing to trust that Bob knows what he is doing."

"Not too promising? What do you mean?"

"Oh, it is just my judgmental side. Don't take it personal."

"How can I help but take it personal? I'm the only one around in this not-too-promising situation. Just what do you mean?"

"I didn't mean to say anything personal."

I go into a sulk. I cross my arms and stare into the ashes.

"I only meant that I've been searching for Nicky for a long time. I've gone on many wild goose chases and never found him. This time Bob has put us together. I don't know why, but I hope Nicky might be at the end of our ride. Not that I love him; I have worked through a kind of weird experience with him and I'm sure more will come."

"Bob sent me, too," I say.

We both stand in silence, gazing into the pit, when I open my eyes and see the tan ceiling of my old Chevy. For a fleeting second, I close my eyes again and stand in front of the smoldering coals. When I re-open my eyes, the tan ceiling appears. I make a number of visual shifts to adjust my double perception. I end looking at the ceiling and realize I'm awake in the back seat of my car. I hear Melinda's breathing. I sit up, rub my eyes, and look over the seat at her. Her pale blue eyes look directly at me. She whispers, as if speaking loudly is sacrilegious. "You were just at the fire pit with me."

Another chill does a time run.

She sits up quickly with a startled expression. "I've dreamt like this many times, I mean being aware in my dreams, but I have never met anyone to corroborate my dream once I awoke. Wow, is this what Bob had in mind when he put us together?"

I'm too dumbfounded to speak.

We both get out of the car and look over a bare part of the terrain. Scraps of paper, old McDonald's bags, and cigarette butts litter the side the road. The pristine bowl of desert we stood in is gone. Once really awake, I'm certain I was in my dream world.

A slight breeze steadily blows out of the west, and a morning chill forces us back into the car.

A feeling of disappointment overcomes me as I start the engine and pull away from the trash-littered spot we called home.

Back out on the highway, driving seventy miles an hour, the landscape returns to its fresh splendor. We pass through a stand of saguaro cactus, when I finally get enough courage to speak. "What do you mean when you say you've dreamt like this?"

Channeling Biker Bob

She turns on the seat and faces me. "I move at will in my dreams. I believe that when we dream, we actually go into another existence. The more I find myself in other worlds, the more convinced I am they exist."

I glance away from the road to see if her expression is serious. "Do you mean Bob's world is a real one?"

"I don't think it's like being awake, but real just the same."

Another familiar chill climbs my back. I'm having a hard time grasping the concept that Bob's world may not be a dream.

"How did we meet in our dreams after Bob left? I feel crazy, like we jumped a couple of cogs or something."

The wind tosses her strawberry hair. She reaches back and rolls her window half way up. "All I know is the rules in Bob's world are different. Heaven sakes, Stewart, don't you see, the fire is a sign. You and I together in that valley means something."

"You got any ideas?"

"Deep in my guts, I'm sure we're going in the right direction. Obviously, more will be revealed when we find Nicky. Something is going to happen, I can't wait to see what it might be."

I have much to think about. We both sit in silence for a few hours while my old Chevy rolls across a warming desert. What Melinda said solidifies many questions that have been bouncing around in my mind since the first night I met Bob.

We pass a junction and drive a mile beyond, before I happen to glance at my gas gauge. I pull a fast U-turn and return to a run down desert station. At a single rusted pump, I turn my engine off, get out, and walk to the dusty little office. When I open the door, a thick smell of fresh cigar smoke wafts out. My eyes water as I look for the proprietor. Walking through the back door, I search the rear of the building. Although the cigar smoke is fresh, no one is around.

As Melinda gets out of the car, I shrug, dig into my pocket, and place a twenty-dollar bill on top of the register. I return to my car and pull the nozzle from a weather-worn gas pump.

After twenty dollars worth goes into my tank, I step around the side of the building and into the most encrusted bathroom I have ever seen. A distinct odor of fresh felt-tip ink permeates the room. At the urinal, having half relieved myself, I stare at a scrawling on the wall. A large, red, felt-tip pen has been scripted over several other messages about where to have a good time and the famous 'F' word. I step back, pull myself into the protection of my Levi's, yank up my zipper, and read the message: "Nick Brown was here."

I run out and drag a reluctant Melinda into the men's room saying, "You've got to see this."

"I'm not interested in seeing the inside of a men's bathroom."

"Trust me, you will be surprised." I coax her into the room and point at the wall above the urinal.

"What?" she says, with a glance. "You want me to see some vulgar adolescent male scribblings."

I stand with my mouth agape, then step to the wall and look closely for any traces of the message.

"The message said, 'Nick Brown was here'." I lean closer to the wall and smell only a scent of old urine and rust. Melinda turns and exits the room, leaving me with my goose flesh.

I get into my car and say, "I swear the message wasn't my imagination. I saw it on that wall in big red letters." I say the words more to myself, than any attempt to convince her. The passenger door closes, I start the engine, and my Chevy glides out of the dilapidated station.

We drive in silence for ten miles, until she speaks. "If you saw the message on the wall, we must be on the right road."

By now, I'm convinced it was an illusion. I glance over to see if she is playing with me. Her face is serious. I cautiously follow along to see where her thoughts are going. "Let's assume you alone could see that message," she says. "Maybe you have an overactive imagination, or maybe not; I'm not sure any of that matters. If you saw something, it's enough to tell us we're going in the right direction."

We ride along for another hour in silence. I'm still considering the message as we come to a junction. The huge overhead sign says 95 South, Blythe. I'm not paying much attention until we are upon it. In a familiar scrawl, this time in orange spray paint, four foot tall letters stand in glaring contrast to the green sign. I slam on my brakes and come to a sliding stop.

"What the hell did you do that for?"

Without saying a word, I throw my shift lever in reverse and race back a hundred yards until I see the sign. I point up. I want her to see the scrawled 'NICK.'

"I saw the message on that bathroom wall," I say, "and it isn't a figment of my imagination."

Melinda stares at the sign. "What?"

I'm flabbergasted. I point at large spray-painted letters. "You can't see the orange graffiti on the sign?"

"What graffiti?" she says in such earnest, I'm convinced she doesn't see it. I look again to make sure. The scribbled letters stand, in tall orange, printed across a green background.

I say weakly, while looking toward her. "The sign says 'NICK' with an arrow pointing south."

She takes a deep breath. "You still see the inscription now?"

"Yes, to the right of the 'H' in Blythe." I get out of the car to have a better look.

Channeling Biker Bob

Melinda follows. "Is this some kind of joke?"

"Look at me," I scream. "Does my face look like I'm joking?"

"You do look pale, but how do you see the letters and I don't? We are looking at the same sign aren't we?"

"I don't know," I mutter. As the message sinks in, I yell, "we're supposed to go to Blythe, not Barstow."

"What?" she yells over a passing truck.

I wait until the diesel fades. "We're supposed to go to Blythe."

"Just like that," she says. "I don't think so. Obviously our destination is Barstow. We have a good solid lead from that biker in the restaurant. We should go to Barstow first. If we don't find him, then we'll go to Blythe."

She looks set in her decision, unshakable, like Renee gets at times. I want to contradict her, but from experience I have learned that when a woman sets her mind, I can do little to redirect her. I want to say that I'm positive south is the right direction, but I get back in the car. Without a word, we continue our westward trek across the desert.

I'm silent, as I usually am, when Renee wins.

"Heaven sakes, Stewart, are you sulking?" Melinda finally asks.

"No!"

"Yes, you are. You better tell me what gives, before we go too much further."

"Nothing is going on."

Renee usually backs off and leaves me alone. I'm expecting Melinda to do the same.

"Look here, pal. Pull your car over right here, and let's get this thing out in the open."

I continue to drive and feel my sulking go a notch deeper. I'm determined not say another word to the pushy female. I'm dumping her in Barstow, and that will be that.

A minute goes by, and I think she has backed off. Unexpectedly, she springs toward me. I flinch, thinking she's attacking. As quickly as she leapt forward she pulls backs, and my engine dies.

"You'll have to pull over now, won't you?" she sneers.

I come out of a flinch to see she has my keys.

"Hey, give me those." I snatch at them with my free hand, but she is much too quick and hangs them out the open window.

My car is rolling up a slight grade, and its speed quickly bleeds off to a crawl. I pull onto the shoulder before we roll to a complete halt in the middle of the freeway. I look out my front windshield without saying a word.

She says, "I'm not interested in being around a person who plays little silence games. I'm not having fun trying to second-guess you. Now, tell me what's going on, and let's talk about it."

"Nothing is wrong, except you stole my keys."

"Don't give me your crap, Buster. Something is bothering you, and it began bothering you before I took your keys."

I sit in silence staring out the front window. I have my wits about me and look over at her to muster a genuine look of acceptance. "Nothing is bothering me. Give me the keys, and let's get back on the road."

With Renee, these kind of conflicts never go further. She wouldn't have taken my keys in the first place. It's easier to let her have her way; our relationship is better served in the long run. My tension melts. The argument is almost over. I relax, knowing the problem has ended. Melinda's next few words make me snap around and look at her in surprise.

"Look here, you wimpy bastard, you ain't getting away with this kind of crap with me. Tell me what the hell is going on, or I'll get out of this car right now and hitch to Barstow. Oh yes, by the way, I'll take your keys with me."

I can't believe she's yelling at me. My stomach tightens. I'm not sure how to respond.

I glare at her. To my relief, after a moment I'm able to smile again. "Nothing is bothering me, Melinda."

I have never been this far in an argument with a woman before. She gives me no choice. I don't know where to go. She holds all of the cards, or in my case, the keys.

"What's bothering you?" she screams.

"Nothing," I snap. Why are we arguing? Can it make much of a difference; certainly not enough to create so much trouble.

"Don't give me any of your bull. Tell me what is bothering you, or I'm out of here."

I think I had better go to my last-resort defense. I have never had to go this far with Renee, but lately my fifteen-year-old Sheila is another story. With Sheila, I can't back down and let her have her way. Like Melinda, she wants an answer. The subject is secondary. "I really don't understand your behavior," I say. "I mean, what is the big deal? Why pick apart something so insignificant?" This works with Sheila; it should work here.

"Look here, buddy, I don't care how insignificant your little gripe is, if we're going to travel together in harmony, you're going to have to tell me every time something upsets you. If you do anything less, I'm out of here."

Her face is a dark shade, closer to the strawberry color of her hair. As long as I keep my attention on her, rather than her anger, I'll be able to make my way through the storm. I smile and feel a calmness come over me. Two veins in her forehead enlarge. The angrier she becomes, the calmer I become.

Channeling Biker Bob

"Well," she spits out the single word.

I have been concentrating on her face so intently that I forgot what had upset me. "Well, what?"

She grabs the handle and nearly tears it off as she yanks back and swings the door open. "Forget you, I'll get to Barstow on my own."

She stomps twenty yards down the highway before I get out of my car. She moves so fast that I have to run to catch up. As I get close, she spins and takes a threatening martial arts position. All of her intent is focused on my destruction. I have a vision of a human chain saw poised, and ready for action.

"Don't you come another step closer, you wimpy bastard." Her hands are moving in a slow rhythmic manner in front of my face. I stop short of her reach and open my arms.

"I'm not going to hurt--."

"You're goddamn right you're not going to hurt me. You come another step closer and I'll chop you to pieces."

I believe her. I have never been so close to having a woman strike me. My stomach rotates a full turn. The acid gurgles.

Something strange happens. I'm all tingly inside. Not the knotted stomach, but a feeling of excited nerves. The tips of my fingers vibrate and turn numb. In an instant the numbness overtakes my hand and travels up my arm.

Oh gosh, will I pass out in front of this human buzz saw?

In less than a second, the numbness travels from my shoulders to my stomach. I don't have time to think about what is happening. My knees weaken. In three seconds, my entire body is numb. I'm left with only my thoughts and a portal view through my own eyes. Even those two senses are not mine, anymore. I'm observing out of two periscopes. Other than the two peepholes to existence, darkness surrounds me.

Melinda and her warrior stance appears far off in the distance. A curious expression comes into her eyes. I notice sudden movement, though it seems like yards below the two portals. A large door opens and a boom echoes through the door. The sound begins slowly. I don't understand the noise, but I recognize the tone. Once it speeds up, I realize that my own voice is coming from somewhere other than my thoughts.

"Melinda, stay with Stewart. You need one another. Kick his ass if you have to, but stay with him."

I'm talking about myself as if I were someone else. Most upsetting, for the first time in decades, I said something vulgar.

In a second or two, I'm back inside my body using my vision, with control of my own voice. All at once, the tickling numbness disappears, and I return to normal. I lift my hands and look at my palms. A feeling of aliveness is back, as if I have just awakened.

I look through my outstretched fingers when Melinda drops out of view. At first, I don't understand what happened. I lower my hands and stare, as she crumples to the pavement.

I'm on my knees and patting her cheeks, but she is pale and not responding. I nervously pat harder. Bingo, she snakes up her right arm, and her little fist lands like a sledgehammer on my left cheek. Had she hit my nose, blood would be pouring all over the pavement. I jump back as she leaps up with a killer's expression.

"Look here, you bastard, tell me what is bothering you, or I'll kick your ass to kingdom come." Her grimace darkens as she regains balance. She moves fast in my direction. I'm back stepping, no, more like sprinting backwards. She's gaining on me, so I turn and seriously sprint away from the road out into the desert. Her footsteps are close behind. Pouring on the juice, I pull away from the screaming nightmare medusa. I twist and turn through the brush. The crazy woman is dangerously close. A memory comes to me, a warning from my father. We sat in his little fishing boat on a hot summer day. I might have been ten. Unexpectedly, while mounting a worm on my hook, my dad said, "Never trust a redheaded woman son; they're crazy." His warning is coming true.

I'm a few hundred yards away from the road and running out of wind. My lungs are collapsing, when I feel a tug at my shirt. A hard yank knocks me off balance. I slide face first into the gravel. I'm fast onto my feet again, but the weight of this female maniac, the wicked witch of the East, amazon woman, pulls me down. I tumble back to the gravel. I'm being crushed into the desert, and all I can do is try to get my wind.

Melinda flips me over like a rag doll. "You tell me what's going on," she screams while drawing her fist back.

I'm lying on my back and can't catch my breath. I'm unable to respond. Her fist hammers toward me. I quickly move my head to the side, but she grazes my right ear, striking the gravel. Her second punch crashes into my forehead.

"Okay, I give," I yell.

"You better give, you bastard." Her face twists. Her mouth sneers. Her eyes are filled with rage.

I better start talking, but I haven't gotten my breath back. I hold a finger up. "Wait."

"Wait for what?" she screams.

"One second."

I'm relieved when she doesn't pull back to hit me.

I'm trying to remember what bothered me in the first place. I cringe while killer woman sits atop me.

Channeling Biker Bob

"The sign had more Nick graffiti," I finally am able to say, and take another gasp. "We're supposed to go to Blythe."

I study her face, sure she'll strike again. In a shift of behavior, like a Dr. Jeckyl and Mr. Hyde, the raving maniac of a woman leans down. I flinch, expecting that she'll smash my nose with her forehead. Will she bite my face? With as much fury as her punch, with as much force as her scream, with a match of the speed she exhibited while chasing me, she plants a wet, full-lipped, tongue-lashing kiss on my mouth. I'm not sure what to do. I'm spellbound. Her tongue forces itself between my lips and plunges down to intermingle with mine. Her thighs, which had been holding me on the gravel, relax and flow into soft, yielding columns of quivering flesh. Her pelvis pushes against you know who. In a split second, my maleness goes from running for his life, shrinking in close for protection, to leaping to attention. She takes a heavy breath, sighs, and wildly crushes my lips again, her tongue searching for mine.

Many years ago, Renee told me she didn't like kissing. She only kisses me passionately when she's been drinking, and she drinks rarely. Kissing has since become a fixation.

As if in a fantasy dream, Melinda's lips hungrily press on mine. The second I respond, she takes me. She tears at me, rips my clothes. She bites and scratches. She is an animal, a cat, a lover I have never experienced. She has her way with me without a word. With much noise and thrashing, we are two wild things coupling in the desert. Being taken by this dangerous and troublesome redhead is a fantasy beyond my wildest dreams. I'm with a woman in the full light of day, clothes torn, buttons popping, and my shirt in shreds. She is a woman who will not let me find my moment until she has had hers repeatedly, until she slumps exhausted onto my chest panting and sobbing.

My dreams are being fulfilled. When I reach my peak, she helps by motoring those luscious hips in a wide, slippery, circular motion. Because gravel chunks bite into my backside, I don't have to pinch myself to prove that I'm awake. This is definitely not a dream. She slumps atop me, and I don't want to change a thing. She moves her body just enough to keep me erect and inside. I'm in heaven.

The sun is high in the morning sky by the time we get dressed and walk back to my car. As we leave our spot of thrashed gravel and smashed plants, the terrain looks as though two big animals have scuffled and fought, maybe to the death. I wonder how long our digging and thrashing of the desert sands will last in an environment where landscape scars heal slowly. A century would be an honorable time to mark such an occasion.

We get back into my car without looking at one another. An awkwardness, maybe embarrassment, has settled between us. I don't know what to say, now that we're not in the throes of passion. I remove my torn shirt and reach for another in the back as she hands me the keys. Wearing a fresh shirt, I put the key in the ignition.

"Stewart, let's talk first."

I knew it. Now comes remorse, guilt, tears; a proper, God-fearing, Christian response to such a spontaneous act. Reluctantly, I release the key. I look out the front windshield and brace myself.

"If you saw Nicky's name scrawled across the sign, I think we should go to Blythe, don't you?"

I'm thrown completely off guard. I can't get my bearings. I respond after a long silence. When I do, I think of nothing more profound to say than, "Sure."

We make a U-turn and drive back toward the Blythe turnoff.

Melinda rolls down her window and leans out. Her thick strawberry hair blows in the wind.

I want her again. I want to pull my car over right here, but I don't have the guts to approach the subject.

It's a hundred miles to Blythe, and I have over three weeks left before reporting to work. There is plenty of time to get where we are going, so I roll along at a poky forty-five miles an hour. I watch Melinda's hair flowing in the hot air and glance at her sleek curves. She lay atop me only few minutes before. I still taste her, smell her scent.

Many miles go by before she finally closes her window and turns to me. "I'm sorry for losing my temper. Something comes over me when I'm not being told the truth."

I immediately try to think of a way to suppress another truth. I want to lie a blue streak, but all I say is a lame, "It's okay."

Why did I say that? Why do I act as if she did no harm? Why am I not stopping the car and taking her in my arms? At least I could tell her how much I enjoyed the experience. Instead, I say, "It's okay"? I should say, "Let's do it again." Something besides just, "It's okay." I'm so nervous that I can't say another word.

"My rage comes from my upbringing with dad," she says. "He used to withhold. I think he withheld to save me from pain, but it used to infuriate me."

"Your dad did that?"

"My ex-husband did it too, and we used to get into horrendous fights over it. With Frank, I got used to being sexual after our fights. We got to a point where he'd egg me on until I came unglued on him. He liked my anger, but for the wrong reasons."

I like her anger too, but I don't say a thing.

"My pattern continued with Nicky," She says. He liked our sex, but he didn't like my rage. When I was with Nicky, I started therapy and began to look at the core of my condition. I don't want the strife, but without it, I can't get turned on. Is that sick?"

Channeling Biker Bob

Jeez, she just revealed more about herself in five minutes than any woman I have ever known. How do I respond to her honesty? My brain speeds along at a hundred miles an hour trying to think of a response, but I have nothing.

"I feel bad, Stewart, you being married and all. I don't want to complicate your relationship. I'm sure you're feeling guilty as hell, so I promise not to do it again, as long as you promise not to withhold. We don't need to complicate matters any more than they already are."

"No, wait," my brain screams. "I want more. Don't stop!"

"Oh," is all my disappointed voice musters.

Should I be feeling guilty? I check my guilt meter, and the needle rests on zero.

Yes, Renee is my wife, and I did promise to love, honor, and obey, but this is the first time in more years than I can remember that I feel like a virile man. Heck, this may be the first time in a long time I feel like a man at all. Guilty? No way!

We drive along for another three miles in silence. My thoughts are racing faster than the car, but I still can't think of a way to respond.

"Heaven sakes, Stewart," she says. "Why didn't you say you wanted to go to Blythe in the first place?"

Because I wouldn't have missed what happened for anything.

"I did," my voice says. I'm too nervous to talk. Heck, I have talked to other women before. I've had great conversations with my wife and with Sara at my office. Why can't I say more than a two-word sentence to Melinda?

She says, "you have to start talking, or I'm going to go crazy talking to myself. If we're going to travel together, we have to talk to one another. Please, tell me what is going on."

"I'm confused." Wow, a two-word sentence. I'm doing great. "Jeez, Melinda, I feel like a teenager."

She snickers. "At least you're doing better than a second ago. Now give me one more statement about how you feel, and I'll stop for a while to let you rest."

Now I'm on the spot. My brain draws a blank. We drive along for another mile in awkward silence. Finally, I have a response. "You are too pretty. I get nervous talking to you."

She laughs. Will she slap me? If she slaps me, maybe we could have more of her unique brand of sex. I find myself looking forward to Melinda's next outburst.

"You must be kidding," she says.

I look away from the road for a second to see if she's joking. In one gigantic flash of insight, I realize that she doesn't even know she is beautiful. "No, I'm not kidding. You are beautiful." Wow, I got a full sentence out.

71

I turn again and see her freckles stand out as she blushes. The fact that she does not see herself as beautiful makes it much easier for me to talk to her. "I couldn't bring myself to contradict you, when you wanted to go to Barstow. I never challenge Renee."

"Well, that is a hell of a statement. You mean to say that you always do what Renee tells you to do?"

"I never thought of it like that, but I guess I do."

"What a yucky thing."

"What do you mean?"

"If you're always doing what Renee wants, how will she know who you are?"

"What do you mean?"

"If you don't declare yourself in different situations, how will she know what you think, what you like, or hate, and what doesn't matter?"

"I don't think she is all that interested in how I think. You don't know Renee. When she sets her mind, nothing will dissuade her. I gave up trying, years ago. I find that life is much easier."

"This much I know for sure," she says. "About the same time you stopped trying, the two of you stopped having good sex."

"Well. . .that is none of your business," I say, but Bob had already planted the seed. Melinda's assessment simply gives the plant a little more nourishment. We ride along in silence for another mile.

I try to remember when sex between Renee and I stopped being good, tapered off, then vanished altogether. Maybe that summer we went on vacation. Mel was three, and I tried to dissuade Renee from going to the Utah badlands during summer. We had a huge argument, and I eventually gave in. The weather turned hot, and she got angry with me about that, too.

"Oh my gosh, you're right," I blurt out after a long silence.

"Intimacy and sex are closely related," she says. "Emotional closeness only works when two people aren't holding anything back. They must be clear about their gripes and complaints."

"It's not easy being clear with Renee."

She looks over. "The more unresolved stuff between us humans, the less intimacy is possible. One of the reasons we had such great sex, is because we have no unresolved issues."

Did she say great sex? I blush and hope she's not looking.

I drive in an embarrassed silence for another two miles. I try to think of anything to break the spell, but I can't organize my thoughts. The idea that she thinks we had great sex, runs five-second laps around my brain. I reach down to turn on the radio. Melinda touches my hand. "No radio now, if you don't mind."

72

Channeling Biker Bob

Another long stretch of silence oppresses me as we roll along the lonely two-lane. I don't think I have seen more than six cars pass since we turned off the main highway eighty miles ago.

Melinda breaks the thickness. "I want to say again how sorry I am that I attacked you. I can't control my rage, just yet. I'm seeing a therapist, but she hasn't helped much."

I say, "I didn't think my wishes were important enough to cause so much trouble."

"Even the smallest thing is worth the trouble."

"Oh."

"All we have to do is be honest with one another and the undermining stuff will not come up?"

"I'll try."

"I've never been with a man who was totally honest, or totally willing to speak when something bothers him. The closest I ever got was with Nicky, but now I'm sure. He probably withheld, too, or he wouldn't have left without at least saying good-bye."

"This is a new concept Melinda. All I can say is I'll try."

"I want brutal honesty. I want to know every time I have done anything to upset you. I also want to tell you every time something happens to me. If we do this, maybe we'll avoid a buildup of resentment."

"I'll give it a go."

"We have a new beginning, a fresh, clean slate. We don't have a bunch of garbage to slog through first, before we get to the honesty. You be truthful with me. I demand it."

"Being direct isn't going to be easy. It's not second nature."

"If we're going to spend time with one another, I want to set one ground rule. Even the littlest thing is worth talking about. I can't have a relationship any other way."

Oh gosh, another new concept. Honesty scares me. The kind of straightforwardness Melinda requires, I have never considered possible, especially with a woman.

My thoughts are bouncing around in my mind while the car bounces along the old road. Time goes by in more silence.

"You know," she says, "Biker Bob came through you back where we got in the argument."

"Really? I thought something strange happened; I just couldn't figure out what."

"I don't know how he managed, but he talked through you. He said we're supposed to stick together."

"Together? Why would he say something like that?"

"I don't know, but this much I know for sure. Bob has put us together for a reason. I trust Bob has my best interest at heart. Maybe we can help one another." She pauses for a long time, then asks sweetly, "Will you help me with my problem, Stewart?"

Help with her problem? I look in the rear view mirror and see a cherry-red bruise the size of Texas cropping up on my cheek. If she is talking about the best sex I ever had, I will help her, all right. I will help her get angry as much as possible. I reach up and touch the tender spot below my eye. My flesh feels puffy.

"I don't want to have to get enraged to have good sex," she says. "I don't want to get enraged at all. I'm asking you not to keep anything from me for as long as we are traveling together."

"That's a tall order, Melinda. I'm not used to the truth."

"I'll ask you to try?" she pleads, "for my sake?"

"Okay, I'll try."

We drive in silence for another five miles before she continues. Deeply involved in my own thoughts, I give her a periodic nod of my head to look like I'm listening.

I don't do it on purpose or to irritate her, but years ago I came to understand Renee wasn't interested in whether or not I paid attention, she simply wanted company. She wanted someone to talk at, not with. As long as I look attentive, Renee is happy to chatter on.

The tactic does not exactly work with Melinda. "Stewart, you're not listening to me."

"Sure, I am."

"Okay, what did I just say?"

Uh-oh, here we go. A part of me shrinks when she demands that I listen. My other, more expectant part, anticipates another blow up, another slugging, a wild chase through the desert ending in you-know-what. A tingle creeps up my right inner thigh.

"You said, well, ummm."

"Obviously you weren't listening."

"Sure I was. I just forgot."

"Stewart, tell me the truth. Were you listening or not?"

Her nostrils flare with the intensity of her demand. She probably has the ability to kill me, yet I look forward to the beating with a hardening manhood. I'm ready to take our little scenario to the next step, ready to push her further. I look forward to her unbridled rage, when I realize I'm pushing her into another sexual frenzy, when less than an hour ago she asked me to help. In a wave of guilt, I say, "You're right, I wasn't listening."

I glance over at her a number of times, sadly watching her transform back to her calm self.

"I'm sorry, Melinda," I say, admitting my secret intentions, my desire, and my lust for her.

She smiles. "You want to have sex with me again?"

Channeling Biker Bob

I answer without a moment's thought. "Yes." It is a good yes. In fact, it is a great yes.

"Heaven Sakes, Stewart, you don't have to get me mad to have sex with me. I liked having sex with you. I like how you make me feel, and I especially like your honesty."

She looks around at the green pastures and farmland we have been driving through for the last ten minutes.

"Too many houses right here, or I would say to pull over right now. We must be coming into Blythe. Let's wait to get a room and get cleaned up, but you might be disappointed."

Disappointed? I think. Unworthy, maybe, but not disappointed.

For fifteen minutes, we drive in awkward silence, anticipating what lies ahead. We come over a rise, and the city of Blythe lays below us, spread out on a wide pan of open desert. After the beauty of a hundred miles of hilly desert, rocky crags, and finally lush farm valleys, the actual town of Blythe is a festering open wound on a parched earth. We come to the first stop light and turn right, heading west. The central part of town runs along one main street. The bulk of shops and restaurants line what looks like the old highway. Less than a half mile to the south, running parallel to the business section of town, is Interstate Ten. The noise of the city combines with the drone of trucks and cars on the freeway. In contrast to the silence of the desert, Blythe is a generating plant for vibration, droning engines, and singing tires on hot pavement.

The freeway sign, with the scrawled letters "Nick" pointing toward Blythe is the only reason I find myself compelled to rent a room in the din of this unsurprising little town. I hope we discover something soon. It has been less than five minutes, and I already don't know how I'll be able to stay.

Cruising the back streets of town, we come across a small motel on a relatively quiet corner. By the time we have showered, I have shaved, dabbed at my growing facial bruise, and applied a little foo-foo juice, my mood has shifted. There is a difference, but I can't put my finger on it. Trying to keep with our agreement of honesty, I tell Melinda that I'm awkward about having sex her.

"Yes, I feel the same way," she says. "Something is different here in town. Maybe too many distractions."

"Vegas has distractions," I say, "but Blythe, I don't think so."

"You might be right."

We giggle.

"How about we walk over to the restaurant?"

"Thought you'd never ask," she says and grabs my arm.

We stroll out of the little motel complex and up the sidewalk toward the main drag.

As we approach the busy street, along a flat beige wall of a hardware store, I catch sight of a scribbled name written in fresh red spray paint. A single word 'NICK' is written in the same scrawling backhand as the other two signs. The extra long leg of the 'K' swings back around under the name. An arrow at the end of the leg points in the direction of a restaurant across Main Street. The scribbled name is the only graffiti on that huge, blank wall. I touch the paint and a little smears off onto my finger.

"Oh my gosh," I say. "Here is the same handwriting."

"We must be on the right track," she says. "Let's go eat; maybe someone waits for us in the restaurant."

I touch the paint again, and in those few seconds, the color has dried in the desert sun.

Racing to the corner, I yell, "whoever painted this did it just before we turned the corner." I look up and down the long busy street. To the east, two women walk side by side pushing strollers toward me. They are paying little attention to anything except one another. I look the other direction and see no one. A quick glance across the street, and I spot an old man sitting on a bench, smoking his cigar. A girl in a summer dress skips away from him.

I expect to see a blue Harley pulling away, maybe Bob's bike with that ridiculous front end, but the only cycle within sight is a Honda scooter being driven by a voluminous man in his fifties.

Melinda catches up and grabs my arm. "Let's go eat."

The stoplight is in our favor, and we start across the street. I look back toward the graffiti and stop in the crosswalk.

"The message is gone," I shout over the din. Melinda spins, has a quick look, then drags me across the street.

"You saw the inscription this time, didn't you?"

"I saw it." She coaxes me into the restaurant.

"What happened?" I mutter, as the street noise dampens when the thick-glass front door closes behind us.

Our waitress seats us in a back corner.

"What happened?" I ask again.

"I haven't a clue." She acts calm, like nothing out of the ordinary happened. "Obviously, Bob left another in a long list of signposts. When I follow his signs, something always happens. Let's keep a sharp eye peeled for anything out of place."

We eat a greasy lunch and wait for two hours. No one slips us a message or drops money. Nothing happens, just a bunch of uninterested, uninteresting people, eating unappetizing lunches in an undesirable little bohunk desert town.

We walk across the street and return to the graffiti. I look carefully for any evidence, but not a hint of red violates any part of the wall.

She says, "maybe the graffiti pointed down the street, instead of toward the restaurant."

"Let's give it a try."

We amble back across the street and walk south. The next business past the restaurant sits a bank; further along an insurance agency; even further, a tire store. For the next quarter mile, the street continues to present one store after another, all the way to the freeway. Once under the overpass, there are only open fields. The road is so straight it disappears in a single line into a painfully flat horizon. Farther down the road, in the middle of a huge open field, stands a white farmhouse with a barn. I notice nothing special about the barn, and the house looks like a million other ancient whitewashed farmhouses. The roofline sags in the center. Like many in the area, the building is old and decomposing. Something about it leaves an indelible impression.

"I'm tired of walking in the sun," I say. "Let's get the car."

Melinda agrees, and we walk back on the other side of the street, in case we missed anything.

Snapshots of the old house keep haunting me. The house frightens me, but I can't put my finger on the feeling.

When we get back to the car, I'm overheated and exhausted. I suggest, "Let's go relax in the air-conditioning of the motel."

Melinda agrees, and we go into our separate cheesy little adjoining rooms. I have a momentary thought of another bout with the wild woman. I'm bushed, though, and I fall asleep before I take the thought into action.

TRIAL BY FIRE

By the time I awake, it's early evening. I take a quick shower, shave again, and knock on Melinda's door.

"Yes," she answers through the locked door.

"Let's go find out what that house has to offer."

Ten minutes later, she steps into my room in Levi's and a conservative peach blouse.

We drive under the freeway overpass and see a sky filled with reddening clouds. In a pre-dusk light, the house looks even more ominous, almost haunted. I drive slower every moment.

Halfway across the open fields, Melinda says, "The place seems more scary, now that it's dark. We better come back in the morning."

The house is nerve shattering, right out of a horror movie. Unlike my normal response, I surprise myself when I say, "Let's do a fast drive-by to see what the place looks like."

"Something isn't right. Do your drive-by, but don't even slow down. I'm getting more frightened the closer we get."

I press my foot on the gas, and pass the building doing fifty, ten miles over the speed limit. When I give the house a quick glance, the structure looks like any other worn-out old farmhouse.

I don't let my foot off the gas until we are a mile beyond the strange house. When the car coasts to a stop, together we turn and look out the back window.

"I don't know," Melinda says, "The place gives me the willies."

Channeling Riker Bob

"From the looks of the road, there is no way to get back to town except to turn around and take another pass."

"Okay, but go fast, and don't even pretend to slow until we're back under the overpass. I'm getting so shaky that I hardly can keep my hands still." She holds up one trembling hand to prove her claim.

"Me, too," I admit, while turning the car around. I gun the engine, and by the time I reach third gear, I'm doing fifty again. A hundred yards short of the old farmhouse, my right front tire explodes. Within seconds, we're thumping along on ruined rubber. My car slows as I fight the steering to stay in the center of the road. I'm determined not to stop anywhere close to that frightening old house, so I gun the engine, ready to ride that flopping tire right to the rim.

My fear meter is off the scale. My shaking hands grip the wheel, but I have no idea why. My foot presses hard to the floor as we approach the house, but the car will only thump along at a creep. When we get across from the front porch, the tire locks up. The car comes to an abrupt halt. We are stuck in the middle of the road, right in front of the rusted iron gate. I press harder on the already floored gas pedal.

"Another ten yards," I yell. "Oh please, just another ten yards."

The engine roars, but my car will not budge.

"Oh shit," Melinda says. "What are we going to do?"

She lets out a short, high-pitched scream when the porch light turns on. She slides low in her seat as an elderly man opens his door and steps onto the porch. He peers right into my soul. He's a devil. My foot is still on the gas. The rear tires are smoking. Billows of thick rubber smoke roll up from under the car. He hobbles to the edge of his porch with a four-prong cane.

Why am I so scared. He couldn't catch us if we hopped backwards on one foot. I get my wits about me and let my foot off the gas. The straining engine slows to an idle and dies. Thick smoke wafts away on the breeze.

"Need any hep' thar?" he asks into the silent evening.

His croaky old voice startles me. For no apparent reason, my hands start shaking.

"No, we're okay." I try to sound convincing. "We just have a flat tire. I'll have the spare on in a jiffy."

He navigates the three steps and hobbles along the concrete walk.

"Ya okay out thar?"

My hands spring into a fresh bout of shaking. His words pierce me. I'm ready to start the engine again, but I have only one option. I have to keep him from coming over, keep him on his side of the gate.

I scream, "No problem, we're okay." He's less than thirty feet away. I get control of my voice. I say more calmly, "Just got a flat. You don't need to worry."

Nik C. Colyer

A trickle of sweat rolls past my right temple. I had better get out of the car and inspect the damage. The old man fiddles with the gate and squeals it opens. The noise cuts to my core.

"Holy moly, he's coming over," I murmur to a huddled Melinda.

She lifts a little to look out and drops back down. She whispers, sliding lower onto the floor. "Get out, Stewart. Get out and meet him halfway. I don't want anything to do with him. Get out!"

"I don't want anything to do with him, either."

As I open my door, I hear its familiar squeak, but it startles me. The entire situation has me unnerved. I get out of the car and stumble on a crack in the pavement.

He hobbles the last few steps, stopping two feet from me. He is too close, so I step back and press against the car.

"Sure yer' gunna' be okay? I could call a tow truck."

"No. . .it's. . .okay." I speak in wavering broken sentences. I'm hyper-ventilating, but I manage to say, "I think we'll change the tire ourselves. We'll be on our way soon." My knees are shaking.

He is not taking my 'no' for an answer. He stands in the middle of the street, facing me. I know he wants me to turn my back on him. Against my instinct, I back step around the front of the car, continuing to face him. On the far side of the car, I glance down to see that the tire has come completely off the rim. It's wrapped around the axle like a rubber band. No way will I be able to get the wheel off. I look back up, and the old man has not moved. He leans on his cane. He looks like any non-threatening old codger. I look back down for an instant to study the situation. My gaze is off him for no more than a half-second. I shift back up, and he has moved. I'm stunned at his speed. He has moved from the center of the street, closing a thirty-foot gap to my side in that instant. I smell the garlic on his breath. I smell the old-manness of him. I look into his face. He is too close. I want to step back and get away, but I'm frozen.

"Sure yer' gunna' be okay?" he repeats his question in my ear, this time so loud that I'm sure my eardrum is blown. I jump back, stumbling over clumps of sod. As I fall backward into the field behind me, I reach for the ground without breaking eye contact.

Horror stricken, I watch his cane melt and transform into, oh my, a shotgun pointing directly at my chest.

"Oh God," I stammer, as I sit hard on the soft earth, crushing two rows of young lettuce.

"Oh shit," I hear Melinda scream from inside the car. The old man, who now seems much, much younger, much more dangerous, gives me a menacing glare. He lifts his gun and points the business end at my head. A sardonic smile spreads across his face. I'm crab walking

80

backwards away from him. I'm scooting over row after row, crushing the immature plants.

His eyes, and I'm positive they weren't like that before, are an iridescent red of cheap cameras when taking flash pictures.

His already too-wide smile widens. His already rabbit-red eyes sparkle. He says in a deep, threatening voice, "All this and more for you, Stewart Chance. Keep your eyes open; the next part will be tricky."

"What?"

He looks down the barrel of the shotgun and broadcasts a deep throated, wolfish howl, not unlike the howl of Beer.

When he finishes, he drops his aim, looks at his gun and says with a titter, "Oh, my gun was only to get your attention."

His gun turns to a long black snake. What I thought was a bad day just got worse, when he throws the reptile at me and vanishes like a puff of smoke. When the reptile wraps around my throat, I scream. The snake tightens, cutting off my wail.

I'm struggling with a monster that I'm sure will strangle me, when I realize that Melinda is shaking me. She must have gotten out of the car. Thank God, she's loosening the grip of the snake? She shakes me harder and gently says my name.

I'm not in the lettuce field, but in my bed in the motel.

After fifteen minutes, my body stops quivering. When I have my voice back, I begin to tell her about my dream.

"Stewart, you don't have to say a word; I was with you."

"What do you mean?"

"I was in our dream."

"Do you remember the old--"

"Yes, I heard the old man tell you something at the end, but I couldn't make out what he said."

"'All this and more for you, Stewart Chance. Keep your eyes open. The next part will be tricky.' What does it mean?"

"Obviously some kind of warning," she says. "What a weird way to give us a warning. I mean, we could have just as easily seen another scribbled graffiti on another wall."

"You saw what he looked like after he changed?"

"Yes, Stewart, like the other day at the fire pit; I saw everything. My question is, what are we going to do?"

"Well, sure as shootin'," I say, "I'm not setting foot outside that door until daylight. I guess we're supposed to go back to the farmhouse, but I'm not going until tomorrow."

"Good plan." A sheepish smile crosses her face. In the half-darkened room, her freckles stand out.

Is she blushing?

"Stewart?" she asks, pausing for my response.

"Yes?"

"I'm scared. Can I sleep with you for the rest of the night? I won't do anything but sleep, I promise."

Uh-oh, she wants to sleep with me and not do anything. I can't think of a worse torture.

She gives me a relieved smile and slips under the covers. Her pajamas are not much help as she cuddles up to my back. I sense her every curve. I imagine her every valley. Gosh, I don't think I will ever get back to sleep, but the morning light leaps upon me. When I awake, she has her back to me, and we're spooning.

After a long while, she awakes and turns toward me. I look at her lovely slender face. She gives a sleepy smile and says, "Morning, you."

"Sleep well?" I ask.

"Once we got past that horrible dream, I slept wonderfully."

As if a thousand spiders have climbed the walls, she shrieks, "Oh Stewart!"

"What," I say, getting ready for the worst.

"Your eye."

"Huh?"

"I gave you a black eye. Heaven sakes, Stewart, I am sorry."

I get up and feel the tender spot on my face. In front of the mirror, I grimace. The upper left side of my face is plum-colored.

After showers and preparing for the day, we walk out the front door of the motel and back to the restaurant for breakfast.

While eating, she asks, "How shall we approach that house?"

"Approach the house? What do you mean? After last night I'm not going close to that house."

She flashes a grimace. "Stewart, we aren't cruising around on a vacation here. Bob has specifically put us together. Our three dreams together is proof."

"Three dreams?" I ask.

"The one in the desert, last nights, and at that motel in Vegas."

"Vegas?"

"You were searching in your car, and I came up from behind. We had sex, I know you remember."

"I thought you were a part of my dream, not actually another person. Did you really come to me that night?"

"Trust me, I was there, not in the flesh, but I was with you."

"Why didn't you admit it that night at Waley's?"

"Embarrassed, I guess. Doing things like that in a dream is one thing, admitting that I had sex with a perfect stranger in real life is another. Plus, I didn't know if you would understand."

"I see your point."

"Not to change the subject, but how are we going to approach that old house?"

"I don't know," I say. "I'm scared to even look at the place, much less go near it. You got any ideas?"

"I'm terrified, too, but I'm sure we're supposed to go."

I'm resigned. "That house is the last place I want to go."

"I think our car experience in the dream is a warning not to take your car. Let's drive to within a few hundred yards of the place and walk."

Reluctantly, I agree. We walk back to my car.

I drive up the street and, at the last second turn left on Main.

"What are you doing?" she shouts.

"Let's get out of here, Melinda. Let's go to Barstow and continue our search for Nick."

"You turn around this instant, Stewart Chance, or I'll, I'll--"

She reaches over and slips my keys from the ignition.

"I'm getting tired of this," I say. Before I lose all forward momentum, I coast into the driveway of a convenience store and park in a stall. "Look Melinda, we have no business at that house. You know as well as I do that nothing good will come of it. Let's get out of here while we still can."

"You coward!"

Did she say coward?

I try to think of a response, a comeback that will cut as deeply. After a long silence, I realize I can't think that quick.

Melinda glares at me. I experience that old familiar buckling of my will. If I'm never able stand up to my wife, I'm sure as heck not going to stand up to this amazon, who is ten times stronger and more stubborn.

Her eyes take on that same penetrating intensity they did yesterday, just before she lost control. One glance makes me shudder with fear and anticipation.

"You're going to the house if I have to kick ass all the way."

I love it when she talks like this.

"Well, are you with me, or do I have to beat the crap out of you right here? This time, no sex, though. I'll leave you bloody on the pavement and go alone. Rest assured I'll leave you bloody."

I throw up my hands. "Okay, okay, okay. I'll go to the house with you, but I sure as heck will not go in."

She tosses me the keys. I turn my car around and head back to the turn at the restaurant. When I make the left, dread creeps in to compound the flutter in my stomach. Once under the overpass, I park, and we sit silent with the car idling.

The small whitewash house, with its barn, sits in the open field as it did yesterday and last night in our dream. I had hoped the building burned during the night.

"I can't go to that house," I say.

"You have to. Bob sent us here for a reason, and we can't turn around now. I'm sure Bob wouldn't lead us into a disaster."

After a few minutes of building my courage, reluctantly, I pull the shift lever, and we slip slowly away from the curb. I'm certain my death, or another horrible fate, awaits me at that house. On the other hand, I agree with Melinda, Bob has never led me astray, so why would he do it now?

I poke along at a crawl until we are within a hundred yards of the house. I switch my engine off, and imagine a low hum.

"Okay, Stewart, here we go." Melinda steps out onto hard-packed dirt. I open my door and stand on asphalt. A car races past us and slowly disappears into the horizon. I close my door, walk to the front of the car and lean my butt against the warm hood. Melinda does the same. We stand for a minute. She snakes her hand down and grabs mine. Both of us are staring intently at the house. Her hand shakes, sweating slightly, as she pulls me away from the hood.

"Let's go meet our destiny," she says.

The second my body leaves the hood, the bent old man, with his walking cane, steps out onto the porch and looks over at us.

I flinch, stop, and try to pull my hand away. I gasp. "It's the same old guy in the dream."

"Heaven sakes, Stewart, what did you expect?"

"I'm not going any farther."

Melinda yanks my arm, forcing me to take another step. My next step is a little easier, as is the next and the next. We are a hundred paces from my car when the old guy reaches the bottom of his stairs. As he turns toward us, my fears are confirmed; he is the same old guy from our dream. I hesitate, and Melinda yanks me forward. Something is very wrong.

Staring wide-eyed at the old man, in slow motion, I watch the house behind him inhale. Is the house actually breathing? Is last night's nightmare coming true?

In a surrealistic impression, I glance over and see Melinda's contorted face. The frightening old man hobbles toward us. He is fifty yards from us. Over his head, I see the bulging walls of that breathing house. I want to turn and run, when the rickety porch yawns. For a second, I find myself mesmerized. Am I imagining this? I'm hoping it's another dream. The next second drives home a horrible realization that our nightmare is true. The old man is real. I look for his cane to turn into a shotgun.

Channeling Biker Bob

Behind him, the glass in every window bulges. I imagine the house staring at me. I blink to clear my head. The second I open my eyes, every window bursts. A dragon's breath of yellow and blue flame blasts from each opening. A concussion knocks me off balance. Heat sears my face. Before I land hard on my back, the old man is projected through the air. His arms and legs are splayed. He flies head over heels until is body bounces.

Melinda lands on top of me. I have a hard time getting my next breath. I feel the heat. The entire porch collapses, throwing tin shingles into the air like playing cards. The thick beams of the porch break into toothpicks, adding thousands of porcupine quills that roll out with the blast of searing air. In an instant, the gust reverses itself and sucks back in toward the building.

Shards and splintered boards tinkle and thump all around me. Other than a few small snicks, nothing makes contact with me.

"You okay?" I shout.

Melinda gets to her feet and shakes particles from her hair. "I'm fine, how about you?"

Forgetting that he was the frightening red-eyed demon in my dream, I get up and sprint to the old man. He lays face down in the dirt. I climb over shattered boards and big sheets of corrugated steel roofing. In the uncanny silence, I hear crunching glass. Melinda is running a few steps behind me.

I reach the old man and slide to a stop in front of him. I'm on my knees, carefully shaking him.

A quiet moan escapes.

"You alright," I ask, feeling like a fool. Of course he's not okay. His home just blew apart and he's been tossed like a rag doll across the yard.

He's trying to speak, but I can't understand.

"It's going to get hot once the house starts to burn. We'll have to move you. Do you feel anything broken?"

He desperately tries to communicate, but I can't make out a word. Melinda picks glass and wood chunks off him. I grab a sheet of corrugated steel from the roof and slide it next to him.

"We're going to roll you over. Let me know if anything hurts." I grab his shoulder, slide my hand under and pull.

He moans, but rolls onto his back without much effort. His left forearm flops, obviously broken. I bend one edge of the tin roofing, grab the folded corner and pull. For a big guy, he is surprisingly light. We pull him back to the car.

"My wife," he chokes.

"Oh my gosh, your wife is still inside?"

He mouths the word, "yes".

85

"Where is she?"

He scrunches his wrinkled face and croaks out two hard won words. "Downstairs bedroom." He swallows and forces another few broken utterances. "To the right. . .back door."

Far off, sirens shriek.

Without thinking, I sprint for the back of the house. My long legs come into play. Mr. Stewart, always gangly, Chance tears up the yard, leaps debris, flies to the back door.

What is left of the splintered back door is a single stick of wood with three twisted hinges still screwed to the jamb. Smoke rolls out from the upper part of the opening. I crouch to get under the dark cloud. Hunching, I penetrate the foreboding back porch and sprint through the splintered inner door. The upper half of the kitchen is enveloped in the same thick cloud. I look to my right and see a half-open door. My eyes are stinging. I'm forced to get on my hands and knees. I enter the bedroom yelling, "Hello, is anyone here?"

I search the room, but she is nowhere. Crab-walking back toward the kitchen door, I spot another opening, maybe a bathroom. I'm on my hands and knees gasping for air. I slide across the floor. One dainty white tennis shoe, with leg attached, peeks out from the bathroom doorway. In a hurry to get back outside before the thick smoke ignites into an inferno, I pounce on her foot and yank her into the bedroom. I get a glimpse of her upturned face before the thick smoke drops to eight inches.

I grab both feet and drag her, head bumping, across the floor. I consider I might possibly pull her hip out, but my options are narrowing. My ability to stay in this smoldering tinderbox will soon end. I must move quickly.

Crawling on my belly, I keep my face in the few inches of non-toxic air. I have both her ankles in one hand. I pull myself along with my other. I focus solely on keeping my grip on her. I'm in a drawn-out crawl over a littered floor, toward what I hope is the door. There is nothing to see but heavy black smoke.

Considering the chaos, the house is quiet enough to hear the woman's head clunking as I pull. The sirens get closer. I'm face down. The floor is now less than two inches from my nose. I still feel the eye-blistering smoke. I push my nose into the floor and take what is probably my last breath of air. I close my eyes tightly, and pull myself half to my feet. Still crouching, I tug her body blindly through the bedroom. I use my free hand to grope the wall, in search of an open door.

I don't dare drop even one of her legs for fear I will not have time to find it again. I mindlessly slide along the wall until, thank God, I find a jamb. I want to gulp for air, but I keep my mouth and nose closed. Finally, I put my arm through an opening. The wonderful door is ajar. I hastily drag her into the kitchen. I crash into the table and stumble over a chair.

The heat of a crackling fire is somewhere to my right. Through closed eyes, I sense its brilliance. I'm running out of breath and time. I scramble back to my feet. I rotate to my left and pull the woman across the slippery floor.

I must be a dozen steps away from the back door. I can almost jump and reach safety, but I slip and crash to the floor.

Is this my last fall? Am I not going to get up? Is this the end?

In automatic reaction, knowing I'm going down hard, I release my grip and put one hand out to catch myself, but I'm too late. The full brunt of the fall crushes my side. Something snaps and I gasp. I know not to take a breath. My body does not agree and I suck in a first hint of hot fumes.

I realize I may not get out alive. Maybe this is the end. For the first time in my life, I do a heroic act, and I'm not going to live to tell about it.

I take a half breath before my lungs expel the burning fumes. Choking is imminent. I want to open my eyes and make my runner's legs sprint for the door. I only have a few yards, but it may as well be a mile. I struggle to my feet. Behind closed lids, I see big yellow spots. I have only a few seconds left. I grab at and find an ankle. I get square on my feet and yank, running blind. In my last-ditch effort to rush the door, though I don't know where the door is, I start across the room. I could easily have been turned around in the fall. With little air left, I charge for what I hope is the door. By a miracle, I brush a jamb, see daylight behind my closed lids, and pull dead weight toward the brightness. I sense a coolness and safety. I want to let go and run. I want to breathe and open my eyes.

The dark cloud clears, and it might be okay to take a breath. I start sucking in fresh clear air, but in a surprising gust, an impact of a bus slams my back. I'm lifted off the ground in the midst of a yellow brilliance. I'm still holding on to something, but I can't remember what it is. The heat is intense. The light dazzles. My skin pulls and crinkles through my thin summer shirt. The flame singes the back of my calves. The ground is somewhere below me. It's coming; I just don't know when.

***

I awake face down in a bed, humped high in the center. My face is turned to the right and all I see is pale green walls. Ten minutes of wondering were I am, a wide-faced nurse wearing a light blue mask bends to look through the railing.

"Where am I?" I ask.

"Burn Unit of San Bernardino Medical," says the nurse in a curt, matter-of-fact tone.

I'm trying to think why I would be in a medical unit, but no answers come to me. "What am I doing here?"

"Well, Mr. Stewart Chance," she snips. "Aren't you just the hero of the day?"

"What do you mean?"

"We'll let the doctor fill you in on the details. He should be around in two or three hours." She lifts back up. I hear her scribbling notes on a clipboard, and I watch two sausage legs covered in light blue waddle out of my view. Her squeaky shoes fade up the hall.

Long before the doctor gets around to me, I remember most of what took place. I remember why I'm face down on this bed. I remember pain, especially when I try to move.

Melinda walks in with gauze wrapped around her head, a light blue gown and her own face mask.

"Hey you! I been waiting for you to wake up."

"What happened to your head?"

"Well, nothing exactly, except my hair took a beating. I look kind of odd with an ultra butch haircut."

"Did the old woman survive?"

"Oh sure, she is fine. She has a dislocated hip, but she didn't even suffer any major burns."

"She bumped around on the floor the whole time. I didn't have time to do anything but grab her ankles and drag her."

Melinda smiles. "No one could figure out why she has so many little cuts and bruises on the back of her head, but she's fine."

"I'm glad. How is the old man?"

"He is a little more banged up. Broken arm, cracked ribs, and a bunch of cuts, but he's in good spirits. He and Mrs. Brown are downstairs. You're not going to believe who they are."

"Mr. and Mrs. Brown, I would assume."

"Yes you're right." She smiles. "Does the name ring any bells?"

I shrug and a sharp pain flares up. The sting along my upper ribs reminds me not to shrug again.

"Nicky Brown's parents."

"Are you serious?"

"We had good reason for being in Blythe, after all."

The doctor walks in. He is a fatherly gentleman with silver flags of hair poking out from his baby blue hospital get-up. From his first words, I like the guy.

"Well, how is our hero this evening?" he says.

He carefully opens my gown from the back and even more carefully un-tapes me.

Channeling Biker Bob

"Things look pretty good, but in case of infection, we're going to have to keep you here for a while."

Melinda's eyes widen. "For heaven's sakes, Stewart, I didn't know how badly you got burned."

The doctor chimes in, "His burns look much worse than they are, young lady. Mr. Chance is a lucky man. I won't have to graft any skin. He'll have some scarring, but things will heal just fine."

While he talks, he packs white cream on the burn and checks the two uncomfortable spots on my calves. "Looks like you've become a national hero," he says.

"What?"

Melinda cuts in, "The media got wind of our story."

A new voice leaps into the room. "Oh my God, Stewart!"

"Renee," I say sheepishly.

"Stewart. Oh, Stewart, what has happened to you?"

I see her blue hospital gown first, before she leans down and looks at me. "You look swollen. Are you alright?"

"He'll be fine," says the doctor. "We'll have him up and out of here in no time."

I wonder what happened to Melinda.

Renee pulls up the same chair Melinda was in and sits in front of me. She leans down where I can see her. The doctor quickly repacks my burns and scuttles out of the room.

"Chicken," I say under my breath.

"What have you done?"

"I'm okay, Renee, just a slight mishap."

"Mishap?" She whispers. "You son of a bitch, the whole goddamn world knows what you did. The whole world knows you slept with that. . .that Chambers woman. I swear, Stewart Chance, you can't treat. . ."

Her demands roll on, but as usual, I tune her out and try to murmur in all the right places. I can't believe she came here to rail at me for being with Melinda. As usual, she can't wait to get in my face with her concerns, her issues. Does she even remember I'm in pain here? For the first time, I understand how Renee Lee Chance really operates.

The life-saving squeak of Nurse Cynic's shoes rounds the corner. I pray she is coming in to save me from the pummeling.

"Well, Mr. Chance." I hear her snippy, gruff voice. I sigh with relief when I see her thick blue covered legs.

"Doctor tells me you need rest, right now." She turns to Renee. "Visiting hours are over for the evening, Madam. Mr. Chance needs his medication. He will be sleeping until morning."

I love her sarcastic voice. I love her demanding tone, her unbending directness.

Renee snorts, raises off her chair. "I'm his wife," she says.

"Sorry, doctor's orders."

I hear Renee huff. There is a standoff between my strong-willed wife and my Gestapo nurse. Finally, I hear Renee's high heels leave the room and echo up the hall.

"Thank you," I say.

"Don't thank me," she says. "The doctor ordered her out."

The prick of a needle stabs my upper hip.

"She your wife?" the nurse asks.

"Yes."

"Hell hath no fury like a scorned woman," she says, and her squeaky shoes exit.

I wake again in the middle of the night when a petite nurse checks my burns and gives me another shot.

The next time I awake, dawn is breaking, and a breakfast cart squeals along the hall outside my room.

After the morning hubbub on the ward, I settle down to get back to sleep, but I hear Renee's clicking high heels. I pray it's a visitor for another patient. As the sound gets too close to hope for anything else, Renee walks in. I have no nurse to save me. I'm on my own. I prepare myself for the inevitable, but I can't think of a word to say in my defense. When I see her nylon-stocking legs peek out from a light blue gown, I cringe and close my eyes feigning sleep.

She noisily pulls a chair over in front of my face and sits. I peek out of slit eyes as she crosses her legs. I hear pages of a magazine flipping nervously. She is here to stay.

Oh well, let's face the music. I open my eyes, and try to think of an easy answer to Renee's obvious question. Why was I traveling with Melinda? I feel a familiar sensation, a tingling at the ends of my fingers. The tingle quickly spreads. I think it's Bob.

Next thing I know, Renee slams her magazine and stomps out of my room. What did Bob say to elicit such behavior. Renee has never shown any fits of anger in public before.

Bob knows what he is doing, I just hope he was gentle. On the other hand, from her uncommon reaction, I guess he wasn't.

Pondering the repercussions of Bob's actions, I hear soft footsteps and see Melinda's freckled legs peek out from another blue gown. I can already tell that light blue is a theme in this hospital.

"She looked pretty angry. What did you say?"

"I don't know; Bob took over. I guess he was hard on her."

"I better get out of here and let you and your wife work things out. The doctor says my burns need checking for a while, but I'm getting released today. I think I'll go back to Vegas."

Channeling Biker Bob

Something happens completely out of character for me. Normally, I let any woman do what she wants. This time, however, I surprise even myself.

"Look Melinda, you dragged me on a wild goose chase in search of Nick. Damn it, you have to stay and see it through. Nick is just around the corner. I'm sure his parents know where his is. I'll ask them."

"I asked yesterday," she says. "They don't have a clue."

"That's okay, we'll find him anyway. Give me two or three weeks to get back on my feet and we'll continue our odyssey. My wallet is in the drawer. Take the cash and go get yourself a room in town. I need someone close by who understands what I'm going through. I'll be out of here in no time."

"Stewart, you said Damn it."

"Yes, I guess I did."

"I thought you prided yourself on not cussing."

I look sideways into her eyes. "Oh well, a first time for everything. Will you stay?"

"Because you put it that way, I have no choice. Guess I'm a sucker for a super hero."

"What?"

"The press calls us super heroes. I've already given about twenty interviews. The mob out in the lobby reminds me of a circus. Camera crews and news reporters are swarming the place. If you could look out your window, you would see what I mean."

"How come all the press?"

"All I know is we got national attention. I suspect that Bob had a lot to do with it. I wouldn't put anything past him."

A familiar click of heels echoes from up the hall.

"Renee is coming, and I'm out of here."

"Coward," I yell, as her wonderfully freckled legs disappear.

"Who is that person?" Renee demands as she rounds the corner and steps into my room.

I'm feeling feisty, though I'm lying on my stomach with my crispy backside vulnerable. Not the best position to deal with a woman scorned.

"Melinda," I say.

"You mean that. . .that Chambers woman."

I have not seen anything other than Renee's blue gown as of yet, but I feel hackles rise on the back of her neck.

"What is that bitch doing in here?"

"If you remember, she saved my life. She also got burned in the process. Don't you think she has a right to be on this ward?"

Gosh, I must be feeling my oats. I have never spoken to Renee like this before. It feels better than I imagine.

She sits and looks at me. "Sorry Stewart. I swear I don't know what's gotten into me lately. Guess I'm feeling scared."

Renee says she is sorry. Somebody give me a calendar so I can mark the date. Better yet, get a tattoo artist and ink it into my forearm.

What do I say? I'm groping for a response when my fingertips tingle. As my consciousness slips, Bob takes over. I must not have been gone long, because when I come back, Renee's hand is caressing my swollen face.

Tears stream down her cheeks. "Oh Stewart, I missed you. When you get out of here, won't you please come home?"

What the heck did Bob tell her? She hasn't sobbed over me in years. Getting Renee to show any emotion but anger is a trick I would like to have up my sleeve.

***

The wind cools my hot back; it rushes through my hair and whistles past my ears.

A rumbling noise consumes me, like a distant thunder rolling across an open plain. Unlike before, I'm conscious of my arms stretched out in front of me. My hands grip around rubber. My right hand twists, and a surge of power thunders under me. The roar quickens with the sound of the wind. Beyond my stretched out arms, white dashes blur by, indicating the middle of a two-lane road. My vision stretches out into the darkness. I look down and see a powder-blue tank. In white script lettering painted diagonally across the tank are two words: Blue Wonder.

Its seat is thick and comfortable; the handlebars are a perfect fit for my gangly arms. My feet stretch out on platforms, just right for my long frame. This bike feels like it's made for me.

I'm admiring the fit, feeling the comfort, testing the power in the throttle as I hear a second thunderous roar coming from my right. In my periphery, a sparkle of chrome spokes gains on me. I let off my gas slightly as a slender front wheel pulls up.

A quick glance away from the road reveals a set of large, bright teeth. I smile at Bob and turn back to pay attention to our precarious position on the narrow road.

We roll along in our side-by-side position in Harley bliss for an hour. When Bob indicates for us to turn right, I let off my gas and drop behind him, instinctively giving him, my leader, first position. He gently bleeds off power and kicks his shifter to third. I follow suit as we turn onto another two-lane road. Far off in the distance a single light flickers. If the road is as straight as the one we were just on, I would guess the blaze is again, right in the middle of the pavement.

Channeling Biker Bob

Minutes later, we drive up to a bonfire, sure enough, built atop the white line. I pull in behind Bob and park in choreographed unison. Both bikes lean onto their stands simultaneously. I dismount as if a dancer on stage, knowing everyone is watching.

I hear a short grunt of approval from my audience. They were more entertained when I stumbled and fell.

Bob and I step as close as the heat will allow. Melinda, now with her blond hair and black leathers, sits across the burning logs from me, but I don't acknowledge her. She is with Nick. The circle is quieter than usual; no one talks. One at a time they nod, as I make eye contact with each of the fifteen people. They do so without a word. I return the gesture, while someone gets me a chilled bottle of water.

"So you're a hero?" asks Dick Pallard, the meanest of the lot.

"I'm sure Bob had something to do with this." I look over at Bob for confirmation.

"All I did was make sure you got to the house on time. You ran into the building."

"You saved my folks; I owe you." Nick raises a can in salute.

"You owe me nothing."

He raises his can a second time and smiles.

I'm being honored by men, something I have never before experienced. They see what I did and show their respect. A long silence follows, while the crowd salutes me, each in their own unique biker way. Uncomfortable from their attention, I'm relieved when Bob breaks the silence. "I knew Stewart could do it; he just needed a chance."

A few guffaws come from the men and giggling from the females. Bob puts up one hand and the noise stops. "We're riding down a road few have gone before. We are moving into groundbreaking shit, and Chance is out on the point. I want you all to support him as much as you can."

Bob goes on with more specifics, but I'm caught on one small part of his statement. What does he mean? Why do I go from prospect to point, all in one leap? What is going on?

When he stops talking, the party begins. Over the next hour, one at a time, each man comes over, puts an arm around me or whacks me on my back. Each gives me his version of what the future might bring. From the array of visions, I gather that generations ago a task had begun. Bob's quest is being played out through me. As the evening wears on and more alcohol is consumed, their pride becomes more pronounced.

Melinda, in her sexy black leather and blond hair, walks up and touches my hand. She steps around to face me.

I ask, "You're a hero too. Why aren't you getting attention?"

"Heaven sakes, Stewart, you are the point man, not me."

Her voice has a sexy deepness. I'm so distracted by how she says what she says that I miss her content.

Nick comes from behind her, snakes an arm around her waist, and smooches the back of her neck.

"At least I'm able to be with him here," she says. He pulls her back into the party.

Bob comes up. I have been waiting to get him alone.

"What is this point man stuff?"

His goofy smile drops to a seriousness expression. "What is this point-man shit!" he says.

"Huh?"

"Hell, Chance, if you're going to be a fucking biker, you got to stop talking like a wimp. Start using the lingo. Point-man shit."

Like someone is pulling my tooth, I force out the single word, "shit," and wince.

Bob goes on like nothing out of the ordinary has happened. "I can't tell you right now, because I don't know much. What I will say is you've been chosen as the pivotal person in a shift that will affect our entire culture."

"What the heck does that mean?

"At least you could say hell."

"What the hell does that mean?" I wince as I mouth the word.

"We didn't come to you randomly, Stewart. You've been chosen to fulfill our mission. Everything that has happened to you is no mistake. Saving Nick's parents was a perfect opportunity to deal the first hand in your card game of destiny."

Not knowing much more than I did before, I ask, "What am I supposed to do?"

"Chill out. Nobody knows for sure what's going to happen next. The media is interested in you, which is a boon for what we have in mind. I've got a plan brewing. For now, do all you can to stay away from those news assholes. Later you'll get in front of the camera, but not now."

***

I'm instantly pulled back into hospital reality when an idiot night nurse comes in and flicks on overhead lights.

"Are you okay, Mr. Chance? You talked in your sleep."

"I'll be okay as soon as you turn the damn lights off," I say, surprising myself with an off-color word.

The next thing I remember, it's morning and a small, pallid woman comes in. My first thought is she needs to spend more time in the sun.

Channeling Biker Bob

"Good morning, Mistah Chance," she says, with a milkshake Southern accent. "My name's Penny Pearl, your Physical Therapist."

Her manner doesn't match the smoothness of her voice. She forces me to get out of bed, not exactly what I have in mind for a morning activity.

"Mistah Chance, since you don't have a lot of burning, getting up and moving about should be easy."

"The skin on my back feels too tight for my body. Every time I shift, even slightly, my back splits."

"Well sure. That fire barbecued your backside, and it'll be feeling like it's splitting for a month or so. Let's just get you some exercise. You'll feel better."

When I'm finally standing, Renee walks in and says, "Your swelling has gone down. I swear, I can actually recognize you."

I greet her, then turn my attention back to my tormentor, the Pearl woman. "I want to lie back down now?"

"No, Sir. Doctor ordered me to walk y'all up and down this here hall three times. You take as long as you like, but bet your bottom dollar, we will be walking."

"I thought I was here for nurturing." Penny Pearl smiles and follows close behind with my IV bag. I'm moving so slowly that I take five minutes to get out the door and begin my first trek up the hall. The hall looks a mile long, and I moan with the thought of having to go that far. My few minor burns shouldn't tap my energy so much, but I'm weak as a baby.

Penny Pearl slides a steel-framed walker in front of me and hangs my IV bag high on a connected rack. She forces me to walk into the waist-high structure and grab the handles, reminding me of the handlebars of my mythical Harley, the Blue Wonder. I want to make a sound like an engine and twist the grips of my walker, but no one would understand.

The first few infant steps leave me feeling odd, and disabled, but since a number of other burn patients are also struggling with the same tortured maneuvers, I give it a try.

I take the better part of an hour to walk that hall three times. I have to stop and rest so many times it's like I'm on a cross-town bus. Renee and Penny Pearl are my cheering section. I realize that I'm the least burnt and luckiest of the walking-burned on my ward. I count my blessings while passing my fellow patients. I will have a minor amount of scarring, but only on my back and legs. Many of these poor souls will wear scars on their bodies for the world to see.

We mercifully return to my room, and I finally get to lie back in my bed. While I get into a comfortable position, I wonder how some of the people on the ward are able to lie down at all.

Once I'm in bed and comfortable, Penny Pearl forces me to roll onto my side, bids us farewell, and leaves me with Renee.

I'm not sure what she will say, so I wait while she sits.

"Your doctor says you will get out of here in a few weeks. In three or four months, you'll be able to return to work."

"Three or four months?" I shout. "I have things to do that can't wait three or four months."

NICK BROWN

An hour after my ordeal, Renee sits next to me quietly reading a magazine. I'm draped across the humpback bed, my mind a thousand miles away. From far up the hall, I hear rattling chain and clomping boots. Steel zings every time one of the boots touches the floor. With much effort, stretching parts of my body that don't want to be stretched, I lift slightly and look over my shoulder. Someone in heavy boots is walking toward my room. It's the sound of a biker, but who?

A thick-shouldered man walks in wearing a well-worn chrome chain, a spiked-studded black leather jacket and leather leggings. A profusion of dark curls bursts from under the edge of a leather bib hat pulled tightly onto his head. Although his face is weathered, it's easy to see that he's in his early thirties. With every step, chains and keys add a Christmas jangle to my room. His heavy boots clunk as he steps over to my bed.

"You Stewart Chance?" he demands in a gruff voice.

I flinch.

His scowl transforms slowly, as if it doesn't shift often. His eyes lighten, and a smile cracks his chiseled face. "I'm Nick Brown," he says. "You saved my parents. I've come down from Barstow to personally thank you." He reaches out his black-leather-gloved hand. The finger-tips of his gloves are missing and grease is caked under his fingernails. When I realize he wants to shake, I tentatively slide my right hand out from under the sheet. "Not real hard. My hands got a bit burned, too."

He hesitates a second, then swings his right hand in a gentle arc across my hand. Our fingertips barely make contact.

"I thought you had red hair." I say. "At Bob's gatherings, you have red hair."

"Well, hell, Chance. Haven't you figured it out yet? At Bob's gatherings, everyone looks different."

"Oh."

"My parents mean a lot to me," he says, before an amazing thing happens. The leather clad, hard-Harley-riding son of a gun, breaks down and cries. He doesn't hold his hands up to cover his face. He doesn't try to hide his tears. He simply stands in front of us and lets his dam overflow. He tries a number of times to speak, but beyond a few blubbers he's unable to form a word.

After some moments, he begins a sentence.

"You saved my parents. I'm forever beholden to you." He wipes his nose on the back of his glove. "My people are forever beholden to you, too. Call me if you need anything." He reaches in his breast pocket and pulls out a slightly bent black business card. As he hands the card to me, Penny Pearl rushes in with a big security cop in tow.

With a scowl on her face, she points at Nick and demands, "Get him out of here, now!"

The cop takes one look at Nick and reaches for his radio.

"This man is my guest, Penny." I say. "I'm glad he came. I've been looking for him for a month."

Nick has already spun and faced off with the cop. He is ready for action, but after I speak, he turns back and looks at me. "What?"

"You're not an easy person to find."

Penny Pearl gives his back a hard glare. "We have procedures in this here hospital, Mistah. Y'all just can't walk in here like you own the place. This is a burn unit, which means we have to be careful about infection. You have to sign in at the desk and wear protective clothing before you can come in here."

"Penny Pearl," I say in my most friendly tone. "Can't we get him a gown and face mask so he can stay? I promise to make him sign in when he leaves. He is the son of the people I saved."

It takes her a while, but she finally says, "Well, okay Mistah Chance. Harm's already been done." She looks at Nick and says, "Don't move another inch, and don't touch anything." She turns to the cop. "Call for a gown, face mask hat and extra large booties."

The cop clicks his radio and in a minute an orderly is dressing Nick while Penny Pearl scrubs down every surface Nick touched. Once she is finished, she spins then exits.

I look back at Nick. "As I said, you're a hard one to find."

Channeling Biker Bob

"I don't know why." He says through the mask. "I've been in Barstow for six months. Thought everybody knew where I was." He finishes handing the card to me. On the front of the onyx colored card, in simple gold block letters, I read "One percent of One percent." Under the lettering next to Nick's name is a phone number. I turn the card and read in red print with a yellow background: Cycletherapy.

Renee's eyes widen. My next few words are going to surprise her even more.

"Hey, I recognize your card. You know Bucky and Twiggy?"

Nick smiles. "Good buds, though I haven't seen them in a while. Where'd you meet them?"

"In a restaurant, I can't remember the town.
Bob says you're building a Blue Harley for me."

His face flushes. In a hushed tone he says, "You're the one?"

"Yes. We met a number of times, the last not too many hours ago at the desert party. I rode in with Bob."

"You're our point man?"

"I guess."

I glance at Renee. Her eyes are wide, but she says nothing.

"Now I remember," he says. "Sometimes those dreams are vague. I woke early and took off before dawn. I was determined to get here to visit my parents and to especially thank you. Could it have something to do with the dream? We honored you for saving my parents and being the Point man."

We are all silent for a moment before he says, "I been building your bike this whole time in Barstow. Bob sent me for that express purpose. The bike is a vintage fifty-six panhead. An old cop bike I got at an auction last year. I stripped it and rebuilt every part. Couldn't figure out why I painted the damned thing powder blue until now. I hate blue. I'm waiting for another half-dozen parts, and your bike will be done."

"Can I ask you to do one more thing?"

"Anything you want."

"In a dream, the words Blue Wonder had been scripted across the tank. Get a sheet of paper and a pencil, and I'll draw it. Will you have someone paint the inscription across the tank?"

"I've already had it done. At the time, I couldn't figure out why, but it came to me in one of Bob's dreams. When messages come from Bob, I don't ask too many questions, anymore. I trust he'll take care of any details. When you get out of here, the bike will be ready. Come by and pick it up."

"I don't exactly have any cash right now."

"Shit, Chance, I'd love to give the damn thing to you for saving my parents. My cash flow is tight, though, and I need a stake for my next bike. I'll charge you exactly what I got in the thing."

Nik C. Colyer

He shifts his attention and acknowledges Renee as if he has seen her for the first time. He turns back to me. "You call me when you get out of here."

He spins on his chain-clad boots wrapped in blue booties and thumps his way out of my room. Metal rattles under his gown all the way up the hall.

Once the sound of his jangling stride disappears, Renee asks, "I swear, Stewart, how do you know these kinds of people?" Her tone is a mixture of surprise and disgust.

"I've met guys like Nick. Lucky he is on our side, huh?"

"Stewart Chance, what the hell has gotten into you? Last I remember, you were a computer jockey at Tridine. Now you're one of those silly motorcycle-riding characters."

"Riding Harleys is not such a bad thing. I'll still keep my job, if that's what you're worried about. I know my responsibilities in our marriage."

She crinkles her eyes. "Damn it, Stewart, don't you know the statistics about motorcycles and fatal accidents? Are you thinking of your kids when you take these chances? Ever think maybe you'll leave them orphaned? How could you hang out with people like that?" She's getting real wound up and I'm getting confused.

Consistent with my confusion policy, I don't say a word. When the tongue-lashing ends, she scrunches her chin as if I'm not only going to disappoint her and our daughter, but every woman who has ever tried to dissuade a man from getting a motorcycle.

"You're actually going to get that motorcycle, aren't you?" It's not a question, but a statement of fact, of warning. Tension builds in her. Her volcano is about to erupt. She wants an answer, but I can't give her the right answer.

My smile fades. I'm ready to tell her that if she doesn't want me to have a motorcycle, I won't get one. I'm ready to acquiesce and avoid an inevitable fight. Standing up for my wishes will not be worth the months of suffering I'll have to endure, the set in her jaw that I will have to look at, the accusatory stride in her walk. Standing firm is not worth destroying even the slightest chance of having sex with her.

I'm ready to give in, to tell her I won't get a Harley. I will do anything to keep her happy, but that familiar tingle overtakes me.

Bob's coming through, invading my thoughts and taking possession of my body. This time, however, he does not actually block me out, but simply takes the helm for ten seconds, just long enough for him to say what he has to say. This is the first time I experience his single-minded intensity. It's all at once frightening and exhilarating. His voice reverberates across the room, much deeper than mine.

100

Channeling Biker Bob

I want to stop his words, but I have no control over what he says. "Fuck, yes!" He/I say. "I'm getting that bike as soon as I get out of here, and you can't do a thing about it."

Bob quickly pulls back, leaving me to face the music.

Renee turns an ashen color. "You. . .you. . .you son of a bitch. If you get that. . .that motorcycle, don't come around my house." She stands, turns away in a huff, and stomps through the door.

***

"I don't know what to do, Katherine. I swear Stewart has gone off the deep end."

"Well, yes I have been asking for changes, but hasn't he taken changing a little too far?"

"No, we didn't get a chance to discuss that Chambers bitch. She is chicken feed, compared to this motorcycle. He wants a Harley, and that is much bigger than a little street tramp. The motorcycle is as big as it gets."

"Yes, I know, he is a national hero, but he has no right to go off and do what he wants. He has no right to abandon his family, because he wants to join some silly motorcycle gang. That hero stuff has given him an inflated ego. It pisses me off and I can't stand him any more."

"No, I don't dare tell either of our kids about the motorcycle. I'm have a hard time keeping Mel from idolizing Stewart, as it is."

"No, I refuse to read anything about Stewart. He is just being glorified for something anyone would have done, given half a chance. The press continues to be silly, splashing his picture all over the newspaper."

"Sure, I know he is going through a kind of bullshit mid life crisis. I have been reading about men doing that same kind of crap. It's so stupid.

"I'm worried for Stewart, though. He keeps talking about that Biker Bob character. You must have a psychological name for what is he's going through; delusions of macho, or tough-guy syndrome."

"No, he's too young for mid life crisis, but I swear he's going through something.

"The other day I visited Stewart in the hospital when a burley biker guy bursts into his room. He was the son of the people Stewart rescued. The guy was definitely weird, but I don't know, in a twisted way, I found him sexy."

"I know what you mean. I probably have a base animal attraction, but his stupid overly macho attitude also revolts me."

"I guess you are right. This is what we've been working on all these months. It is kind of familiar that he repels me, and at the same time makes me kind of tingly. I wish I could feel that same tingle toward Stewart. He doesn't turn me on anymore."

"Yes, yes, damn it, but I have a bit more to say about Biker Bob before we go on.

"Nick Brown walks in and thanks Stewart. They talk like they're old pals. The Nick guy tells Stewart that he dreamt about Biker Bob, too. Bob supposedly led Brown to Stewart's room. Now get this, Stewart told that greasy biker that he had been looking for Brown for weeks.

"Like it's common knowledge, they agree that Biker Bob led them to one another."

"At first I thought Stewart was just kind of spooky, but now I swear he's really flipped.

"If I could get him in here, I would. I'm afraid he got burned so bad that his doctor wants to keep him in the hospital for two more weeks. I'll get him in here as soon as I get him home. I hope you can help."

"I know what you mean, it's more than simple mid life crap."

"Okay, okay, I know, I said the word crap. Far be it that I put any words in your mouth."

***

I have been in the hospital for two excruciatingly painful weeks. The doctors and nurses have poked, prodded, and scraped me until I can't stand another attentive person. The hardest part of my stay is Penny Pearl. She demands that I call her by her full name. One would think she would be gentle, kind and attentive, but she is the worst. With jailhouse tactics, she forces me to lap the hall fifteen times during my waking hours.

Renee has not shown her face here since the day she stomped off the ward. She calls every other evening, though, but lately all we do is get into fights.

I never used to argue with her. I guess I'm standing up for myself more, these days. Going through that fire and surviving has tempered me, made me stronger.

Melinda has been my beacon of light in my sea of misery. Without her cheerful eyes, I would be depressed and lonely. Without our endless games of two-handed solitaire, Scrabble, and Yahtzee, I would be extremely bored. She comes in early in the morning and stays until they kick her out at night.

I have grilled the doctor about my release, but he won't commit. "Any day now," is all I get.

Although I can't see the burns on my back, yesterday while they changed the dressing, I glanced at my calves and almost threw up. My

Channeling Biker Bob

doctor says they don't look bad, but in my limited experience, I have never seen worse.

Two days ago, they moved me to the less critical ward. Melinda and I have played cards for hours. I'm thoroughly bored.

We force some chuckles while trying to outmaneuver each other. Our next hand of cards is almost laid out. I catch Melinda's glance. She makes a face as a familiar clack of distant high heels rolls, like a jack-hammer, from far up the hall. I recognize the purposeful stride. I'm able to pick that sound out in any crowd: click, click, slight pause, click click. The sound gets louder as Renee gets closer. A terrorized look flashes into Melinda's eyes. She quickly pushes her chair back, ready to bolt from my room before the marching heels get too close.

"Please stay," I ask.

She nervously looks at the door, then back at me. She pulls her chair back up and continues to deal me a hand both of us know we will never finish.

Renee turns into the doorway and stops short when she sees Melinda. Renee glares at her and pirouettes in an automatic reaction, ready to leave.

"Hey, Mel," I shout. My son steps from behind his mom.

"Hey, dad."

"Come on in here. I haven't seen you in a long time. What the heck you been up to?" I look directly at him as he takes five steps toward my bed. The two women are sizing each other up. I sense hackles on Renee's neck.

She turns and grabs Mel's arm, "We're getting out of here."

For years, Mel was a mama's boy, which I feared would be a problem when he got older. To my delight, once puberty set in, he has developed a rebellious streak a mile wide.

He pulls his arm free of Renee and says, "I'm staying." He has never been much for words, but every word he says counts.

"I swear," Renee says. "I'll be in the waiting room."

I listen to spike heels hammering their way up the hall as I call him over. "Hey kid, what have you been up to?"

"Oh, going to school, you know, all the boring stuff." He steps closer, but not close enough that I can reach out and touch him. Heaven forbid I show any signs of affection, especially in public.

"Did you do the stuff the papers say?" he asks.

"I'm not sure. I haven't read any papers."

"I mean about the fire. Did you save those two old people?"

"Melinda and I did." I motion toward her. "This is my son, Mel Chance. Mel, meet Melinda." They tentatively greet.

103

"Melinda saved my life when the building blew the second time. She dragged me out of the fire and watered me down. If it wasn't for her, I'd be burnt toast."

"Thanks for saving my dad." He chokes his words.

"He's worth saving."

"Yeah."

"The two of you have a lot of catching up. I'll wait outside."

After Melinda leaves, Mel, in his unique bluntness, asks directly, "You coming home after you get out of here?"

Heck, I don't know what to say to the poor kid. Maybe he has a different view of his dear old dad; a spark of admiration. Mel has never even given me the time of day, well, at least not since puberty kicked in. Now he wants me to come home?

"I don't know, Mel, your mom's mad at me for traipsing off like I did. I guess she will have to decide. I guess you're pretty angry too, huh?"

"First I was, but I don't know anymore. I wish I could take off like you. Mom hasn't been happy since you've been gone. She's kind of, you know, extra moody."

"Boy you got that right."

I want to explain. I want him to understand what I have been going through. He should know what has been going on, so I tell a long story that involves Bob and my search for the blue Harley. I also tell him the truth concerning Melinda, leaving out the sex part, of course. I explain why Bob put us together. I tie in Nick Brown and how the fire connects everything.

When I get to the part about the Harley, his eyes perk. "You going to get a motorcycle?"

"Not just any motorcycle, son, a Harley. I don't know how your mom is going to take it, but I've wanted a bike all my life."

"Cool! You'll give me a ride?"

***

Ten more days pass in card-playing hell.

Melinda comes in the night before I'll be released and, not until she starts speaking, do I realize this is her last visit, maybe the last time we will see one another.

"I saw Bob last night," she says. "All I know is he says my business with you is over, and I should go back to Vegas."

Nothing I say will dissuade her. In such a short time, probably because of the experiences we share, she has become a part of me. With tears in both of our eyes, she plants a longing kiss on my lips, hugs me as well as she can, considering the circumstances, turns, and walks out of my life.

104

Channeling Biker Bob

In the morning Renee comes in and signs me out of the hospital. Penny Pearl pushes me through the front doors and up to the car. She gives me a hardy handshake. "I wish you well, Mistah Chance."

"Thank you, Penny Pearl, for putting up with me."

"It's my job, Mistah Chance. The goal of my job is to get you out that door. I believe I've accomplished my task."

"Yes, but lately I have been a bit of a pain."

"In my experience, everyone is a pain."

"Thanks for taking such good care of me."

"Good luck, Mistah Chance."

She helps me lie face down on the back seat of the car, the only possible position, considering my healing wounds. I'm lying, staring at the carpet, when three reporters race up.

"Mr. Chance, will you continue your search with Chambers?"

"What I plan to do is none of your business."

Renee tucks in the last of my long coat and slams the door much harder than necessary. The reporter shoots questions at her as she rounds the backside of the car. A camera pans in the windshield, Renee starts the car and races away.

The oppressive silence in the car far outweighs the reporters' stupid questions. Five Arctic-cold, unyielding minutes pass before I venture forth and ask about her silence.

"Are you going to continue your silly search with that woman?"

"No." I say, omitting the fact that Melinda decided to go back to Vegas. "My adventure with Melinda is over." Instinct tells me I'll be better off if I act like I made the choice.

"Are you going to see her anymore?"

"No!"

I lift myself and look over the seat into the rear view mirror. She still doesn't smile, but our pea-soup tension has thinned. I've satisfied her for the moment. She turns on the radio. Soothing classical music blankets the noise of the rental car. I'm glad she didn't ask if I still planned to get the Harley.

Forty-five minutes across a bustling city and we are at the airport. An hour later, we descend below the clouds into Sacramento metro. Within the next hour, we have passed through the main part of the city and climb the long slow grade into the hills. It's a relief to see familiar landmarks.

I'm exhausted by the time Renee pulls into our driveway. A computer-generated banner hangs diagonally across our front door that reads, 'Way to go, Maxi-balls!' It looks suspiciously like my son's handiwork. Renee rips the paper down and wads it.

We walk in our front door and find a small welcome-home party. Three of our neighbors, the postman, and the Feltzes, our friends from

105

Placerville, are waiting. I'm cast into the middle of hoopla as everyone helps me get situated.

My daughter, Sheila, bless her heart, has made a tray of cheese and crackers. Chairs are pulled around me. Funny stories are passed around, and I laugh in all the right places. I agree at all the right moments, but I'm tired and want to rest. No one notices that the party goes on with memories of good times and tired old jokes, the last vestiges of a coherent crowd trying desperately to have a conversation. They have an all-around festive hour. No one gets near the subject of either Melinda or my search for the motorcycle.

A grueling ninety-three minutes, three trays of goodies, and friendly, but cautious, camaraderie goes by. The party dies of its own inability to sustain itself at a time when honest, straightforward conversation is needed. Once everyone leaves, Renee leads me into the spare bedroom and tends to my dressings more tenderly than I was ever treated at the hospital, and more tenderly than she has ever treated me. It feels good to have her rub on the white goo and re-pack my burns. When the final layer of gauze is in place, she helps me back into the most uncomfortable part of this whole business. I have to wear a special expando shirt every day for the next six months. It looks like tights bicycle riders wear, but much tighter. It's so tight I'm hardly able to move, barely can breathe, especially because every breath cracks another of thousands of those healing potato chips on my back. My doctor says the suit will keep my scars from rippling. The thing is hot and uncomfortable, but he has shown me pictures of burn scars that hadn't been treated. No matter how uncomfortable, I'm wearing the expando top and Ace bandages on my calves.

***

"I don't know, Katherine, though he is weak as a kitten, something inside him is stronger."

"I guess you're right, he is a little scary. My wimp of a husband has come home with a cockiness I don't understand. Something happened in that fire, because he acts different."

"No, damn it, I don't like the difference. He's bothersome now. He demands things."

"You want an example? That's easy. The other day, he asked for a sandwich. I had been taking care of the laundry, so I guess I snapped at him. Instead of backing down and getting his own sandwich, now get this; he asked me what was going on. What's it been twenty years, and he has never once asked about me. I about fell over."

"No, I didn't tell him. It pissed me off, because he pressured me. We got into a big fight, and that wasn't the only fight, either. We've been in more fights since he's come home, than we've had in eighteen years."

"What do you mean 'good?' It's not good at all. I yelled at him, and he yelled at me. After almost an hour, I broke down and cried. It was the only thing that stopped the argument."

"I guess you're right, I have been asking for Stewart to stand up for himself and stop being a mouse, but I didn't mean in an ugly, ill-mannered way. If he can't control his anger, I don't want him to change. I would rather have my old Stewart. Even worse, I know that illusionary Biker Bob guy is behind all of this."

"He claims that Bob comes to him all the time. Stewart probably has a personality disorder, and I'm trying to adjust, but scary things have been happening. Stewart has been saying some pretty crass things to me, especially when we argue. I'm talking about a God-fearing guy who not once in his whole adult life used a cuss word. I swear, last week he slung a series of cuss words that would make a sailor blush."

"What do you mean, nothing to worry about? I'm very worried. What if he starts cussing in public? How will it look?"

"Yes, the network people called twice last week. Can you believe it? They want him to appear on Murry Podich. I hope this celebrity crap doesn't go to his head, because he's just a little computer nerd."

Chapter 5

HAWG HEAVEN

I'm sitting in my living room late on a sunny morning. I'm having a hard time staying with the plot of a questionably written mystery novel. I'm in my pre-noon gloom. Too many hours before my kids get home from school and too much time on my hands.

I have been sitting at home four long, cold months, and I'm going out of my mind. I want to go outside to the garden, but my patch has been tilled, furrowed, and planted. Unless I want to go pull weeds with tweezers, I have nothing to do except wait for the seeds to pop their little heads above ground.

I stroll out to the porch on an unusually warm spring day. My stretchy expando top and bandaged legs incessantly itch from the heat. I make a comfortable spot on the porch swing, settling into watching an occasional passing car. I bide my time, whiling away boring hours.

I wonder how Melinda is doing, and what Nick is up to. My bike must be ready and waiting. A dozen times in the last four months of endless recuperation, I've met Bob in my dreams and we've ridden together over miles of backcountry roads. I'm reminiscing about fantasy rides when I hear the distinct rumble of a Harley downshifting at Peterson's corner. "The bike is coming," I say aloud as I perk up. The sound gets louder until the rpm's bleed off and the engine slows. From what I know of our neighborhood, with just the sound of an approaching Harley, phones are off hooks and fingers poised to dial 911.

Channeling Biker Bob

The driver finds first gear as I stand. The engine lumps into an idle and I step off my porch as the machine comes around the tall hedge at the front of our property. The color of the big bike is desert-sky blue. Long leather tassels hang from the ends on each side of bullhorn handlebars. The chrome spokes sparkle.

Holy schmolly, it's Nick. He has come all the way from the desert to deliver my Harley. My jaw hangs as he unfurls the kickstand in the grand tradition of his biker group. He leans the bike over when the engine comes to a full stop. Nick steps off the bike so smoothly that I'm afraid I may be dreaming, after all.

He takes three strides and enters the shade of my tree. He holds out his hand, slapping my outstretched fingertips.

"Hey, Chance, how you doing?" He turns and we both stare at the gleaming blue Harley. Like in my dream, the words Blue Wonder are scripted diagonally across the gas tank.

"What do you think?" he says. "Ain't it a beauty?"

Except for a momentary glance at Nick, I can't keep my attention off of the blue Harley. It is an exact duplicate of my dream bike, even to the chrome ring around the speedometer.

"Finished this baby four months ago, and it's been sitting waiting for you. I decided to go for a final long distance run. Figured I'd deliver it to you at the same time."

Finally, words escape from my lips. High-pitched squeaky words, but I manage to speak. "For me?"

"This is the bike you wanted?"

My head bobs as I walk over. Reaching down, I stroke one of the small leather tassels hanging from the handlebars. I stroke the polished chrome handlebars themselves and run a finger around the speedometer ring.

"Hell, man, you might as well sit on it. I'll take you out and show you its quirks later, but for now, see how she feels."

Long-held tears of expectation, tears of joy, also tears of forgotten disappointment, well up in my eyes. I look away so Nick can't see as I step over the wide seat, grab the handlebar grips, and pull the bike off its kickstand then sit.

"Pull the clutch in, Chance, and hit the starter."

I follow his instructions and the engine instantly comes to life. With the idling engine rumbling under me, I give the throttle a rev for effect and turn the key off.

"Let's go inside and take care of your paperwork, so you can take it for a putt," he says.

I lean the bike back onto its stand and dismount.

"I wasn't exactly prepared for you to show up here today. I don't have any money transferred from my savings, but I can write you a check dated for tomorrow?"

Nick grimaces. "Look here, Chance, nothing to do with me trusting you or not, but I'd prefer cash. I got stuff doing with the IRS. If I put a check in my bank, they'll snatch it pronto."

"I don't have that kind of cash lying around. I'll have to draw it out of my bank in Sacramento."

"Hey, that's okay. I brought an extra helmet so we can ride together. On our way, I'll show you the finer points of your bike."

"Let's go," I say, hoping I have enough money in my savings.

"Let's sign over all the papers, first."

When we finish, I get sunglasses, and we go out to the bike.

After instructions about the choke and checking the oil levels, he finally says, "Okay, let's go."

I stand back to let him start the bike.

"No, Chance. You're driving me into Sacramento."

"I've never driven a Harley before."

He smiles. "No better time to learn than now."

I mount my bike and start my engine. I'm in a dream. Following Nick's instructions on shifting and weight distribution, I turn the bike around, and he climbs on the back. As I pull out of the driveway, I almost lay my new bike down in the dirt. After a last-ditch save, I find myself out on the road making a unsteady left turn. Once on straight pavement, I twist my throttle, and my machine responds like a jackrabbit. When I reach third gear, we're traveling sixty, and I let off the throttle to shift into high. The rumble of the engine softens, and we float along in my lifelong dream, a longing fulfilled. I'm in hawg heaven.

Although I make endless mistakes, Nick doesn't say a word. By the time we start down the hill toward Sacramento, I have a better feel for driving. I shift smoother and feel a little more confident about getting to my bank without crashing.

With the real wind in my hair and the sun on my shoulders, life is just beginning.

Pulling into my bank parking lot, I again nearly dump the machine, but by the thinnest margin, I manage to keep six hundred pounds of metal and rubber upright. Thankfully, my passenger says nothing. After I park, my entire body continues to vibrate. On wobbly legs, I lead Nick into the bank.

While scribbling in a date and signing the withdrawal slip, I ask, "How much do you want?"

"Hey, man, you saved my folks. They're important to me, and I'm forever in your debt. If I was a rich man, I'd give you the bike for nothing, but all I can do is the next best thing. Like I said in the hospital, I'll

110

sell the bike to you for exactly what I got into it. My labor will be your reward for saving my folks. Thirty-nine hundred is what I have invested, and that's all I want. Your money will stake me for the next one."

I write a withdrawal slip for forty-five hundred, a quarter of my savings. We walk up to the teller together. After checking my account and my identification, the teller counts forty-five one hundred-dollar bills over to me. I thank her and count forty-five hundred dollars over to Nick at the counter. He stops me at thirty-nine and explains that he would be insulted if I try to give him a penny more. He means it, so I put the remainder in my pocket.

He splits the cash into two wads and stuffs them into each of his front pockets.

We spend the next two hours standing in line at the Department of Motor Vehicles. At 5:30, we get back on my bike and drive over to my favorite restaurant, where I treat him to a celebratory dinner.

After dinner, I drive Nick to the airport. Once we say our good-byes, I'm free to do what I like. I want to ride for the next ten hours, maybe the rest of the night, except for one little glitch. My dressing change is three hours overdue and my itch is getting worse. I could go to an emergency room to get changed, but the only realistic place is home, where Renee or one of my kids can help. I want to ignore the irritation and ride all night, but past experience tells me that the itching will just get more insistent.

I'm sure Renee will flip out when she sees my new bike. An argument is a certainty. I would like to have time alone before I face another barrage. On the other hand, Renee has been acting different since I got out of the hospital. I'm hoping her deference toward my healing will help in our bike-or-no-bike debate. She is a headstrong woman at the best of times, and this will not be one of her best of times.

Many thoughts go through my mind as I roll toward home on my dream machine.

A hour and a half later, wind-blown, sunburned, and buzzing with engine vibration, I turn into my driveway and pull around, facing the bike toward the road, a last-minute safety position, in case I have to make a quick getaway.

By the time I turn the bike off and unfurl the kickstand, Mel is standing next to me.

I'm pulling my helmet off as he says, "Hey, dad, where'd you get the cool motorcycle?"

I'm ready to tell him, when I notice Renee on the porch in her familiar, arms-folded, toe-tapping stance.

"I can't talk right now, Son."

My dismount is flawless, but no one in present company can appreciate it.

"Hi, Renee." I'm trying to sound self-assured, but I hear that little catch to my voice when I say her name. It is a slight hesitation that most would not notice, but I'm sure she notices, and she knows what my minute hic-cup means.

Without saying a word, she turns, stomps across the porch, and disappears into the house.

Once she goes inside, Mel repeats his question. "Hey dad, where'd you get the bike?"

"Bought it this morning, son. What do you think?"

"It's very cool. Take me for a ride?"

"I will, but not until I'm more used to riding. It's a pretty big bike, and I'm still awkward."

"When?" he asks.

I ignore his question and walk toward the house pulling off my wonderfully bug-stained shirt.

"Can I sit on it?" Mel asks.

I'm already focusing on the storm brewing in the house and answer with a distracted, "Sure."

Renee has disappeared, I assume upstairs, but Sheila sits in the living room watching TV.

"Will you change my dressing?"

Her eyes make a momentary flicker from the TV. "Okay, Dad, but give me a few minutes till the commercial."

In the bathroom, I begin an agonizing process of unraveling myself from my bindings. This part I'll do myself. The part I can't do is apply the cream and re-bandage. Except for the constant itching, the relief of being free of bandages feels good. I turn to look at my back in the mirror and see rippled flesh, with excruciatingly new pink skin covering the two patches, but it doesn't look nearly as bad as photos I saw in the hospital. A more pinkish skin around the main burn area is healing well, but the two patches look inflamed.

Sheila comes in and helps me apply the cream, then hurriedly wraps me without saying more than ten words. Her rushed exit leaves me reconnecting the ends of bandages; difficult, but not impossible. Do I expect more from a fifteen-year-old intent on getting back to her program before the commercial ends?

From many years of experience, I have learned to leave Renee alone until she calms. She needs time to digest the newest member of our family. She is pissed; the only question is how pissed. The longer her silent treatment lasts, the angrier she is.

I'm preparing to sleep downstairs. I have spent most of the last four months recovering in the spare bedroom, anyway. I'm also preparing to weather the Renee-silence storm, however long it lasts. Whatever happens, I can always jump on my bike and go for a ride. I have an escape from the hurricane destined to roar through our house.

Knowing she has cordoned off the entire upper level with her silence, I don't even attempt an exploratory foray upstairs.

I sit in the living room watching the eleven o'clock news. The kids have long since gone to bed and are surely asleep, when Renee startles me. She steps across the room in front of me, calmly turns off the TV, and sits as far away from me as possible.

Only three hours, and she has broken her silence. I try to give her my friendliest smile.

"Katherine suggests I let you know exactly how I feel, instead of holding my anger in," she says in a sing-song, I'm-doing-what's-right, holier-than-holy manner.

She scowls and begins a careful dissertation on the dangers of motorcycles. I've heard this particular monologue once, in the early months of our relationship, when she first got pregnant. She recited her tale again two years ago, when Mel wanted a little dirt bike. Her last discussion came in the hospital last winter.

My face has not changed expression. I have not interrupted by trying to defend myself. Kathrine taught us the technique last year, and now is the perfect time to use it. She talks for five minutes. Although I have heard everything she has said before, I listen.

When she seems finished, I wait for thirty seconds to make sure, before I go into the second part of Katherine's communication technique: reflective listening.

I carefully step back through a minefield of Renee's monologue, reflecting her every point, making sure she knows I understand. At each juncture, I pause and wait for her agreement that signals that I have, in fact, understood her statement. If I don't understand, she comes in to correct me. When I reach the end of my reflective listening part, I pause and wait for her final consent. When she gives her agreement, I have the floor while she is supposed to sit quietly and listen.

"When we met, I wanted a motorcycle, but having a family came first, and I put my dream aside."

"Yes, but our fam--," she interrupts.

"No, Renee, it's my turn to talk, your turn to listen." I surprise myself at the intensity with which I say it.

After a moment, I continue, "as I said, our family came first and I put my dream aside. Our family has grown now and--"

"Our family isn't g--"

"Shut up!" I scream at her. I have never screamed at Renee. Inside, Bob cheers me on. Something about running through that blaze and making it, gives me an inner strength.

Her face darkens, but she shuts up.

"You know owning a bike has been my dream for more than twenty years. I gave up my dream eighteen years ago, when you got pregnant. I didn't mind, but now my family doesn't need me in the same way it once did, and now is the time for me to live out my dream."

She is ready to interrupt, and I jump to my feet. "Don't do it," I growl. "It's my turn to talk and that means you shut up." Her mouth opens, but she doesn't say a word.

I sit. "Anyway, this bike is my dream. The bike stays, and that's all I have to say."

I watch her mouth open and close as if she is talking, but no sound comes out. I feel good. Not once in eighteen years have I said such a statement of finality, a statement that leaves no room for discussion. A big part of me feels the unfairness of my statement, but Bob is in the background trying to stomp that feeling into the carpet. He cheers my firm stand. I want to jump and whoop for joy, but Renee is still sitting with her mouth twitching.

She leaps from her chair so fast I'm sure she's attacking. "The hell with you, Stewart Chance," she says and storms off, disappearing upstairs again.

***

"Katherine, thanks for squeezing me into your busy schedule. I swear I won't take but a few minutes."

"The Biker Bob fantasy has gone too far."

"Yes, yes, you have said he might be going through a midlife crises. Sure he may have a split in his personality, but his last move takes the cake. Yesterday he went out and bought a motorcycle, a Harley-Davidson no less.

"Damn it, I don't know what to say to him, anymore. Last night, though he is still bandaged, he rode the bike into Sacramento and didn't get home until after nine."

"Sure, he has been healing, but if he can ride a motorcycle all day, I think he could help around our house. I swear, Katherine, I can't keep the guy in line."

"You're damned right, I'm mad, I'm fuming. What should I do? I can't control him any more, and I'm scared. That's why I needed this unscheduled session."

"What am I afraid of? Since that other woman came on the scene, I'm scared he'll leave. I'm also frightened he'll turn into an old greasy biker, who rides Harley-Davidsons."

Channeling Biker Bob

"I guess your right, he is a bit more desirable in his new role, but that is no reason for him to go off the deep end. I have been with Stewart too long to have him change overnight."

"Emerging maleness? Damn it, I call what he is more like emerging madness, and I'll fight him every way I can. Why would you want me to support him in this. . .this infantilism?"

***

This is my first day at work in six months. My back is healed, so I don't need the bandages, but the itching drives me crazy.

Last month, after leasing a small cabin five miles north of town, I rented a trailer, towed my personal possessions and the Harley to Barstow.

My first day at the job and Steve Sinder knocks then steps into my office. "How you doing Mr. Chance?"

"Stewart. Call me Stewart."

"You raised quite a ruckus when you saved that old couple.

"The newspaper people lined up at our front door within hours of your accident. The next day, TV crews and radio personalities rang our phone off the hook. They know you're back, so I'm sure you'll be fielding calls from the network guys soon."

"Those people never give up. They have been trying to contact me for months, but I'm not interested."

"They don't want to let it go. You're going to have to talk to them sooner or later."

"Later would be better."

He smiles and catches me up on inner office business.

My secretary, Sylvia, buzzes me.

"I've got Martin Vander of BCS news on the line, Mr. Chance. He wants to make you an offer."

"Stewart. Call me Stewart. What kind of offer?"

"I don't know Sir. He mentioned an offer."

"Please don't call me Sir. I hate that kind of nonsense. Find out what he has in mind and get back to me."

"Yes, si. . .Stewart."

My line goes dead and I turn to Steve. "The circus has begun."

"I don't think they're going to leave you alone."

My buzzer goes off again, and I push the intercom button.

"Mr. Chanc. . .I mean Stewart, Mr. Vander is on the line and wants to offer you twenty thousand dollars for a TV interview."

My jaw drops. "Take his number and tell him I'll get back."

I release the button. "What'll I do now?" I say, not to Steve, but to the universe.

"Hell, twenty grand for a simple little interview ain't chicken feed. I'd jump at that kind of money in a second."

"I can't go in front of a TV camera. I freeze when a video camera is on at home."

Steve stands. "I got to get back to work, but if I were you, I'd go for the twenty g's. Who cares if you freeze up? For that kind of money, you could buy a pretty nice car or put a down payment on a house." He turns to go, hesitates, then turns back. "A guy could even buy a Harley and have change for a trip."

He disappears through the door. I smile, knowing why I like him. Of course, he is a Harley rider! Well, at least, a want-to-be Harley rider, and that's good enough for me.

By noon, Sylvia has fielded calls from the big three TV networks, seven regional stations, and five major radio personalities. Each has an offer for exclusive rights to my story. Why am I still hot news? Bob must be behind this.

By afternoon, Vander has called three times, upping his twenty thousand each time. He finally offers an added incentive through Sylvia. "I can put him on Daniel Leatherman's late night talk show."

I can't think of a worse fate.

The fourth time Vander calls, while I'm trying to figure out how to organize the mess Layton left behind, Sylvia clicks through. "Mr. Vander is on the line and he's insistent. He offered me a hundred dollars if I could patch him through to you personally. His offer has nothing to do with work, but I could sure use the money. Won't you speak to him?"

She presents herself so sweetly that I automatically pick up my phone. "Mr. Vander." I'm ready to tell him to leave me alone, that I don't want anything to do with news media. I'm ready to lay into him about bothering people, but a familiar tingling sensation begins at the tips of my fingers and quickly moves toward the center of my body. I want to slam the phone, but Bob has already gained control, and the receiver remains against my ear. I'm powerless to stop the coming event. I'm a passenger in my own body and someone else is driving.

"Look here, Vander," Bob says. "If you're interested in Stewart's story, I suggest you stop pussy-footing around and make the real offer you called to make. Leatherman is good, but if we're going to do this, I suggest we do a tour of all of the talk shows.

"Who is this?"

"Just call me Bob. You might say I'm Stewart's agent."

"If your client is willing to sign a binding agreement with my company for all rights to his story, including movie and book rights, I have been authorized to offer him seventy-five thousand."

"Make it a hundred, and we split book and movie rights."

Channeling Biker Bob

"I'll have to check with my superiors. I'll call on you tomorrow to work out the details?"

"Stewart looks forward to seeing you. I'll give you to Sylvia to figure out a time."

As the phone touches the receiver, Bob disappears. I'm left with a calm body colliding with my scattered and frightened mind.

I click the intercom and tell Sylvia to hold all incoming calls. To steady myself, I dive back into the job of trying to figure out what Layton left behind. The day quickly comes to an end, and I drive back to my new cabin.

With the remainders of a sandwich in my mouth, I turn the key and push the starter button, feeling my thunderous engine come to life. After a warm up, I shove the rickety garage door open and jump back on my blue machine. I push my toe on the shift lever and hear a familiar and satisfying clank as the transmission snaps into first. Letting the clutch out, I feel a soothing raw power between my legs. I slowly pull the bike past my little house and down the gravel road.

Out on the highway, I twist the throttle and the machine moves. The wind flies past my ears. The desert sky is huge and I feel free. With screaming whoops of joy, I ride until after dark.

At ten o'clock, I turn off the highway and drive back up the gravel road to my house. Satiated with the wildness of riding, I pull into the garage feeling exhausted.

***

Unlike when I first started having my dreams, and found myself at parties of drunken bikers and their women, now I sit in somber circles of men, talking about serious personal issues. Most times, like tonight, our meeting is held in the desert.

I have gotten used to listening and speaking. Tonight I talk about my new job and how good it is to be back at work. I also speak about missing my wife, my children and my home. As real as it seems, I'm in a dream. I'm safe knowing whatever I say will not go outside this closed circle of men. I feel secure knowing that I'm in a group of men. Not that I don't like women, but since I have been in these men-only meetings, I realize when women are around, men act different.

After everyone has finished saying their piece, Bob looks over at me. "What are you going to do with these TV dicks, Chance? You going to go through with being on Murry Podich and Leatherman, or not?"

I'm not prepared for Bob to single me out. I stammer while trying to think of an answer. With nothing solid to say, I eventually respond with a wishy-washy, "I don't know. What do you think I should do?"

117

Bob stands, towers over me, lifts his arms and spouts off like a Bible thumping preacher. "The fifth century philosopher Atnov said; 'there is a moment in every man's life when he must stand and be counted. If at that moment he does not, he will be crushed under the tyranny of his own impotence.'"

He shifts his stretched right arm and points directly at me. Now is your moment Chance. Take it or throw your life out for fish bait.

I expect the men to laugh. Although these are the same men who jeer and shout into the night, this evening they are a much more serious bunch. I look around and find somber faces.

"What do you have in mind for me on TV?"

Bob looks at me slyly. I have gotten used to his coyote grin. Whenever he sports his look, I'm in for a surprise.

"Like I said some months back," he says, "you're our point man. You've been chosen to go out and give what we're doing to other men. The TV thing is perfect."

"I never did understand how I got chosen," I whine. Whenever I hear I have been chosen, I get angry. Anger is not an emotion I express too often; whining is my normal response. "I never wanted a front man position. Who picked me, anyway?"

"You are the oracle." Bob says.

"What the fuck is an oracle?"

Bob's coyote grin widens and he bursts into laughter. The other men are snorting and guffawing.

"What?" I shout, as the roar quiets.

Tears rolling down his face, Bob says. "You said fuck."

"I what?"

"You said fuck!"

"So?"

"You haven't said fuck since you were a kid."

"How do you know?"

"Accept that I know, Stewart. You've said your first fuck in thirty years. I thought your nice-guy act would never crumble."

"What do you mean by nice-guy act?"

"You're always nice, even when you don't want to be."

"I mostly want to be nice."

"I don't think so. You have been trained."

My face must have dropped, because he says, "don't get all worried, Chance. All of us have been trained. As boys, we learned to roughhouse with other boys. We cussed, spit, and squished frogs just to see what would happen."

"I never did that."

"Whatever."

"Well, I didn't."

118

Channeling Biker Bob

Bob gives me an all knowing smile then goes on. "You probably didn't notice, but during those times not many girls hung around. The girls we all called tomboys also liked to roughhouse and squish frogs."

"I never--"

"Don't deny anything; remember I know your past. Don't feel alone, either. It happened to most of us. By the time we were in our teens and we wanted girls around, things changed. None of us noticed the change, but stepping on frogs and pulling wings off flies were big no-no's with most girls. By the time we got interested in girls, we learned to keep guy activity among guys."

He's right as usual, but I'm not saying anymore.

"At sixteen you met Susan. Being a normal teen, you wanted to get closer to her than you had ever been to a girl before. With Susan, as with most women, you had to abide by her unspoken rules to stay on her good side."

"It wasn't her fault," I say.

"These facts don't make women wrong, it's just one of many differences between men and women.

"Unspoken rules include no squishing frogs, no farting contests, no spitting, and no cussing. The list is endless."

His words hit me. As usual, Bob is right. Women I've known have unspoken rules.

"Don't feel bad, Chance; we still do it. Hell, man, the only way to get next to most women is to abide by their rules. At nineteen, sex was all we had on our minds. Whatever we could do to get sex, we did it, right?"

I hear a chorus of grunts. I look up from my embarrassment to see every man agreeing.

"Oh shit," I say. "I thought I was the only one."

"You're not. We all did it. Even now, many of us still participate in the nice-guy syndrome."

"The problem occurs when we adjust our basic male behavior to be, and I love using one of your computer terms, user-friendly. We became so friendly, we forgot who we really were. We forgot how much we liked squished frogs."

"I never liked squished frogs."

"Of course not," he says. "I'm using frogs as a metaphor.

"Anyway, because we began our relationships with the opposite sex by giving up our inherent male instincts to squish frogs, it stands to reason we were willing to give up other parts of ourselves, for the good of the relationship, that is."

"What you're saying is men give up their basic maleness to be with women when they're young, then forget how to be men when they get older. Your version seems awfully one sided."

"I'm not saying women don't give up a whole hell of a lot for men, too, but for right now I'm concentrating on men and more specifically you. Differences being what they are, I'm amazed that relationships hold together at all. If everyone gives up their basic selves for the good of the relationship, no wonder we are a bunch of zombies."

He takes a drink from a bottle of orange juice and gives me one of his toothy grins. "Cussing is one of the first things most men give up for women. For you to start cussing around us is a sign that you're feeling safe enough to reintroduce your primary maleness." He points at my chest. "User-friendly Stewart Chance, meet fucking Stewart Chance."

***

The morning sun slips over a flat horizon and in my window.

I'm considering Bob's statement, and realize, as usual, he never answered my question concerning the oracle. He is a sly one. I make a mental note to ask again next time I see him.

After showering and getting dressed, I have a strong urge to get on my bike and ride to work. I unlock the garage side door and gaze at the blue machine sitting next to my old Chevy. I walk over and pat the seat of the Harley. "I'll be back."

The drive to work is broken by my usual stop at a cafe for breakfast. I walk out burping cheap cooking oil mixed with whispery coffee.

At the office, Sylvia hands me a copy of my itinerary. I scan the single page and find Martin Vander's name penciled in at one-thirty. Out of a whole day of meetings with different company managers, Vander's meeting leaves me the most reluctant.

Steve Sinder pops his head in the door. "Want to have lunch?"

"You're on. How about Bill's Hof-Brau?"

He closes his giant fist, puts a thumb in the air, then quickly closes my door as he leaves.

Some of the people who come through my door are interesting, but most are entrenched bean-counter-lard-butts, individuals who drag a company down and moan endlessly when things are not getting done. I meet with each, ready for a new complaint to grapple with.

By noon, I'm exhausted. I sneak out my back door to avoid seeing even one more person.

I walk fast to my car and slip out the back gate. A five-minute drive to the restaurant allows me time to recoup my wits. When I walk in, Steve's huge arm waves from the back.

While eating, he says, "Hear you bought a Harley."

"Yup."

Channeling Biker Bob

"Always dreamed about a Harley myself. That and a fishing boat." Steve sports a winsome smile. "You know, the kind with all the fishing bells and whistles."

We talk for a while until the subject comes around to Vander and his talk show offer.

"I heard something coming down the pike," he says. "The grapevine works pretty fast here. You going on Leatherman?"

"Heck, Leatherman is only one. They want to put me on all the talk shows. I don't understand why I'm so special. Anyone else would have done the same, given the same conditions."

"I don't think I would have had the courage to get close enough to the house to help the old man, much less go inside the building after his wife."

"When I look back, I realize it was a stupid move. I could have died. If not for Bob, I would have never gone in."

"Who is Bob?"

I tell a long, edited version about my biker dreams. I explain Bob's help through the quagmire of my misplaced manhood. I recount the story of meeting Melinda and saving Nick's parents. I finish my story telling about Nick dropping the motorcycle off and almost giving it to me. When I'm finished, Steve sits slack-jawed.

"Biker Bob sounds like your guardian angel."

"More like a guardian Hell's Angel to me."

We both snicker.

"I've got a problem, though."

"From your story, I wouldn't think you had any problems."

"I'm deathly afraid of being in front of cameras. The thought of being viewed by millions of people nauseates me."

"Oh, you're right; that could be a problem."

"The network people are coming to my office after lunch. They want me to talk to a bunch of famous people. I don't think I can."

Steve looks at his watch. We both stand and walk toward the cashier. "Hell, man, you got through a burning building. With the help of Bob, you should be able to get through camera shyness. Let Vander know about your phobia. I'll bet they have a class or instructions that'll better prepare you for being on stage. Sounds like Bob is helping you out. If he's directing you, I'd do it."

I slip in the back door and sit at my desk for a minute before I buzz Sylvia. She sends Vander in. We sit in chairs on opposite sides of my desk.

"I've checked with my superiors," he says. "We're ready to honor yesterday's offer if you're ready to sign over book, and movie rights, then go on tour for a month."

121

Nik C. Colyer

I'll die in front of cameras for a full month. I'm going to have to think quickly to ward off his offer.

"I have a job, Mr. Vander. I don't think my boss would be too happy if I took another month off. I've just returned to work."

Vander grins. "Last week we contacted the president of Tridine Industries and gave him our offer. After a bit of maneuvering, he agreed to let you go, if we plug Tridine when you're on camera."

"Oh."

"Because of your heroics and blind luck, you've become a household word. The name Stewart Chance is on everyone's lips. Although you haven't wanted to talk to us, the nation wants to talk to you. You turn us down, and you let America down. They want to know who you are and how you think. They want to know what you eat for breakfast and what kind of sneakers you wear."

"Oh," I say again, this time deeper in anxiety. I thought my work excuse would give me an easy out, but he has me painted into a corner.

"Mr. Vander, I'm afraid of being in front of a camera." I hope my revelation will slow him a little, but he doesn't skip a beat.

He goes into a long explanation concerning training classes and coaches. Halfway through his explanation, I realize that Bob won't let me slip out of this. Being the point man is coming true.

After I agree to take their classes, Vander slides a thick stack of documents across my desk.

"Have your lawyers check the contract before you sign."

He looks sheepish, then says, "I'd like to meet your friend Bob. Can't you set up a meeting with him?"

"I have no control over Bob. When he wants to have a meeting with you, he'll show up. I'm sorry; I can do nothing to help."

He stands with his ever-present, camera-ready smile, gives my hand a hardy shake and leaves my office. My head reels. My teeth chatter. I'm so scared my bowels loosen, and I have to move fast to the restroom.

My afternoon is filled with endless meetings of which I halfheartedly attend. Sylvia sits next to me taking notes. My mind is filled with network contracts, and TV cameras.

When I get home from work, I call Renee and tell her the horrible news. I leave out the hundred thousand.

"Are you going to do it?" she asks.

"I guess. Bob wants me on TV."

"Bob wants you on TV! I swear, Stewart, what about you? Do you want to make yourself available for the whole world to see? What the hell does Bob have to do with your decisions?"

I feel her bites slide through the phone line.

"Damn it, Stewart, you have no good reason to go on TV."

122

"I have one good reason to go on camera," I say.

"What possible reason would you do such a silly thing?"

"Well," and I pause for effect. "They offered me a hundred thousand dollars to go on a month tour."

During the next fifteen seconds, the line is dead and I hear nothing but broken breathing.

"Renee, are you still there?"

"Yes."

It's the shortest sentence she has ever spoken.

The wind is out of her sails. I hear a shift, a resolution in her voice. A hundred thousand dollars is not enough compensation to subject myself to so much strain for an entire month, but in Renee's world, money talks.

After my conversation with Renee, after each conversation with Renee, my anxiety meter flies off the scale. Lately I have found a way to counter the unsettling feeling after dealing with my demanding wife. I jump on my bike, pull out onto the highway, and ride until long after sunset.

When I get home, I come across the one-percent-of-one-percent business card. On a whim, I make the call.

"Hey, Twiggy," I say when he answers.

"Yeah, what the hell do you want?"

"This is Stewart Chance?"

"Who the fuck is Stewart Chance."

"We met at a restaurant some months back. You told me to call and go riding with you when I found my Harley."

"Oh, you're the guy who pulled Nick's parents from the house."

"Will this hero stuff follow me forever?"

There is a moment of silence before he changes the subject. "I guess you got your bike."

"Oh yes, and it's a beauty."

"Lucky you called. Our group will be meeting Friday evening. Let's putt together over to Bucky's."

"Sure, where does he live?"

"Victorville, but we'll meet at the taco stand in Garden Valley.

"Which taco stand?"

"Hell, Chance, Garden Valley is a dinky little town with only one taco stand. You can't miss it."

"What time?"

"About 6:30." After a short pause, he says in a cautious voice, "Look here, Chance, it ain't like a party or nothing. We get together to work shit out, you know, like when Bob has men's gatherings in his dream world."

He could have told any other person on the planet and not been understood, but I understand.

"Okay," I say. "This is just what I've been searching for."

We talk for a few minutes and hang up. I don't need to mark my calendar. This will be a memorable occasion.

It is 11:00 before I climb into bed and 6:30 when the buzzer gives me my next conscious thought.

I walk into my office and find, as usual, a stack of phone messages from every network in existence. I also find six letters from department heads of news companies and a single white rose in a vase. A small canary yellow card hangs from the stem. In familiar longhand script, I read: "Just wondering how you're doing. I'll be passing through next week on my way to Los Angeles. Thought we might have lunch. I'll call your office in a couple of days. Melinda."

I click the intercom. "Sylvia."

"Yes, Stewart?"

"On Monday my friend Melinda will call. Patch her through, no matter what I'm doing. If I'm not around, take a message and give her my home number."

***

"Katherine, I'm sorry to call you at home, but I need to talk for just a minute or two."

"Thanks, I appreciate your patience."

"I swear, Stewart has gone off the deep end again. Susan Olsen and Murry Podich want him on their show, and damn it, he's going to make a total fool of himself."

"You might think he'll be alright, but I know Stewart. He's a dope in front of a simple flash camera. He'll screw things up, and I'll never again be able to show my face at another social gathering. How do I stop him?"

"Of course I have to stop him. He's wrecking my life. He's going on TV, for god's sakes, and he'll make a laughingstock of himself and our family. I can't allow his foolishness."

"What do you mean, I've been asking for him to stand up and act like a man? Yes, I want him to act more like a man, but sweet Jesus, not in front of the whole world.

"What? Support him? I thought you were on my side. I thought you were my therapist. Sounds like you're working for him."

"No, Damn it! I will not support him. This is the most foolish thing I have ever seen him do. He'll fall flat on his ass, and I'll never be able to show my face again."

124

"Well, yes, I like it that he's acting more manly these past few months. He is certainly sexier, but the stuff he does with his new manliness is not exactly what I had in mind. If he would come home and cut our lawn occasionally, I would be much happier."

"All I know is he hasn't come home in a month and a half. I'm positive he's seeing that woman again. I have a mind to go to Barstow, kick her ass, then give him a piece of my mind."

"Okay, okay, I promise I won't go. I'll wait here like a good little wife for my wayward husband to come home."

"Of course I'm getting sarcastic. Hell, my man ran off with another woman. Who knows, he'll probably go on TV with her."

"No, I won't do anything crazy unless I call you first.

Chapter 6

A BRIGHT AND SHINING STAR

Steve walks in while I'm on the phone and sits across from me. When I hang up, I say, "Once everything is signed and the courier leaves, I guess I'm committed."

"Yes, you are, and what a commitment!"

"This will be the biggest thing I have ever done."

"A piece of cake, Stewart."

"Bob says he'll be around, but in what capacity, I don't know."

"Once you get out on stage and get over your first few minutes of nervousness, you'll do fine."

"I'm guessing I'll pretty much be on my own, maybe a few gooses from Bob, if I lock up."

"You're lucky to have him."

Periodically, throughout the rest of the day, I find myself sighing and repeating a mantra, "I guess I'm committed."

At eleven the following morning, Sylvia buzzes me. "Stewart," she says, "Melinda Chambers is on the line."

I grab the receiver. "Melinda!"

"Stewart!" she shouts.

"When are you coming into town?"

"I'm an hour east of Barstow. I'll meet you for lunch?"

"Sure, how about Tanger's? It's a small restaurant off the main drag." I tell her how to get through town before I reluctantly hang up. I twitch and turn for the next hour, trying to get work done.

Channeling Biker Bob

Minutes before the regular lunch crowd jams up traffic, I slip out the back door and drive off Tridine property.

Sitting in a back booth, I fiddle with my silverware for twenty minutes, just enough time to settle the butterflies in my stomach. The moment she enters, my butterflies return.

I haven't seen her for six months. I don't remember her being so lovely. Shit, she is a goddess in a tight dress. Immediately, I'm scheming a way to get her angry, but I catch myself.

Hell, I'm a married man with two kids. A big part of me longs for her attack. I don't care one bit about marriage vows. I haven't had sex in so long that I can't even remember what it's like.

Melinda walks down the aisle toward me. Her smile widens as I slide out of the booth and stand to meet her. Her pace quickens. We collide into one another and embrace. Her wonderful body conforms to mine; I have my arms wrapped around her slender waist. All I think of is sex, and more pointedly, sex with her.

She pulls the upper part of her body back and looks at me. "How have you been?" She speaks, but my mind is on her lower half that is pressed firmly against me.

I'm in heaven. Please, no one wake me.

Once we sit and get settled, I begin to come out of the clouds. I hear a murmuring of what she says. So far, I'm lucky, because everything she says needs no response. I squirm, trying to get comfortable without actually reaching down and adjusting my newly sprung crotch. Maybe if I concentrate on baseball, but I can't think about baseball. I think only about Melinda.

"You okay?" she asks. "You don't look all here."

"I'm okay. I'm just happy to see you."

Oh damn, what a lame response.

"Well?" she says.

"Well what?"

"What have you been up to? Are you sure you're okay?"

"Yeah, I'm okay, maybe a little distracted."

She giggles. "Heaven sakes, Stewart, what the hell is on going on? If I didn't know you were a married man, I would think you had sex on your mind."

A blush spread over my face. I open my mouth, but for fear of blundering, I don't speak.

After mustering every ounce of courage my engorged manness has taken from me, I say, "Sorry, Melinda. I'm momentarily confused, but I'll be okay in a minute."

She smiles, and we sit in silence until I get the courage to say something else. Grabbing at anything, like a drowning man might grab at a straw, I say, "I got my motorcycle a few months ago."

"You must be kidding," she says, still smirking. "Is it the motorcycle Bob had Nicky build for you?"

"The exact one. Nick made a personal delivery to my house in Sacramento. I've had to go to his shop for adjustments a number of times, but the bike has been running great."

There is a shift in her demeanor, a change in expression.

"Have you seen him?" I ask.

"Not yet."

"Like we always thought, his shop is here in town."

I see another slight shift in her facial expression, a twitch under her right eye. The corners of her mouth drop a little. She looks sad, or is it anxious.

"I have to go back to work after lunch, but if you want to stick around, I'll take you over to see him after I get off at five."

Her face shifts again, this time to a more confused expression.

Our waiter steps over with obvious expectation. His stance demands that we order. Always obliging, I scramble to order, giving Melinda time to look over the menu. Once finished, he turns on his heels and marches off.

"Little bit huffy, aren't we?" I whisper across the table. Melinda giggles and looks over at him.

"Cute butt, though," she says. We sit quietly chuckling as he stomps through the swinging doors into the kitchen.

The snooty waiter has broken my spell. Both Melinda and I catch up on the last six months. I recite parts of my long, boring healing process and she tells me about her new job. We swap tales of our lives, laughing and guffawing more with each telling. Mr. Tightass returns with our food. As he sets the plates down, Melinda gives him a big smile, slips her hand back and pinches his butt. The waiter jumps nearly a foot in the air with a gasp the entire restaurant hears. When he lands, he gives her a glare.

"I'm giving you a reminder to lighten up, pal," she says.

He nervously spins and scampers off, not the forced march of before, but with furtive glances over his shoulder.

"Melinda, what got into you?"

"I don't know, Stewart, it was a good idea at the time." She smirks and breaks into a quiet, but uncontrollable laugh.

The hour of being with Melinda has gone by in a second.

"I have to go. If you want to stick around, I'll give you directions to my house, and you could hang out until I get off. Maybe we could go for a ride on my Harley?"

She accepts and I sketch simple directions on the back of a napkin. "If you get lost, call me at work."

Channeling Biker Bob

As I throw a twenty on the table, she pulls money out of her purse, places a five under her dish, and says, "It's the least I can do for embarrassing him."

I think it's a chauvinistic thing to do, but I don't say anything. Secretly, I wouldn't mind being pinched by her.

We go outside, she gives me another huge full-body hug, and we go our separate ways.

As soon as I sit at my desk, with a never-ending pile of papers, my randy thoughts disappear.

At three, Vander calls.

I realize, of all the things I told Melinda, I had forgotten to tell her about the TV deal.

"Mr. Chance," he says.

"Call me Stewart."

"We got your signed contract yesterday. I'm happy to have you on our team. We will have to work out schedules together and see when our tour might take place."

"I talked to my boss." I say. "He says we have a big push for the next two weeks, but after that, I'll have time."

"For us, the sooner the better, but I don't think your popularity will fade in two weeks."

"Popularity?"

"Mr. Chance, your heroic act of saving those people has taken the country by surprise. Usually this kind of thing blows over after a few days, but you have captured the hearts of the nation. Since you have refused to show yourself on camera, everyone is curious. They've made you a folk hero. Hell, man, three songs have been written about what you did. Don't you watch TV or listen to the radio? Seven months after the fact, and your picture is still on the screen almost every day. For some crazy reason the public wants more of you, and we are going to give them exactly that."

We finish with niceties and say good-by.

Five o'clock rolls around, and I'm through the front gate without even slowing. I race for home to see Melinda, but more to get on my Harley and into the wind.

The little house has been lonely, lately. It's nice to know someone will be waiting.

I turn up my gravel road, then after a half-mile, into my driveway. The back door opens and Melinda pokes her head out. I get out of my car, bounce through the back door and into a house filled with smells of cooking. I'm in her arms hugging.

When we separate, and Melinda turns toward the refrigerator.

"Since I was here, I made you a meal." In a wink, she removes two bowls with salad and two frosty non-alcohol beers, then sets them on the table. She sits across from me and we do our little eating ritual. Her salad is great, the beer good, but the company is best of all.

I go through all the formalities about how she shouldn't have and she didn't need to, but my house has not had anything warm other than toast since I moved in. I like how a place brightens when a woman is around. In a few hours, Melinda transformed my stark cabin in the desert into a comfortable little home, and I don't think she has changed one thing.

She serves a simple spaghetti with red sauce and garlic bread.

Halfway through our meal, I tell Melinda about my TV contract. Her eyes brighten and she says, "I knew it, Stewart!"

"You knew what?"

"Bob told me once that he had been looking for someone to go on national TV with his message. He intended to find someone acceptable to middle America to pull such a thing off. When you came on the scene, he was excited you might be the one. Bob has done it again."

"What do you mean, done it again?"

"Bob has a way about him. He is able to foresee events and guide whomever he wants into those events. I mean, look at us, for instance. Bob first guided us together, and then to Blythe on the day of the explosion. You have to agree, he definitely had something to do with us being around when the explosion happened. Although you were heroic to go into that burning house, why did America pick your one act to obsess on? You're almost a folk hero now. How do you, in a country where heroes surface every week, get not only media attention, but also capture the imagination of the whole country?"

I shrug while she goes on. I'm getting a feeling she will answer her own questions.

"Obviously, Bob has his wonderful meddling hands in it. His fingerprints are everywhere."

"I'm not interested in going on national TV. I get so nervous that I nearly pee my pants every time I think about it."

Melinda smiles. "I think Bob has a plan for you. Personally, I like what he has in mind. Look, Stewart, I have been on local TV a number of times. I admit, it wasn't anything national, but television, just the same. After a dozen times, you get used to it."

"A dozen?" I say. "By that time, I will have made a complete fool of myself on Leatherman, Jay Leno, Murry Podich, Sally Jessy-Raphael, and more importantly, Susan Olsen."

"He has you booked on the Susan Olsen show?" she has a surprised look on her face. "I love her show. Susan Olsen is the only talk show I will even give a second glance. She talks about real issues, however controversial. The others seem nothing, compared to the subjects Olsen covers. Now I am impressed."

"You won't be impressed when I fall flat on my face in front of Olsen and the rest of America."

She laughs as she collects the dishes and puts them in the sink. "You'll do fine," she says. "Remember, this is Bob's show. I'm sure he won't let you fall on your face."

I get up and clear the table as we talk about less frightening subjects. Once the dishes are washed and the kitchen is clean, I suggest, "Let's take a ride to Nick's. I called him earlier, and he said he'd be around."

Melinda's face drains. "Stewart, I'll need support when I see Nicky. Please stay close when we go into his shop?"

I agree as we walk out to the garage. I open the double wooden doors and my blue dream machine sits waiting. Even Melinda is impressed. "What a beautiful bike. The blue color works well with all the chrome."

I'm beaming with pride as I swing a leg over and sit on the seat. I lift my bike off its kickstand, pulling the stand in with the toe of my boot. I press the electric start, button and the bike springs to life with a lump-lump-lumping sound.

Melinda gets on the back. I nudge the bike into first, and we slowly idle down the driveway to the gravel road.

We haven't reached the end of the gravel, and already I feel the exhilaration of being in the wind, smelling desert sage, and seeing the colors of a late afternoon sky.

Turning onto the highway, I twist the throttle slightly, and my bike leaps. I go through the gears and find fourth at sixty. Melinda squeezes herself against my back, her arms wrapping tighter around my stomach. Riding alone has been wonderful the last few months, but the experience triples with someone on the back. A big part of me wishes Renee could be here. We move across the desert as Melinda points out landmarks.

On a hill overlooking Barstow, she yells for me to pull over. When the bike is off, she says. "I don't know, maybe we shouldn't go see Nicky. It's a nice night; maybe we should let dead dogs lie. I don't need to see him."

"You're the only one who knows what is right," I say.

"I don't know Stewart."

"Face the old ghost."

"Maybe facing Nicky isn't necessary."

"I'll be close by in case you go into a tail spin."

"You promise to stay close?"

"Yes."

She gives me a frightened smile, "Thanks Stewart. Okay, let's go face the music."

We ride into Barstow, and I'm wondering if I might be holding a devastated woman through the night. I'll have to put aside my sexual desires and support Melinda through a sorrowful period. Who knows? I'm ready for the possibility that I might also be driving home alone.

Since I've been there many times, I have no problem finding the battery building. I pull up and turn off my engine. Nick swings open his weathered garage doors and pokes his head out.

I park my bike as Nick goes back inside. Melinda and I look at one another. She takes a deep breath, grabs my hand, and we walk through the half-open wooden doors.

Nick's latest creation sits on the first block, a canary yellow machine with red-orange flames on the tank and rear fender. The all chrome springer front end sports a slender twenty-one-inch wheel. A long sleek machine, it's as trim as a sailing ship. Unlike my bike, every part is absolutely necessary; no tassels, no saddlebags, not even a speedometer. I step over to have a closer look at the progress. I have seen this machine five times, each time a little closer to completion. The bike is nearly finished, a work of art on wheels, sculpture in the truest sense of the word. The only difference between this bike and a fine piece of sculpted marble or bronze is that the motorcycle is kinetic. Not only will its owner be able to look at it, but he will also be able to move it through space. The bike is sleek and clean; it will surely take prizes at any motorcycle show.

I'm ogling the machine, my mind distracted. Nick is bent over in the back, bolting an engine into a freshly painted black frame. He stands, flashes a guarded smile at Melinda, and wipes his hands on a shop towel. I look at the new additions to his yellow marvel. He shifts his eyes to Melinda. I'm not paying close attention, giving them space to approach one another. Melinda moves as if a mountain lion on the hunt and rushes over to him.

I'm expecting a long anticipated reunion, tearful hugs, soulful kissing. I'm ready to turn and depart while two lovers reunite. I'm ready to leave her here. I will go home alone. I'll feel happy for her. I want to cheer their reunion.

Melinda charges over to Nick. He lifts his arms. I think he will embrace her. I concentrate on the yellow Harley, but my gaze momentarily shifts to them. Melinda, point blank, without hesitation, clips him under the jaw with a wicked right uppercut. Her left comes in as quickly and tags his right eye. I get my wits about me and rush over as Nick's knees unhinge. His body makes a slow spin toward the dirt floor. I'm barely in time to catch him. At the last possible second, I nudge his head away to miss the corner of his workbench. I partially break his fall, but can't get enough of a grip. He hits the floor hard.

"Jesus Melinda, why did you hit him?"

Channeling Biker Bob

"The bastard deserves it." Both her hands are fisted.

I drop to my knees and try to help Nick up, but he's out cold. I turn him on his side and make sure he is still breathing. I look up at Melinda standing over us. Her face is rage contorted.

"Shit, Melinda, you didn't have to knock him out."

"Trust me," she screams. "I wanted to get in four or five good ones before he went down. I should have slugged him in the stomach first and worked him over on his way down."

When Nick wakes up, she might finish him off before he has a chance to defend himself. I've got to stop her.

"Christ, Melinda, will you calm down? I didn't bring you over here to kill the guy. I thought you two would make up."

She's breathing hard, stepping from one foot to another. She is ready to take on the world. If Nick wakes now, he may take another beating. I look down at him. His head is cocked to one side. On each exhalation, he blows a small puff of dust across his floor. It's better to get Melinda out of here. I stand and gently herd her toward the door.

"Come on, Melinda, leave him alone until he wakes up. Let's go outside." I reach out to gently touch her arm and she yanks back at my contact. "You leave me alone, you bastard. I'll get myself out if I want. I'll stay, if I want to stay."

"Yes, you can," I say, backing a step. "I won't have you hurting Nick when he can't defend himself though. Let's go outside until he wakes up. Once he is on his feet and coherent, then have another go at him if you want, but not until then."

Her face is scarlet from rage. Her fists are clenched. Her stance is such that I'm glad to not be the recipient.

"Melinda, let's go outside." As I coax her back, I look as friendly and non-threatening as possible.

She hasn't stopped her intense staring at the prone man. She looks up at me and says, "Let's get out of here, Stewart. This place makes me sick."

"Good suggestion."

She turns, takes five long strides, like preparing to jump a high hurdle, and disappears out into the darkness.

The second she disappears, I hear a groan from Nick. I reach down and pat him on the back. "I'm right here, Nick."

His next groan is louder, loud enough to carry outside the garage into the quiet night air. Expecting to have to defend him from a second charge, I go outside to meet her. I simply close the doors behind me. Once the doors are closed, I look over at my bike and see her leaning against it. I sense she has calmed a little. I walk over and touch her shoulder. She melts into my arms sobbing. I never know what to do. I simply hold her for five minutes while she cries. I experience an intimacy in the moment, and I'm closer to her than I ever have been. Tears form in my eyes, but I brush them away.

She calms and says, "Oh, Stewart, he hurt me so much when he left. I hadn't realized it until I saw him again." She leads herself into another bout of tears, which has me holding her until she pulls away and looks at me.

"Let's go home," she says, laying a long, sexy, soulful kiss on my lips. Her tongue reaches in, searching out mine. When the kiss is over, and by no means am I trying to rush it, she pulls back and repeats, with a bit of a gasp, "Let's go home."

"Okay," I say. "Let me check on Nick first. You wait here."

A flash of rage flares in her eyes. I step away and walk back to the double doors. I pull one open and look in. Nick stands over the filthy shop sink toweling his face with a wet rag. "You okay, man?" I ask.

He glares through the mirror. "Just get her out of here."

"Sorry." I close the door.

Melinda sits on the back of my bike. I lift my leg over, pull the bike upright, and hit the starter. The second the engine catches, I pop the clutch and we move through the alley.

Oh my God, she has her hands under my T-shirt. Oh my God, she bites at my neck and nibbles my ear. Oh my, she unbuttons my pants. She slides her hand inside. She grinds her body against my back.

Before we're out of the alley, she pulls the back of my shirt out of my pants. She lifts it up to my armpits. I can't figure out what she is doing, until the warmth of her bare breasts push against me and she drags those expressive tips across my back.

I pull onto the main highway with her hand buried in my jeans, her body pressed hard against my backside, I wonder if we're going to get home at all. Will she take me again in the sand, like she did before? I hope she will do something wild. I hope she will simply take me while we're moving. She doesn't do any of these things, but she still rubs every part of my body she can get her hands on. One hand is under my shirt grabbing at my chest, while her other squeezes my sprung maleness, trying to pull him free.

My bike is thrown horribly off balance when she tries to reach the upper part of her body around in a thwarted attempt to take me in her mouth. I counter balance as we wobble through the streets. Unable to complete her maneuver, she resorts to kissing and biting my back.

Finally, and I can't believe I made it, I turn onto my gravel road. The woman is all over me. She raises on the back seat; her hair in my face. She attempts to reach her entire body around to kiss me. I try to keep my attention on the road. I'm not complaining, but driving is difficult.

We turn up my driveway and into the garage. She slides her whole body around under my stretched-out arm. She works her way around with her teeth. She bites me hard. Her lips kiss me softly. Her tongue licks my belly button. She works her way downward. All the buttons on my Levi's have long been undone. She has had my hardness out in the wind, protecting him with her hand, for the last three miles. Now her entire body slinks, around. Her mouth encompasses mine.

Oh my God, I think, as I reach over and turn the ignition off. The throbbing of my engine stops, leaving only the other throb in my ears. Melinda, wild woman, touches my hardness with her cheek, her neck, her tongue, kissing, licking, and biting.

Ten minutes later, we get off the bike. She drags me into the house and throws me on my bed. "Oh my God, oh my. . ."

***

The next day at lunch I slip away from my office and go to Nick's. When I walk through his dilapidated garage doors, Nick gives me a wince and looks beyond me for Melinda. He reaches up and rubs the puffy plum colored skin around his eye.

"Geez, Nick, I'm sorry I brought her here."

He sits in front of the black frame and picks a wrench. He returns his focus on the bike. I'm used to him turning bolts while he talks. It's the only way he can talk.

"That's the reason I left her," he says. "The only thing I'm disappointed about, is I got the beating, and you got the great sex." I stand stone-faced, not wanting to acknowledge that Melinda and I slept together.

"Look, man," he says, "she must be violent, to get wild enough for good sex. I know what happened last night after you left. The fact is, she can't help herself after she gets violent. Once her clock gets wound, she is a maniac. Remember, I lived with her. We had an incredible time, but after a while, I realized my body wouldn't hold out over the long haul. She's just too violent."

Too violent? This revelation comes from one of the toughest bikers I know.

"How could she be too violent for you, Nick?"

"Give yourself time, pal. Soon you'll be sporting one of these and wondering what happened. The funny thing is you'll look forward to the next black eye or bloody nose. She is amazing when she gets all lit up, but someone has to get hurt to fire her libido. I miss her wild sex, but I don't miss the beatings."

***

"He's with that. . .that slut again. I sense her in my bones. I have a mind to go to the desert right now."

"What do you mean? Of course I'm positive. For one, he hasn't called in more than a week. Once he moved to that shitty town, like clockwork, he called every third day. Only one distraction would make that wimpy son of a bitch guilty enough not to call and she has strawberry blonde hair."

***

Six days after the Nick incident, Melinda and I are riding in high desert up the Owens Valley. After a wonderful cruise to Lone Pine, I reluctantly turn my bike around and begin a long drive back to Barstow. Since the night Melinda slugged Nick, we agreed to only talk about sex, not act on it. At first, talking is awkward, but she continues approaching the subject, and I'm forced to respond with more than a simple yes or no answer. Once the talking-frankly-about-sex barrier is breached, a dam breaks. Every chance I get, I spill the most intimate parts of my life to her. I don't understand it, but this is my first true friendship with a woman.

Melinda has stayed through the weekend, but early tomorrow morning she will go on to Los Angeles. Her new job demands she be in her manager's office before nine o'clock.

***

The network guys rented studio time with a local television station. They hired an instructor to help me adjust to being on camera. I have an appointment to do a mock interview every afternoon after work. I can't believe they are going through such pains to help me get over my phobia.

I've been training for a week, but I can't get the hang of TV.

My trainer, Bill, has been patient, but whenever the indicator light goes, on I freeze and stutter through my simple lines. With less than two weeks before I go on Susan Olsen's show, I'm getting discouraged.

One day at work I pick up the phone to field another of a hundred phone calls.

"Mr. Chance," Vander says.

"Stewart. Call me Stewart."

"We will pick you up Monday morning at eight. Just bring your personal items.

"Personal items like clothes and--"

"No, Mr. Chance."

Channeling Biker Bob

I want him to call me Stewart.

"Nothing except your lucky rabbit's foot and contact lenses. Everything else will be furnished. We will fly you into New York where Susan Olsen broadcasts live. You will be staying at the Hilton, and we will take you on a shopping trip to get you ready for your unveiling."

"I'm not a painting. Why would I be unveiled?"

"You're the best thing that's hit the screen since TV was first invented. When you debut, all of America and half of Europe will be watching."

Oh great, now I'm better. Now I'm more confident about getting in front of a camera with not only a million people, but two hundred fifty million people to watch me stumble and stutter.

"Can't we start with a smaller audience for practice?"

"Mr. Chance, you won't need any practice on the Olson show. We'll talk more when they pick you up." He abruptly hangs up, leaving me with shaking hands and a dry mouth.

Monday morning comes much too soon. I find myself awake before dawn. Because I'll be gone for a month, I want a last ride on my bike. I drive to the top my favorite bluff that overlooks town. The opposite view is of the endless, untouched desert hills to the north. I park and sit straddling my machine for a meditative half hour. My frayed nerves calm as I look at the expansive beauty. Sleep came to me last night, but not much, and only after hours of tossing and turning.

Television is not going to be easy.

Chapter 7

THE CIRCUS

I start my engine and slowly glide onto the highway leading back to my house.

As I turn onto my gravel road, I notice three TV vans with their antennas high in the air. They have taken a long time to find me, but if insanity must begin, I guess a good place is in front of my house. I savor the last half mile of quiet as my magical machine lub-lubs at an idle in first gear. Cameras and crews are in my front yard. Six or eight suits are milling around on my dinky porch. When I get close enough to turn into my driveway, I spot Vander standing with the others. They all turn to face me as he waves. I scowl, and pull into my open garage. By the time I reach down to switch the key off, the crowd rushes in and surrounds me. My loping engine does a good job of drowning out the mayhem. I give my throttle a sharp twist and rotate the key. My engine revs slightly, then unwinds. Once it dies, I hear the din of six reporters asking questions.

I glare at Vander. "Did you invite them here?"

He shrugs. "Good publicity."

"Mr. Chance. How does it feel. . ."

I don't catch the rest of the first question from the woman to my right, because a large ape-like figure shoves a microphone in front of my face and asks, "How do you like being a hero?"

Channeling Biker Bob

The cameras are on, the tightening pressure returns. I had better speak quick or suffer the embarrassment of getting so nervous that I'll start stuttering.

I fall back on a line that Bill taught me at the station. I get a practiced annoyed look on my face and say, "If you have intelligent questions, I'll answer them. Until then, I'm going inside." I look over at Vander and my scowl deepens. "You come inside with me, but no one else."

I lean the bike on its kickstand and dismount. I've made it so far without stuttering.

I step quickly, Vander close on my tail, in the direction of my house. A narrow corridor opens for us to pass. I leap two steps in one hop and push my back door open. Once inside, my tension subsides, and I breathe again. Vander slips in behind me and closes the door. I give him another sharp scowl. "Why did you tell the reporters where I live?"

"I had to. My boss would have fired me if I didn't."

"Okay, then during the month I'm gone, you're going to have to keep a guard on my place."

He smiles. "I think we've already arranged security. Tonight on the news, your face will be plastered all over the country. This is the first part in letting people know you'll be on the Olsen show in the morning."

"In the morning?"

The limo is parked out front. Vander signals the driver. "Get your stuff together. We've got a flight to catch."

I jump into a one-minute shower, dress without shaving, and grab a suitcase.

"Forget the suitcase," he says. "Get personal stuff and let's go."

My gaze rests on a small framed picture of Renee and the kids. I grab the photo and keys to my bike, then follow Vander out the door through the crowd.

"Mr. Chance, what do you plan--"

"Mr. Chance, where will you go--"

"How do you explain your--"

They all talk at once. I don't catch a single question as I push my way through the crowd.

The back door of the limo opens. I follow Vander inside. The driver closes the door, and the din lessens.

"Geez," I say. "They're mobbing us."

"Get used to it," Vander says. "You're a national figure now. For a while, at least, you're going to have to dodge an endless line of cameras and reporters. Until you cool off with the media, you'll also have to evade the public."

I lean back in the white leather seat. The car pulls away from my house. Two photographers run alongside the car snapping pictures as they jog. Once we pick up speed, they fall behind and we're alone again.

The ride to the airport is awkward. Vander and a young woman sit across from me in silence. Once I'm secure inside the car, they begin talking about the upcoming series of events.

A six-seater Beachcraft split tail, engine running, waits for us at Barstow airport. We board and the plane immediately takes off. Although I don't say a word, I wonder if we are going cross-country in this cramped little plane. Once the plane is in the air, to my relief, the pilot circles the airport and flies due west, the opposite direction of New York.

Twenty-five minutes later, we land in San Bernardino and taxi over to an idling Lear jet.

The second we are on board, the plane pulls out onto the active and bullets into the air.

The plushness of the interior, the comfort of wide swivel seats, coffee and breakfast, all add to ultra first-class flying.

After a few minutes in the air, Vander says, "We'll be flying into New York at 6:45. You'll be taping your first show with Olsen tomorrow morning at nine. We'll take you out on the town after the show, so stay inside tonight and get some sleep."

The rest of the flight is a blur while I watch six months of news clips and read newspaper articles telling stories concerning my family, my job, and me. They have documented my entire life. Melinda is included, but they don't have much on her, thus a great deal of speculation flies about. I already see where tomorrow morning's show will be headed, and I'm scared. As we descend, I look out the window and see New York.

On the ground we're hustled into a waiting limo and driven downtown to the Hilton. My suite is expensive and plush, but I'm so exhausted that all I want is a place to sleep.

***

The next thing I know, I'm moving down a highway on Blue. The engine humms between my legs. The wind flows through my longer hair, and I'm free again. The skinny all-chrome spoke wheel of Bob's bike comes into my periphery. I turn and see his ridiculously long bike, then his gleaming teeth.

His smile is infectious. I break into a grin myself.

We ride until he motions me over into a gas station.

I slow and make a long arc into the station. I'm not surprised when Bob leads me through the station and around back. I realize I'm at the original shop where I first saw Blue. The doors are closed and no one is around. We pull up and turn our engines off. Once our bikes are parked, Bob directs me around to a back door and steps in like he owns the place. He flips the lights on and walks me across the bike-parts-filled shop, through another door and into a dingy little apartment, obviously set aside as a place to crash and prepare food, but that is all. In the middle of the room sits a table and a few greasy chairs, and in the corner a dirty mattress lays on the floor. Bike parts are leaning against walls and strewn around the room. Greasy hand prints and wild graffiti cover the walls. Spots of motor oil and bearing grease dot a bare wooden floor.

Bob leads me through a small doorway and carefully slides over an open newspaper cluttered with a disassembled carburetor. He removes a wildly painted rear fender slung over one of two chairs and sits me down. He hasn't said a word. Once I sit, I notice, hanging on the far wall, a gas tank that matches the fender. An entire freshly chromed, springer front end leans against the wall under the tank. Except for the frame, engine, and wheels, most parts of a complete motorcycle sit within my reach. The larger ones are on the floor, while smaller pieces are scattered on the counter, in the sink, and atop a rank refrigerator. Dirty dishes tell me that food is cooked in this kitchen, but I don't know how.

"Chance," he says. "Let's have a pow-wow."

I wonder what I did to have Bob single me out like this? I pick up a brass carburetor body and nervously chip at flaking army-green paint with my fingernail.

"You didn't do anything wrong."

I'm always amazed how easily he reads my thoughts.

"I have been waiting forty years for tomorrow."

Bob doesn't look forty, but am I going to remind him? No, I'm not even thinking about his age.

"I'm much older than you think, Chance."

"What do you mean?" I ask, this time out loud, though I don't know why I bother to speak.

"The latest me died in 1952 when a truck plowed into my bike on Pacheco Pass, fifty miles east of Monterey. At the time of my untimely demise, I was in the middle of a life long quest, the reason why I'm still hanging around."

I believe him when he says he doesn't have a living, flesh-and-blood body.

I put the carburetor back on the newspaper and grab an ugly plastic salt shaker. Absently, I shake a little into my hand. I'm surprised when white crystals sprinkle into my palm.

"What kind of quest?" I ask lifting an open palm to my outstretched tongue. I take a tentative taste of the white crystals, ready to spit out any questionable findings, but I taste salt.

"When I died," he says, "I'd been gathering information on men. How men are the workhorses of our society. Men are used and discarded when they are no longer useful. My father was one of those men. I vowed to get to the core of the issue. Once I started down the path, hundreds of other men's issues cropped up. Once I got some answers, I wanted to tell the world."

"How did you plan on getting the word out?"

"How do I plan would be better put. At the time, I didn't know, but I was hell bent on broadcasting my message, when my time on earth abruptly ended. Shit, man, I had just gotten started, and my life came to an end. I guess I'm so set on completing my task I've been hanging around all these years trying to find a way to finish, until you came along."

I put the salt shaker on the table. "What do you mean?

"You are perfect. With my rough attitude and scruffy looks, I would be laughed out of any studio long before I ever got on camera. My message would never be heard. You, on the other hand, have a Jimmy Stewart, guy-next-door kind of look. I've learned one lesson the hard way. When it comes to cameras, it's what a person looks like that counts."

"Now hold on for one darn minute. What do you mean, Jimmy Stewart, guy-next-door kind of look?

He smiles, reaches out and twiddles the salt shaker. "Hell Chance, you even sound like Jimmy Stewart. Everything that has happened to you has been toward the completion of my master plan. Being a national hero has all been part of my strategy."

"What do you mean? How do I fit into your god damn plan and what about that oracle?"

"Hey, that's great, Stewart, you're cussing more these days."

I blush. "Seems to pop out in the oddest places lately, like I can't help myself anymore. But don't change the subject."

"Remember months ago when I called you our point man?"

"Yeah, sure, but what does—"

"A psychic from Nevada City contacted me. When Madam Pickering said you were the one, I set up the entire TV deal."

"Is Madam Pickering the oracle?"

"No, you are the oracle, Madam Pickering simply channeled your energy. It took a while to find you, but I had time."

"I thought you didn't have a body. How could she contact you?"

He grins. "Through her dreams of course.

Channeling Riker Bob

"Once I got you and Melinda in place for your act of heroism, I set my sights on network executives, especially one Phillip G. Underman. He is a top executive at BCS. He is also a man who has been living under his tyrannical wife for twenty-five years. He responded wonderfully. The lesser guys followed suit. They kept you in the limelight and in no time, you're a national hero."

"Do you mean you had the whole thing planned?"

He shows his famous toothy smile.

"If this set up is your plan, what do you have in mind for me?"

"Tomorrow is our big day, a day I have been waiting for since my dad died in 1948. All I want you to do is take it easy once you're in front of the camera. Just relax, and I'll help. You don't have to worry about stuttering, I'll be close to help you through any tight spots."

"Really?"

Bob smiles. "No problem."

"You don't know what a relief that is. I have been afraid to blow the whole thing by making a fool of myself in front of the entire civilized world."

"I'll be around, Kid. Don't you worry."

***

I awake in the most comfortable bed I have ever slept in. The clock reads 6:25, minutes before my wake-up call. I could easily get used to this kind of living. Five minutes later, I hear a soft tinkle of my phone. I grab the receiver.

"Mr. Chance, it's time to wake up."

"I'm awake."

I get out of bed and saunter into a luxurious shower. Some time later, I dry off while sipping coffee. A man comes in with an armful of clothes.

"BCS did the honors of getting you three changes of clothes for today. I hope this will suffice, Sir."

He lays my clothes out on the bed. I immediately reject a gray suit, with a light blue sport coat as a fast second. I decide on a pair of slacks with a herringbone pattern and a short-sleeve shirt.

He suggests loafers, but I'm set on the tan sneakers for comfort. I'm shaving my chin, when Vander blasts into my room.

"We've got a great breakfast downstairs, then we're off to the studio for make-up and sound checks. Come on, Mr. Chance, don't dawdle. We have a big day ahead of us."

"Stewart," I correct. "Call me Stewart."

We go to a private corner in the restaurant where three people are seated in huge leather chairs.

143

Vander introduces me, "Mr. Underman, I would like you to meet Stewart Chance. Mr. Underman is president of broadcasting."

Oh, this must be the guy in Bob's back pocket.

"Mr. Chance, pleased to meet you." The gaunt man rises and leans across a highly polished table to shake my hand. I reach out and he grips me like a vise, gives two precise shakes, and releases me. For a man obviously in his late sixties, his hair is too black, his pencil-thin mustache too well manicured. Wrinkles around his eyes are too few.

The other two men are introduced, but I'm so nervous that I forget their names before introductions are over.

"We hear you're the hottest thing since the hula-hoop," Underman says. The other two give mandatory snickers.

"News to me, Sir."

"He is hot," Vander jumps in.

"Well, I hope what you say is right," says Underman as he stares at Vander. "We have a great deal of money riding on him. He had better deliver."

"Look, Phil, you give us enough room, and I promise we will deliver. Today on the Olsen show you'll see."

A staring match goes on for another five seconds. The waiter, dressed in a tux, delivers a breakfast I have only dreamed of. He sets my dish down and the smell alone is satisfying.

While I concentrate on slowly savoring each bite, the other four get into an active discussion about the business end of television. I'm glad to be left out of the conversation, as the food takes every bit of my attention.

When the meal is over, Vander signals me to follow. We go out of the hotel, step into another waiting limo and slip away into New York traffic.

In a short time, our limo pulls over to the curb. We walk across the sidewalk, up a flight of wide concrete steps, and through huge double glass doors into a corporate foyer. We make our way through the throng to a private elevator; up three flights, then step out onto a lavender carpet.

HELLO, BIKER BOB

A knock sounds outside my dressing room door, "One half hour, Mr. Chance," calls the attendant.

I think, Bob, where are you? I get no answer. You'd better show up and now is a good time.

Although I have never held one, I want a cigarette. Maybe I'll take up smoking to get through this insane morning.

Bob, where are you? I'm running out of time here. I haven't heard a peep out of you. For the hundredth time, I pull my hand through my hair.

Bob, you better show up. My time to go on is too close.

I've always heard that, when you are having fun, time speeds up, and when things are boring, time slows. No one ever says how time reacts when one is anticipating being hanged at the gallows, getting married to a woman you don't want to marry, or going on nationwide television.

Knock, knock. "Ten minutes, Mr. Chance." The attendant chimes his musical refrain. Ten minutes left. Bob, where are you?

Vander opens my door. "How you doing, Mr. Chance?"

"Call me Stewart. I don't know if I can do this."

"You'll do fine. Remember, Susan will be asking all the questions. All you have to do is relax and answer." He turns me toward the mirror, massaging my shoulders.

"Take deep breaths like the instructor told you. Calm down and re-lax; Remember, we're only doing television. You aren't going on stage in front of a thousand people."

Bob, where are you? Bob, if you're coming, now is the time.

The shoulder rub calms me. Once I start breathing deeply, I calm more, but Bob hasn't shown. I may have to go out there without him.

Vander's constant, camera-ready smile widens. He gives me a gen-tle slap on my back. "You'll be okay. Just remember to keep breathing. I'll be directly off stage. You'll see me the whole time. If you lock up, look over at me. I'll help you get started again."

Knock, knock. "Two minutes Mr. Chance," says the warden. How could eight minutes have gone by so fast?

Bob, if you're playing a joke on me here and waiting till the last sec-ond to come out, come out now.

Inside my quaking mind, I don't hear a peep from Bob. There is no tingly feelings to warn me that he is ready to come forward, no numb-ness at my fingertips; nothing.

Maybe Renee is right; Bob might be a figment of my imagination after all. Maybe he is a dream, and I'm going to have to go on the talk show from hell on my own.

I'm breathing and breathing, getting as much oxygen into my cells as possible.

Knock, knock. "You're on, Mr. Chance."

Oh, God help me.

Vander pulls me to my feet and straightens my shirt collar. Like a mother hen, he gives me one last inspection, pulling specks off the front of my shirt. One last concerned look and he says, "Break a leg."

He hustles me outside the protection of my nest and through nar-row corridors filled with wires and props.

Like a light at the end of a long tunnel, there is the proverbial stage left, from which I'm supposed to enter.

Where are you Bob?

"Okay, Mr. Chance," says an older man with a horribly chewed, unlit cigar that hangs limply from the right corner of his mouth. I met him earlier during the first run-through, but I don't remember his name. In fact, I don't remember much of anything.

"Olsen will introduce you," he says. "When she speaks your name, step out, shake her hand, and sit as quickly as possible, just like we did earlier. Mr. Chance? Mr. Chance?"

He lightly slaps on my right cheek. I come around to see a worried face and that bedraggled cigar.

"Mr. Chance, are you still with us?"

"Yes, yes. As soon as she says my name, I go out, shake her hand, then sit."

Channeling Biker Bob

His worried look turns to a grin. "That's right, now get ready."

I watch Susan Olsen joke and laugh with her two guests. I wish I could magically be sitting in my seat without running the stage gauntlet. She shifts the subject. My butterflies turn to vultures. Oh shit, she is talking about me.

"Get ready, Mr. Chance," says Cigar.

My vultures circle in. She tells a short version of my explosion story. The last thing I hear is her say, "Let's give a big hand for Mr. Stewart Chance."

My prompter pats me and pushes me forward. "Break a leg," he says, as I stumble past the curtain, and out onto the stage in front of a room of applauding onlookers. My forward movement turns to a stick figure walk. I step out into blinding lights. I'm silently screaming for Bob. Thank God I can't see the audience. I continue moving across what looks like a mile of stage.

Out of my blue fog, a small feminine hand grabs mine, and I gladly follow her lead. I look for anything that resembles a chair, but her hand, gripping me like a vise, holds me in place. The din slackens. A million hands clap, a thousand, a hundred, finally only three coming from opposite ends of the hall. She grabs my other hand and turns me. "How are you doing, Mr. Chance?"

I'm not sure if I responded. I hear a squeaking sound coming from inside me, but I don't recognize my own voice. My heart beats too loudly. I look over as the woman is trying to get my attention. She looks into my eyes and motions me to sit. Relief beyond relief, I spot the chair. I find myself sitting.

"They tell me that you work for Tridine Industries?" She starts with her first easy question. A simple yes is enough.

"What do you do in your job, and what does Tridine do?"

Oh, I remember now; the mandatory Tridine plug, two on every show. I can't think of a thing to say. Susan asks more yes or no questions. She gives a synopsis of my computer company and what they do before she gets down to business. Once she finishes with Tridine questions, the room is silent, an even more frightening response than the heart-stopping applause.

"Mr. Chance, how did you happen to be in Blythe?"

Yes and no have been my only responses so far. I can't think of another word, so I say "Y-yes."

I'm chiding myself for starting down the long dark road of stuttering. I want to get up and run. I look toward the stage exit. Vander stands with his ever-plastered, smile. Worry lines around his eyes are apparent. He waves me to continue. His prompting helps me remember what I'm supposed to do.

"Y-yes, I mean. I-I was looking fo-fo-for Nick Brown."

I look back at Susan Olsen. She smiles, and I feel relief in my guts. My vultures are shrinking back to butterflies.

"Nick Brown is the son of Mr. and Mrs. Brown?" she asks.

"W-well, yes, but I-I didn't know a-at the time." I finally get a sentence out. I have given up on Bob showing his face. I'm pissed. He promised to be here. For the first time since I have known him, he has not done what he said he would do.

"How close were you when the building exploded?" Olsen asks, bringing me out of my internalized Bob rage.

"A hu-hundred feet." I'm getting more comfortable. My confidence returns. The next question floats across the room and ruptures my eardrums.

"You went inside the building by yourself and pulled both Mr. and Mrs. Brown out, before the building burnt?"

"Well, no," I hesitate a moment. "Melinda was with me. She helped me get Mr. Brown away from the explosion before I went in alone to get Mrs.--"

"Mr. Chance," Olsen interrupts. "I thought you were alone."

"Melinda was with me."

She gets an all-knowing smile on her face, turns in her swivel chair to face me and asks, "Melinda. Is she your wife?"

I understand where she is going with her line of questioning. I've dug myself a deep pit, and I'm being led to the edge in front of the whole country. I'm not left with many options except tell to the truth. Not the whole truth and nothing but the truth, but I hope a smidgen of the truth.

"Melinda Ch-chambers is a fr-friend. We w-were in Blythe that day." Oh no, I'm stuttering again. My confidence isn't lasting as long as I'd hoped.

"What is your wife's name, Mr. Chance?"

Olsen is not helping; she digs deeper into my personal life. I look at Vander and see his attention is on me. His brow is deeply furrowed, and little beads of sweat are dripping down the side of his face. I get no sign of suggestions or help from him.

"R-R-R-Renee," I answer.

The rest of Susan Olsen's line of questioning I don't hear. I'm in overload. My circuits are smoking. My intellect has given up. I'm ready to sprint for stage left, safety, home, but the second I push myself up to run, a delightful, life-saving thing happens. I begin to, ever so lightly, feel the tips of my fingers go numb. With relief, I relax and welcome a familiar feeling of non-reality.

"What took you so long?" I ask as darkness surrounds me.

"I'm here, Chance. You've done well, but she needs to be knocked down a few pegs. Let me at her, I'm ready to kick some talk-show ass."

Channeling Biker Bob

My fading consciousness smiles. With a definite familiar snap, I thankfully drop back into the passenger seat of my own body. Like I have taken nitrous oxide at the dentist, my physical form is not exactly a well-defined outline. My hands and arms push me upward from my chair. I spring to my feet. Where I stand, I don't know, but I'm aware that I still have a body. Off in the distance, controlled rage boils in my face. I sense Bob speaking, and thank God, I don't have to figure out what to say.

Bob/I say, "Why do you media jackals have to find the most private place in a person's life and dig?"

***

Up until my last question, I have a frightened and controllable Stewart Chance. I have him in the bag. Chance is dog meat in my hands, but what happened. Just as I'm ready leap in for the kill, he responds with an off-the-wall question of his own. I have to think fast. The cameras are running. The ball is in my court, but I'm good at thinking fast. BCS pays me almost a mill a year to think fast.

He started out demure and pliable. In seconds, he looks like a Marine sergeant. What happened? He is so much bigger.

"Answer the question, Mr. Chance," is the best response I come up with. My brain is going a thousand miles an hour. I'm trying to think of a great comeback. I need to cut my new, worthier adversary back down to size.

"I'm not going to answer your silly-assed question," he says. "If you ask a question with merit, I might consider answering."

Silly-assed? He can't say ass on camera. He certainly can't stand until the interview is over.

"On the other hand, Ms. Susan Olsen," he spits my name out like a cuss word, "I might ask what gives you the right to pry into another person's life on a whim? Are you doing a reporter thing, or is it the only question a female in our twisted culture is able to think of?"

"What?" My one-word question blasts out of my mouth. I want to say, I'll dare you say one word against women. You are only a man. You have no right to question what any woman says. I have been waiting to say this ever since I joined my feminist sisters. I have wanted to say it a million times to my bosses, to my father, to my husband. I hold my tongue. I'm on national television for God sakes, the worst place to consider saying anything this controversial.

"Sir, my job as a reporter is to--"

"That is bullshit, sister," the bastard says. "Let's talk about why you would think I, as a man, have no right to question what women say?"

Holy shit, he said it. How does he know what I'm thinking? I'm completely confused. As a last resort, I look at the prompter.

"He is leading you." I read.

Well of course he is leading me, you idiot. I glanced at the prompter for help, not confirmation.

I regroup my thoughts and get ready for another blast. "You, or any man for that matter, has no right to question what women have to think or say." I spit the words back at him and watch him smile, but he wears a wider, more self-assured smile.

I can't believe I've finally said it. I can't believe he's smiling. He has something up his sleeve and I don't trust him. For the moment though, I have taken my show back.

"You're right," he says.

I'm right? I know I'm right, but it's the last thing I expect him to say. The little wimp, turned monster, is agreeing?

"I am right?" I say with as much self-assurance as I can.

He swings a hand up and points at the ceiling. "Men have no right to question anything a woman says. Men and women think differently. We approach problems differently, we live entirely different lives, sometimes under the same roof, so why would a man have any right to question a woman?"

"Yes," I say in complete agreement. I'm ready to go on to explain my position, but he takes over again.

"Okay," he says, "then you might agree that a woman has no right to question what a man says, thinks, or does, either." He drops his hand and points at me. "My question, Ms. Olsen, is why do women think they have the right to meddle in men's affairs?"

I'm flabbergasted. I stumble on his question. I look at the prompter and, luck of the Irish, read aloud, "We're going to take a moment to have a word from our sponsors." The applause sign lights and flashes, but the usual clapping from the audience is missing. My cheering section is stunned into silence.

The camera light blinks off. I stand and walk around my desk and off stage. As I pass, he sits with a smirk. "Come back after break, Olsen. I'm ready to go another round."

I find myself spinning on my heels to face him. "Look here, you bastard. I'll be back when I'm good and ready."

***

"I can't believe it Katherine. Did you see him on Susan Olsen?"

"Yes, then you saw him almost expire from nervousness, then Susan asks him the one question everyone knew she would ask."

"Oh, sure, it just gives me one more reason to kill the weasel son of a bitch the second I see him. In front of God and the whole goddamn country, he answers Susan's question like he was telling yesterday's news."

"Oh sure, and I'm glad he stuttered. He looked like a fool. I can't wait to see him; I'm going to cut his balls off up to his elbows. I can't believe he would embarrass my family and me like that on national television for god sakes. He is dead meat."

"What are you talking about. It is not better to have everything out in the open. I'm going to waste him when he gets back. That jerk has embarrassed me one too many times."

***

"Holy shit, Mr. Chance, do you know what you did?" says Vander, once I step off stage. I hear him from a long distance away, but I can't respond. Bob has a firm grip on the situation, and I'm glad to give him the helm.

"I know exactly what I'm doing, dick head," Bob says. "Just sit back and enjoy the ride." Again from a long distance back, Vander's ever-smiling face darkens. I don't exactly know what Bob has said to insult him, but Vander's demeanor shifts from a worried, friendly helper to angry, unwilling participant.

I'm not sure what Bob has in mind, and I'm sure if I'll have to pay later. For now, I'll enjoy the ride.

***

I come back to the smart-assed twerp and sit across from him without saying a word until the cameraman signals me. His smirk has not disappeared, so I lay into him in a collected voice.

"Mr. Chance, you asked the question 'why do women think they have the right to meddle in men's affairs?' Just have a look at the world around you. Men have tinkered with everything, bringing our planet to near destruction. Who decided we needed protection and built the atomic bomb? Did they stop? They didn't have enough bombs to destroy our world, hundreds of time over, so they built thousands more.

"Men decide when a war will happen and what country to invade. Mr. Chance, our culture has been under the influence of the patriarchy for the last two thousand years. If you count the crusades and dark ages, don't you think men, with their mine-is-bigger-than-yours attitude, have screwed things up?"

I got him! His shit-eating grin disappears. I'll revel in watching the little worm squirm. The longer his silence, the better I feel. I don't want to

151

sneer at him, but his silence is heart-warming. I can't remember any-one, much less a man, who has thrown me off on my own show. I'm back in the driver's seat.

Ten seconds goes by, much longer than I like being silent on cam-era, but I let him sit in his awkward silence without saving him. He pre-pares to speak, and it's about time. Billy, my ear prompter, has been screaming for me to fill in.

"You are absolutely right, Ms. Olsen. The juvenile way men have acted for the last two millenniums has been unconscionable."

Did he say juvenile? Again, it's the last thing I expect him to say. I was so sure he'd defend men's positions and point out the wonderful advances men have made. I'm prepared to counter any example he presents. I have a half hour worth of examples where men have screwed up the works, but he agrees. Damn him!

"That's not what I'm talking about, Ms. Olsen."

"What are you talking about, Mr. Chance?" I sense a curve ball flying right across my plate. I get a feeling he'll regain control, and the com-mercial isn't scheduled for another seven minutes.

"Many women meddle in men's affairs by trying to get them to ex-press their feelings like women.

"Mr. Chance, don't you think men need to get more in touch with their feelings? Aren't men an epitome of blocked emotion?"

"Most men are, Ms. Olsen, but should they find their emotions through a female model? Much of western therapy uses a woman's approach to reach emotion. Why do women and traditional therapy assume the female approach to feeling is correct for men?"

"You have to agree, Mr. Chance, when a man opens to his emo-tions, he is better off."

"That is bullshit. When a man reaches for a female model of emo-tion, he does find some of his feelings, but only soft female ones. A guy becomes safe for women when he finds those feelings, but at a cost of losing his maleness."

"Better a soft male than one who can't feel emotion."

"Better for who? Better for women perhaps. Safer for women I'm sure. I'm not sure the soft male is better for society.

"From my point of view, a wimpy man is like a puppy. He is cute and cuddly, but entirely useless. When he piddles on the floor, women clean up after him. I'm hoping for the day when the puppy grows up. Under a veneer of puppy-dog emotion is a vicious Doberman pin-scher. Men's emotions are different."

He gets all worked up about male issues. I'm not sure if I want to fuel the flame or throw water on it. He definitely is not a wimpy male. There is something exciting and at the same time repulsive about him. I decide to slow him down before his Doberman does come out. "How did you think of that interesting conclusion, Mr. Chance?"

"How I came up with it is of little importance, Olsen."

The bastard called me Olsen.

"The important thing to recognize is under a soft veneer of modern man is a killer, ready to strike out at any moment. Repressed emotions of men are what most women are afraid of. Isn't that why you're trying to sidetrack me from my point?"

"Sidetrack you?" I say.

He leaps to his feet again, swinging his arms, taking three steps away from me, pulling the spotlight away with him. When he turns, he yells, "Get off it, Olsen, and stop bullshitting around. Stop trying to slow me down. If you have the balls, get your butt into this dog pit with me, and let's scrap."

"Mr. Chance, I wouldn't go anywhere with you. All I want to do is to call security."

He steps back, and sits. "My point exactly!" he says softly.

"Exactly?"

"A man in his wildness scares women, who in turn want to keep men from feeling wild and unruly, crazy and sexy."

I open my mouth to counter, but he continues.

"When a man refuses to become friendly with his wildness, someone else must fill in for him. The reason war and murder run amuck is because most men are too afraid to touch their dangerous side. Have you noticed the big gap between hawks and doves? Hawks, under the guise of protecting us, play out society's inability to deal with rage. Hawks get to run roughshod over the rest of the world because most men in our culture don't want anything to do with anger. Our system is built to keep men disempowered, so hawks can run with our unexpressed fury."

"If I'm hearing you right, you're saying men should go with their killer Doberman. Doesn't that sound a little scary to you?"

"No, Olsen, it sounds scary to you. I'm not saying men should act on their killer instincts, which is what men have been doing since time immemorial. What I say is instead of hiding that wild part of them, men need to become friendly with that side of themselves. They need to bring that side of themselves into their living room and introduce it to the family."

I can't believe what he is says. Sure, it has merit, and I know where he's going, but I'm still cautious.

"You say men should bring their Doberman home and let it lose on their family?"

"Come on, Olsen, not let it lose, introduce, keeping a short rein, so that no one gets hurt."

"So far you have been speaking in metaphors. What does your theory look like in real life? What would a man do, for instance, in day-to-day life, to introduce his killer to the family?"

He swings his head away and looks directly at the camera, like he is speaking to all of the men in television land. He gets a serious expression and says, "A man needs to consider what I'm about to say as dangerous work. It should be approached slowly and with caution. He must gradually unravel old ways, slowly introducing the new. The process could take twenty years."

"Twenty years, Mr. Chance. That's a long time."

He doesn't turn his head to look at me, but maintains his focus on the camera. "If a man does things too quickly, he can easily destroy his family, his career, maybe everything around him. Sometimes that kind of destruction is mandatory for a man to find himself again, but it is not always necessary. To make a careful start, find a place in the relationship where you feel resentment."

"You mean like he resents the woman because she doesn't like to sleep with him?"

"That is not a small subject Ms. Olsen. That one could be saved until the family gets used to the gradual changes, and sees that the changes aren't going to destroy the family. Start small."

"What do you mean then?"

"A man could refuse to do dishes if he resents doing the dishes. A man who mows the lawn because he is supposed to could decide he is not going to ever mow another lawn. It could be washing the car, if that is where his rancor lies. Each man has his own place where he has been bending over backwards to appease a woman or his family. Some men might have to quit their destructive jobs and do something creative or more interesting. The list is endless."

"You're advocating that men stop doing things for their family?"

"Only if what they do brings them resentment. Unresolved resentment kills relationships, not the Doberman itself."

"Don't men and women have resentments they have to live with? Isn't this simply a fact of life?"

"Anger is a fact of life, Olsen, but it is pure bullshit. The less bitterness a person is forced to live with, the longer and happier he or she lives."

"Mr. Chance. Do you live in a fantasy world. We just can't end resentment. Some resentm--"

"Resentments can't be helped, but most are either self-inflicted, or worse yet, self-accepted. Many men are forced to deal with women who are resentful, like you, for example, but most resentments are easily dealt with by being ruthlessly honest."

I snap back at him, "what do you mean, I'm not resentful."

Channeling Biker Bob

"Oh, get off it, Olsen. You're the worse kind, because you have candy coated your resentment to look like you're being helpful."

"Mr. Chance, I nev--."

He holds his hand as if to shush me, then leaps to his feet. Again, the cameras follow him as he walks away from my desk out to the middle of the stage, taking the spotlight with him. He looks over the crowd.

"Many men refuse to say they're sorry, but I believe a larger portion of our male population wants to appease their women. They are the first to apologize, often without an apology in return.

"Those men need to make an agreement with their women."

I glance at the small screen on my desk, as the camera pulls in for a close up of him. Like he is personally talking to every man watching my show, he says, "Make an agreement that you won't say you're sorry for a year or two, just to break a pattern."

"Not say they are sorry?" I shout as I stand and walk over to him. This is getting interesting, and I want the cameras on both of us. I'll be damned if the bastard will steal my limelight.

He has just walked down the wrong path. He made a fatal mistake, and I'm getting ready to chop him to pieces. "Mr. Chance, if a man has done something wrong isn't his responsibility to apologize?"

"I don't mean he shouldn't be accountable. He must admit his error, but just not apologize. Remember, this only applies to men who constantly find themselves apologizing."

I can't say this on the air, but I think all men should apologize for more than what they have done. They need to make up for all the wrong done to women by men throughout history.

He screams, "No, Ms. Olsen, men should not apologize for more than what they've done. They don't have to make up for all the wrong done to women throughout history."

I'm speechless. How does he read my thoughts like that?

His tone is lower, but still loud. "Yes, men have raped and murdered their way through history. Millions of little Genghis Khans cloud every historic moment, but they are clearly only one type of man. Women will never get even a hint of an apology from those kinds of men. Those men have a shell that is nearly impossible to crack. Your job is not to hold responsible the millions of men who are approachable, who would never harm a hair on anyone's head, much less a woman's. Usually these men get most of the flak for the others. Safe men, the ones who are more good-natured and more easily held responsible. They are also men who are willing to accept responsibility, though they clearly are not the perpetrators."

155

Nik C. Colyer

What he says goes against every fiber of my womaness, but I find no holes in his statement. He has no loose ends that allow me to slam him back to his former Mr. Stewart Chance, the stuttering wimp.

He looks bigger and bigger as moments go on, and I don't like what is happening. No one is supposed to look better than me on my television program.

I try to think of a way to wedge myself between the man and his philosophy. I don't notice him turn his back to the camera. He reaches his hands over mine. In shock, I pull back, but he has a firm grip. He leans over and whispers in my ear. "You don't have to hate men. Many of us are okay."

I find myself leaping back and yelling at him, "Get your hands off of me, you asshole."

Oh shit, I said one of the seven deadly words on the air. In horror I watch him strut off stage.

My ear prompter is silent. The video prompter is blank. Is the camera still running? I look at the camera, shift from my look of horror and attempt to pull the corners of my mouth up into a smile. My smile finds its place as the red indicator light blinks off. My face returns into a twisted grimace. I walk back and plunk myself into my chair, then look out and see that the entire audience is again silent. My other three guests are silent. The room has not made a sound since Mr. Chance left the stage.

***

Since Bob took over, I have a vague recollection of what happens while I'm on stage, but I have no specific memories. A hazy feeling of doom persists all the way into my dressing room.

Someone knocks at my door.

"Come in," I say. My voice is still shaky.

Vander steps in with a worried frown and says, "I don't know, Mr. Chance, you might have blown the deal. Olsen isn't happy."

"Oh my gosh, what did I do?"

His expression shifts as he snickers, "You ripped her heart out. You probably blew the deal, but for the first time since she came on the scene, you put that snippy bitch in her place. She has been a thorn in my ass for years, and you are the first guy to ever get to her. For that one reason alone, I salute you. At the same time, I have the rotten job of informing you that we will probably lose the contract with the network."

"Lose the contract," I say. "That's great! Being on camera takes too much out of me."

Vander doesn't like my response.

156

Channeling Biker Bob

Within the next thirty minutes, seven men knock on my door, each one with a congratulatory thumbs-up for getting to Olsen. I'm accepting cheers and salutations, but I still don't know why I deserve all of this attention.

At the top of the hour, as I'm ready to vacate my room, a real live executive enters. It's Underman, the guy I had breakfast with, the guy under Bob's influence. Tension in the air is thick as he steps in with a knife-edge smile. While only looking at me, he asks Vander to leave.

"You had many interesting things to say today, Mr. Chance," he says without emotion. "I've always been the one to apologize first in my marriage."

He's embarrassed. With great effort he continues.

"I'm always the only one to apologize."

I try to figure out why Mr. Executive has come into my room and unloaded his family secrets on me. I want to find a reason why he is here, but I can't.

"I want to stop doing that," he says. "Any suggestions?"

Do I have any suggestions? He's asking me? What the heck do I look like some kind of guru?

Bob's voice deep inside me says, "Tell him to write down three or four of his latest experiences. Tell him you will get back with him in a day or two."

I relay the message.

He nods apprehensively and backs out of the room.

"What the heck was that all about?" Vander asks after he comes back in and closes the door.

I shrug.

"Shit, Mr. Chance, that was Phil Underman. What you said out on stage, in one way or another, struck home for most of us men."

"What did I say?"

He looks at me. "You don't know what you said?"

"Bob speaks through me. I'm hardly ever around."

He turns pale. "That was your buddy Biker Bob? All along I thought he was a friend of yours."

"Well, in a sense he is a friend. He's a troublesome spirit who comes through me."

"Jesus, man, you are hotter than I could have ever imagined."

Another knock comes at my door.

I ask Vander if he would get me a copy of my fifteen missing minutes. I want to know what Bob said. He agrees and lets in the next of an on-going line of men.

Twenty minutes and five more congratulating men later, Vander returns with the tape and locks the door behind him.

"You'd better listen to what Bob said and to what is being said about you on the noon news." He plugs in the video cassette, and I watch Biker Bob talking through my mouth.

It's weird seeing myself talking on subjects about which I know nothing. The strangest thing is, everything Bob says is true. I'm the wimp he speaks of. I'm the man who gets to my feelings using a female model.

When Bob's performance ends, after a second or two of blank tape, the anchor of a local television station comes on. "Mr. Stewart Chance gave a heroic talk this morning on the Susan Olsen show. He was. . ."

The newsreel continues, but after seeing what Bob did, I don't need to hear a commentator recap the event. I turn the set off and look at Vander.

"Do you give me a ride home, or am I on my own from here?"

"Ride home? Mr. Chance, I don't think you understand. At first, I thought we were finished when you murdered Olsen. From all indications, everyone likes what you, I mean, Bob had to say. Well, at least every man. Except for Underman, I haven't gotten any concrete message from the top, but from what I have seen, I'm sure they'll want you to continue with the tour. Not only are you a hero, but you are also a controversial hero. In the television industry, you're a dream come true."

"Oh?" I say, "I looked forward to going home."

"Sit tight, pal, in four hours they will be taping Leatherman. I need to talk to management, but I'm sure they'll want you on tonight's show."

As Vander leaves, I hang a "Do-not-disturb" sign on my door and take a nose-dive onto an uncomfortable little couch for the express purpose of re-gathering enough guts to go on Daniel Leatherman. Now that I'm sure Bob will take over, I relax, but how long must I be on camera before he shows up?

It's only mid-morning, but I desperately need a nap. Although I slept well last night, I fall asleep almost before my head rests on the rigid arm of the couch.

***

Bob sits on the end of my couch. "Don't worry, Chance, I'll help you get through the interviews, if you help me by continuing to do them."

I lift my groggy head and glance at him wearing full-dress black leather riding gear. His wrap around shades and silver-colored studs running along sleeves give him a look of an Egyptian scarab.

I'm reluctant to awake, knowing I need to rest for Leatherman.

158

Channeling Biker Bob

"Hey Chance, you're still resting. I'm in your dream, and I want to talk to you. Open your eyes." As if commanded by his simple suggestion, my eyes flash open, and I bullet into a sitting position.

"That's better," he says. "Now here's what I want you to do."

Twenty minutes later, I awake. I reluctantly roll off the couch and onto my feet. The large lighted mirror reflects an image of a haggard prune-face with hangover eyes. The sink in the corner of my room is a welcome sight. I splash an ample amount of water and scrub sleep from my eyes with a stiff towel.

The clock on the desk blinks little red numerals: 1:15. I have an hour and forty-five minutes before I'm in front of the camera again. The water helps, but the mirror still says I look like death warmed over. A quick walk in fresh air might help.

I reach for my jacket and walk out of the room into chaos. Twice as many cables as I remember snake along the hall floor. I'm forced to step on several of them to find my way to the back door. An old security guy with a paunch the size of Iceland, stops me as I reach the stage door.

"I'll be back in twenty minutes," I say.

He acknowledges me with a yawn, as I push through the door and out onto a steel landing three flights over a back alley. On the other side of the door, I trade the noise of the set for a roar of the city. I descend the stairs and find myself stepping out onto a busy boulevard. I'm not thinking about which way to go. I don't even think about what I'm doing on the streets. I'm simply on a stroll to loosen my body from sleeping on a couch of concrete.

I turn at a corner and the light is with me, so I cross the street. A throng of humanity swallows me as I zigzag through shoppers, hoppers, and bippers. By the time I reach the next corner, I'm asked for spare change seven times, and two different men try to sell me something from inside their coats.

I turn the next corner, intent on making a loop back to the alley and my dressing room before they call me for Leatherman.

Dodging the shoppers and boppers, ignoring the hustlers and spare changers, I turn left into a small shop. I have not even looked to see what kind of shop, before I'm through the glass door that rings a little bell above my head. A young woman dressed in skin-tight black Lycra, and sporting silky long black hair stands in front of me.

Her eyes brighten like she recognizes me. I turn to see if someone else has walked in.

"Stewart Chance." she says.

"Yes? How do you know my name?"

"I'm watching you right here on Susan Olsen." She points to a monitor above my head. I turn and see myself standing over Ms. Ol-

159

sen. My voice is so loud that I'm nearly yelling at her. She turns ten shades of red and snaps a response, but I'm not listening. What I'm listening to is a few sound blips every sentence. I must have used an abundance of cuss words.

"I like what you had to say about men," she says. "My boyfriend could use your philosophy."

"Thanks." I have a hard time pulling my attention from the lines of the Lycra-enhanced woman. She stares at the screen above me. I turn away from the she-spectacle and glance at merchandise. The small store is filled with steel studs and leather biker gear. On the walls are riding chaps, saddlebags, gloves, fully spiked jackets, and knee-high four-inch spike-heeled boots. The boots are much like the ones Miss Lycra wears. Three glass counters are filled with buttons, badges, and knives.

I wonder what I'm doing in here as I glance back at the shapely young woman. She is still glued to the TV. As if not knowing what I'm saying, my mouth spews out a demand, "I want a full set of leathers."

Her eyes flash from the screen for a split second.

"Give me another minute, until the commercial."

Consciously pulling my gaze away from her amazing form, I concentrate my attention on the contents of the glass cases for five minutes, until the commercial blares into the shop.

Her face lights and she has a wide, full-lipped grin. "Damn, Mr. Chance, you nailed her. I've watched her show since I started working here, and no one has ever got to her the way you did."

I want to say it wasn't me, but from experience I'll be here a week trying to explain my relationship with Bob. "Thanks," I say.

"You want leathers, huh?"

I can't believing I have even formed the idea of leathers, much less walked into a store and requested them.

"Black, I assume?"

I agree, then follow her to a chrome rack of black leather.

"What size are you?"

I shrug.

"Most guys don't know their size." She starts into a long dissertation concerning men and their size, as she expertly pulls a cloth tape from behind the counter and measures my shoulders, chest, waist, hips, and inseam. She only interrupts her incessant chatter to call off each measurement, as if someone else is in the store writing the information. Once a number is cast adrift, without missing a beat, she continues with her chatter.

My first impression of her as a silent, sultry dominatrix is blown as she shifts, non-stop, from one subject to the next.

160

Channeling Biker Bob

As her incoming oral tide rolls through the store, she expertly slips me into a jacket. I look in the mirror at a perfect fit. No studs or tassels; this one has been cut to look good either on a bike, or at a gathering of business executives. Well, okay. We won't go that far, but friendly business executives, after work.

I'm still admiring the jacket while she helps me slip into pants.

I wonder why I'm buying leathers? What has gotten into me? I continue a biker dress rehearsal and find myself out on the street wearing a black T-shirt with the golden-winged Harley-Davidson logo plastered across my chest. The black leather jacket hangs comfortably from my shoulders. My leather pants are a little stiff, but the calf-high boots with a Harley logo embossed in the tread and black Harley socks, make up for the rigid new leather. I carry a pair of long-skirted Hap Jones leather gloves in one hand and wear a black duck-billed cap on my head. My new look is finished with a gold-plated Harley wing pin in the center of my hat, just above the bill.

I look at my reflection in a window of a department store and see a ridiculous walking advertisement for Harley-Davidson.

When I arrive at the stage door, the guard doesn't recognize me. I have to take off my hat and jacket before he lets me pass.

In my dressing room, I sit in front of the mirror and look at a want-to-be Marlon Brando. I like the look, and I love the hat.

"You're on in ten minutes Mr. Chance," I hear after three quiet knocks at my door.

I'm ready to disrobe and resume my old life, when the door bursts open and in walks Daniel Leatherman. He gives me his famous goofy grin and walks over with his hand out to shake.

"Hey, I hear you gave Olsen a run." He grabs my hand and gives me two quick wrenches. "She needed a worthy adversary."

"Thanks," I say.

"Hey, your gear looks great. You going to wear it on the set?"

"No, I just bought it down the street. I'll take it off before I go in front of the camera."

"Hell, man, you look grand. Kind of gives you a biker mystique. Go ahead and wear it, you'll be a great show stopper."

"You think so?"

"Wear them, your clothes will be perfect."

In the same manner he busted into my room, he says, "See you on the set," and exits.

I stand in stunned silence until I hear a knock at the door. "Five minutes, Mr. Chance."

Here come my butterflies turned to vultures again. Here comes my hurricane of self-doubt. Here comes that insane stuttering. Although I have yet to say a word, the fear monster creeps up from my guts.

"One minute, Mr. Chance."

I make another death march following Vander down the hall. I stand, watching the Leatherman show with a live audience, shaking in my new Harley boots, waiting to step on stage and be introduced.

I'm in front of the camera, answering two of Leatherman's questions in my stumbling, stuttering, blanched-faced manner. I think an hour has gone by, but the big clock on the wall says two minutes. To my utter relief, Bob takes over. I'm in the background and hear what is going on. I almost come forward and engage in the conversation myself, except I'm frozen with stage fright. To have a ringside seat in my own body is an odd sensation. I come up with questions and answers, while my mouth speaks on entirely different subjects.

"Men in our culture!" Bob says after he has taken possession.

Leatherman's face changes as Bob shifts from my squeaky tenor to his powerful baritone.

"If we are going to have meaningful relationships, us men must learn how to re-engage with our women. Our culture is set to disempower everyone by keeping us separate: Men and women, blacks and whites, Catholics and Protestants, Jews and gentiles."

Bob is winding up for his pitch and I get a strong feeling that it will be a doozy.

"We're kept separate by continuing to use everyone else as our scapegoats. Too many negative things are said about others, whoever they might be. For now, I would like to concentrate on men and women."

Leatherman leans back in his chair. He looks like he's hunkering for the duration as Bob steam rolls into his next subject. "Now is the time for those men who have aligned themselves with women, at the expense of themselves, to find their masculinity."

Leatherman says a quick, "What do you mean?"

"Too many men have turned into unfailing nice guys. It's not a bad thing, but working from within the mandates of the feminist movement, in the face of female intensity, many men roll over like puppy dogs. I'd rather see men stand and make their own masculine needs be known. Many men shrink under a threat of women's rage. I believe we need to figure out how to love a woman, while holding our ground and our own points of view."

"If what you say is true," Leatherman says, "and men are giving away the farm, what can we do?"

"We need to take our stubbornness back, practice being unaccommodating assholes again."

Leatherman winces, glancing at the cringing producer.

"Women don't emasculate men. Men who don't stand up for themselves allow their own balls to be cut. Often a man will think that taking a stance with the feminine is just not worth the trouble. Trust me, if the subject is important enough for her to hold her ground, you better make it important enough to maintain your opinion and not allow yourself to be emasculated."

Bob pauses to let that last word sink in. So far, as usual, he's talking about me.

"The intensity with which a strong woman will maintain her position, not allowing any dissenting remarks, is an amazing thing. The problem comes when a man isn't willing to stand in the face of adversity, with kindness in his heart, and say he has a right to his opinion, too."

Bob looks out at the audience. "That is to say that we need to maintain a warrior's love while we are engaging in battle with our women. If we lose that edge of kindness and let the killer Doberman lose, all is lost. Not only do we allow our balls to be cut, because we lose control, but we also act like jerks or abusers in the process."

I get a strong feeling that he is ready to leap to his feet and take over the show, but, though he grips the arms of his chair, he holds himself back and continues. "Only a strong man maintains his opinion, while also honoring his adversary's voice. Opinions are like assholes everybody has one. The job for both men and women is to make room for other views. Often, men and woman have opposing points of view. We see our worlds differently. No one has to accept the others opinion as fact, but we must make room for contrary views.

"If either sex gives in even once when an opinion issue is up, it is easier to buckle a second time, and a third. As time goes by, the person can forget that their opinions matter. Forgetfulness happens to a man as well as a woman. This is one place festering resentments come from."

"That's all good for you," says Leatherman.

I'm ready for him to counter Bob's monologue.

"But, my opinion is that we need to go to a commercial."

The audience whistles and applauds as the indicator light on the camera dies.

Leatherman leans over. "I like what you're saying, but you've got to let me speak too."

"Sure," Bob says. "Just jump in."

"You must leave me space to jump in, or we will look like we're fighting. Battling for the floor is not good on camera."

"Oh," Bob says. "I'll toss the subject over once in a while?"

"Makes for a better production."

"Okay, no problem."

"You're on in ten, nine," the production manager says and wags his finger with the passing of each remaining second, until the camera light blinks back on.

"You talked about maintaining our opinions while in discussion with women," Leatherman says.

"Yes, but let's talk about the other side of this issue, the patriarchy. In the sixties, the women's movement made an amazing and desperately needed shift for our culture. Women got together to take their power back from a two-thousand-year-old patriarchy. I applaud them for taking on that honorable task.

"I want to make myself clear; patriarchy and masculinity are two different things."

"Oh, how is that?" Leatherman says. He isn't going to get a word in, but that doesn't slow Bob.

"Patriarchy is a system of defined rigidity, usually controlled by men, but either a man or woman can choose to be part of the controlling patriarchy.

"One patriarchal myth is that women need protection. In giving them the protection we think they need, we disempower them. The chauvinistic, sexist, controlling, men who continue to perpetuate the patriarchy are usually not available to even hear what women have to say."

Bob leaps to his feet. He steps forward a few paces and looks out into the audience. "Men are aware of the changes women are going through. Those who listen to your demands for equal rights and treatment, know the balance between men and women is way off. Some men instinctively understand the justice in women having equal rights and equal pay. Many of those men bend over backwards to accommodate women."

"Are you one of those men?" Leatherman says.

Bob ignores his question. Without skipping a beat, he continues. "To compensate for an unfair system, many men have learned to be nice, sometimes too nice. They have done the nice act so long they have lost focus on their own masculinity. They lead their lives being entirely considerate of women, with little consideration for themselves. Women are not to blame for this."

Bob takes a breath, gathers his thoughts, and gets ready for another salvo.

"We men have been leading our lives in fear of women's wrath, too long. We need to take our maleness back. The wrath of a woman frightens us, because it's dark and mysterious. We must respect feminine darkness, but we don't need to take it on."

He walks along the stage. The lights follow.

"Our biker sons of bitches need to come back out. We need to take the part of ourselves back that the feminist movement has been holding for us all of these years."

"What has the feminist movement been holding?" asks Leatherman from back at his desk.

"Our bitches!"

"Bitches?"

"It means taking our rage back from women, the cranky or spiteful parts we don't want, the snippy parts we definitely don't like, or even as small as those ugly little thoughts we don't think we have. If we don't own that dark side of ourselves, without thinking, we ask our women to carry it for us. Unconsciously, too many women agree. If you look closely at a man who has asked his woman to carry his bitch, you may find an unusually nice guy. Everyone will say, that Harry is so nice he would give you the shirt off his back. When you meet his wife, you might find a short-tempered, snappy, shrewish sort of woman, ready to bite off anyone's head."

"You're generalizing aren't you?"

"Yes, but it happens too often, and the unfortunate woman probably carries her husband's dark side. Many call it the witch. Because Harry is such a nice guy, and few want him to be different, someone else must act out his masked behaviors."

I realize that Renee may be carrying my bitch. It could explain why she has been so angry. Have I been overly nice?

While I have my revelation, Bob continues, "That unfortunate women is forced to carry two people's unruly parts inside of her. A balance must be achieved. If a man is unfailingly nice, his wife, or one of his children, may have to carry it. It may be left to the family dog, but trust me, someone has to carry the pent-up anger. Isn't it time that men take responsibility for our own rage."

Bob steps back, settles into his seat, then looks straight into the camera. "Now is the time for us men to take our bitches back."

Leatherman, in his unique goofy way gives his wide-gapped toothy grin and says, "I don't think I've heard that many cuss words in one program in my life. We're making television history."

The audience laughs and applauds. When things get quiet again, Leatherman asks, "Mr. Chance, what do you mean by--"

"First thing I want to say," Bob interrupts, "I am not Stewart Chance. Because I don't have one of my own, Stewart has been gracious enough to loan me his body. Call me Biker Bob."

Leatherman's expression shifts. His look is transformed.

"Okay, Biker Bob," he says cautiously. "Do you mean to say you're inside of Stewart Chance's body?"

"In a sense Stewart has accidentally channeled my frequency, and I come through him from the other side of the veil."

"Do you mean you're dead?"

"I didn't come here to answer questions about how I happen to be inside Stewart. Let us just say that I am and call it a day. I came here to say that it's time for men must stand and be counted without joining the patriarchy and overpowering the feminine."

Leatherman looks confused or cautious, but he takes the revelation in talk-show-host stride and moves on. "What did you mean when you said earlier about taking our bitches back?

"A man must make an agreement with his family first, then begin a daily practice of not being nice. If he has found himself apologizing too often, he might stop saying he's sorry for a year or so. One can admit to being wrong without saying he is sorry."

"Not being nice?" Leatherman asks.

"Try getting a little cranky when you feel irritated. Don't loan that lawn mower to your neighbor, if you don't feel like it. You don't need any reasons. Let yourself be a small-minded asshole from time to time. Practice getting angry."

Leatherman leaps in, "getting angry around a woman is not that easy. They take it so personal."

"You can't let go with women around, because at first most women can't handle masculine fury. It's too frightening.

"Find men who understand, and let your unbridled rage out with them. Get a punching bag and beat the shit out of it. There are as many approaches to getting the anger out as there are humans on our planet."

"You're advocating abandoning the nice guy?" Leatherman says. "Doesn't being pleasant to one another make our congested, chaotic plant livable?"

"I'm not saying to make an about-face with everyone you come in contact, though some men must, to purge themselves. Find places in your life that are safe enough to consciously let your monsters out. Hire a therapist who specializes in rage work. Go alone into the forest, or along an abandoned shoreline, and direct your screaming at who-ever you are enraged with until you lose your voice. Get an ax and split cordwood, putting on the wood all of the faces of people who have ever wronged you. Rage at that person, as you split that particular piece of wood. As you can see, there are many approaches."

Leatherman grimaces. "Sounds a little frightening."

"At first it will be, but get creative. Doing these things won't be easy, but reward far exceeds effort. Remember, you can't purge yourself all in one attempt. This kind of work takes years, sometimes decades. It's a slow unraveling."

"I have to admit that your concept takes a little getting used to, but what reactions will our families have?"

Channeling Biker Bob

"It's unfair to do most of this work around your family. They wouldn't understand. But, it won't take long before they'll start asking you what happened. Soon they will feel the relief of you beginning to own the not-so-nice side of yourself.

Chapter 9

LETTERS

I'm back in my dressing room before I'm fully myself. My face feels foreign and still numb. I dip both my hands into a pitcher of water and experience a soothing coolness on my estranged fingers. Scooping the icy liquid in both hands, I splash and rub water on my face. During my second dip into the water, my attention is drawn to the right end of the table.

I dry my hands and pick up the envelopes. My name is scrawled in black felt-tip ink across the face of the first, a manila oversize. Its inscription is thick enough lettering to see from twenty yards. Mr. Stewart Chance/Biker Bob, the cover reads. The letter has obviously been hand delivered, because there is no stamp. I flip the back envelope to the front. In neat, well-spaced, script I read Mr. Biker Bob.

I tear a strip off the end of the big yellowish envelope and pull out two sheets of plain white paper.

Mr. Chance/Bob,
I'm watching you speak on Leatherman as you tape for this evening's broadcast. I can't help but realize that I too have been suffering from acute nice guy.

I appreciate your candid and fresh views on the subject and look forward to more about repairing this weakened part of myself. I believe I have also given my masculinity over to women; first to my wife, but also to my daughter, and last, but certainly not least, I daily give my

168

power over to the three women who work under me to produce this show. I understand now I have been such an overly nice guy that I've given women around me no choice but anger. I look forward to hearing more.

Thank you for helping me understand a fundamental flaw in my relations with people. What I'm going to do about it now is another guess. I will watch and hope you will address this critical question for me on the air.

Thanks again

William G. Flanders
Production Manager

The second letter is much less formal, yet well scripted. On a postcard-size piece of card stock five words are printed, all in caps: KEEP UP THE GOOD WORK!

In the same neat pen, at the bottom of the card, he has signed simply, SOL.

I don't know, is this fan mail?

Leatherman bursts into my room.

"Hey, Chance, that was amazing. Where did you think up a character Biker Bob?"

"I didn't think of him. He just showed up one day, and my life hasn't been the same since."

"Come on man, he can't be for real. I mean the stuff you had to say is pretty good, but Bob can't be real?"

"I'm afraid he is, and I'm afraid he is here to stay."

"Oh," says Leatherman. He gets an odd look on his face. "I hoped he wasn't for real, because he scares me. The stuff he says is bone jarring."

"He scares me, too. My life is a shambles because of Bob. Would I do it all over again? No hesitation."

"You come on my show again. We'll talk more about men."

"Whenever you'll have me."

"I'll talk to my producers and see what we can cook up." He takes a furtive glance at his watch. "Got to get back."

When he leaves, I look back at my two pieces of fan mail.

***

"Katherine, I couldn't believe it, that. . .that son of a bitch went on Leatherman dressed in black leather biker clothes. He has gone over the edge. I was forced to get used to him owning that motorcycle after he became a national hero, but now he wears that leather getup on Leatherman?"

"Oh, no you don't, Katherine. He has gone way over the line. You can't write his actions off as midlife crisis crap. He has got shit to pay when he gets home, if he ever comes home. He hasn't taken the time to call his wife and family in more than a week. When he calls, I'm going to read him the riot act."

"What do you mean, it is no wonder he doesn't call? I pay you to support me, not my son of a bitch husband."

"You can't support my anger! Aren't I here to get to my anger? Now that I'm pissed as hell at Stewart, you say you aren't going to support me?"

"What? Why should I take responsibility? He has abandoned his family, leaving all the responsibility of running our house on me. He's having sex with that. . .that slut. I have a list as long as my arm. On top of everything, he's talking about men's crap on national TV where everyone and their sister watches. After Leatherman, I got sixteen messages from my girlfriends alone."

"Yes, I know he is on top. Unfortunately, everything is pretty sweet for him, now. Things won't be so sweet when he gets home."

"Chase Stewart away? You don't know Stewart like I do. He sticks like glue."

"Yes, yes I know. He finally went away like I wanted, and I'm still no happier."

"Yes, I guess I miss him. I wish he would just come home and be who he used to be."

"I guess. Now look, you've made me cry."

"I do miss him. Maybe he'll never come home again. I worry now that he is a national hero. . ." Sniff, sniff. "I worry he'll run off with that slut and never come home."

"Yes, though he is a jerk. . ." Sniff, sniff. "He is my jerk, and I want him back. I miss him."

***

I look at my watch at 10:30 and dial Renee from a pay phone outside of an all-night diner on Fifth Avenue. It's the first chance in three days I have gotten to do anything except be shuttled from set to set.

Except for Leatherman, who had no agenda, they all are too happy to take shots at me. They have all done their homework, but Bob has destroyed each talk-show host. Including radio interviews, the count is seventeen and zero. Although, thank God, I don't participate in the interviews, I watch while each new talk-show host bites the dust.

It's late and I'm tired, but I have been warned not to use the phones on set or at my hotel for fear of the press pinpointing my calls and harassing whoever I call.

"Hello, Renee."

"Stewart?"

"How have you been?"

"Where are you?"

"New York."

Silence.

"Listen Renee, I thought Friday you might fly out. We could spend a romantic weekend here in the Big Apple."

"Look here, you son of a bitch, if you've cooked up some kind of ploy to get me back, it's not going to work."

"Get you back? I didn't know you had gone anywhere. All I'm doing is inviting you to come out so that we might spend some time together without the kids."

"What would you have me do with our children?"

"I don't care what you do with them." I want to apologize for being rude, but I sense a nudge from inside; a Bob nudge.

I take a breath, put the terminal nice guy aside and say, "Getting someone to watch our kids is something for you to work out. I'm inviting you to come out and stay with me in one of the better hotels in New York. These TV guys are treating me like a king. I would like to share my kingdom with you."

She shouts over the line. "You can't talk to me that way. Your job is to take care of our kids just as much as mine is."

She's starting down a long winding path of rage, and she wants to take me with her.

"Renee!" I shout at her for the first time in our relationship. The three-thousand-mile gap between us makes my response easier. "Stop screaming. Either you come or not; it's up to you."

She stops her ranting and launches into a other kind of intensity I'm well used to: silence.

In the dark space, I calm and gather myself. I begin again. "I'm inviting you to come to New York for a romantic weekend. You work out how you are going to accomplish the task. I'll call you tomorrow to see if you're interested."

She starts back into another rant.

I quietly replace the receiver.

It feels good to hang up on her, but my guilt weighs on me before I have taken ten steps. I nearly turn to call her back. I want to apologize for being crass, but Bob rips at my gut to continue walking. I force myself to put one foot in front of another with guilt twisting at my guts. I turn back toward the phone booth three times before I reach the end of the block. Each time, however, I continue. When I step through the double glass doors of my hotel, I'm elated. I made it. I didn't buckle.

In the morning, I awake to a knock at my door as a young man rolls in an early morning wake-up tray. A smell of coffee brings me around enough to open one eye. It isn't long before I pull up and sit on the side of the bed, stand, then amble into the living room to a tray of croissants, bear claws, and fresh fruit. Coffee is my main objective. I fill the dainty cup to the brim. With coffee in one hand and a bear claw in my other, I walk over to the table and look out over the Hudson River. From my perch of thirty-five stories, far off to my left, I see the Statue of Liberty. The sun peeks over the buildings as I take my first bite.

Five minutes of early morning bliss passes before my phone rings. I know who it is. I have gotten the same call every morning for the last month. He thinks he is giving me a you-are-going-to-do-fine-today-Stewart wake-up call. I don't want to answer the phone, but it will continue to ring until I do. I reach over and grab the receiver. "Good morning Mr. Vander," I say in my most cheerful voice. The more cheerful I am, the fewer pep talks I get.

"Stewart?"

"Renee?"

Butterflies from last night return and flutter into my mouth. I can't deal with Renee's anger so early. I look over and the clock reads six-thirty. I realize it's four hours earlier in California.

"Stewart?"

I'm not hearing the voice of the shrew I hung up on last night. I hear a woman I married many years ago. I haven't heard her in more years than I remember. Does her change have anything to do with me getting angry last night? Am I really beginning to take my bitch back?

"Renee?" I say again.

"I haven't been able to sleep since we talked." She says. "I thought about your offer, and I'd like to come to New York for the weekend. Will you book the flight for me?"

In a million years, this was the last thing I ever expected her to say. Berate me, belittle me, control me, and try to make a deal with me, yes, but accept my offer?

"Sure, Renee. I'll get your ticket today. I'll call you tonight with the times and flight numbers."

"I. . .I love you, Stewart," she says tentatively.

I haven't heard those words for many years. I'm so unhinged from her declaration that I don't know what to say. Before our almost perfect conversation is ruined with an argument, I want to hang the phone up. I want to completed one conversation in the last year without a cross word between us, without one disagreement, not even a hint of resentment.

"I'll get the tickets and call you tonight. I have to go now," I lie. "They want me on an early set."

I disconnect and give a whoop. "We did it!"

I'm joyous, elated beyond belief. As I get into the shower, I sing an old Beatles hit, "When I'm Sixty-four."

I think about wearing leathers again today, but remember how hot they are under lights. How good I feel in them is almost worth the heat, but I put on a pair of Levi's and a Hawaiian sport shirt the network left for me.

At 8:30, the limo is at the front door. I get on board still floating from my conversation with Renee.

At lunch, I call and book a flight, writing the time and flight number on the back of a studio business card.

"Renee," I say to our answering machine at three in the afternoon. I give her the flight information and hang up before she gets to the phone. I don't want to risk disrupting my euphoric feeling from our earlier conversation. As I turn from the pay phone, I face a group of five men who want my autograph and advice. I try my hardest to convince them that Bob is the one to talk to, but no one listens. They all want to talk to me. Once the growing New York crowd realizes I'm not going to answer any questions, things take on a more aggressive nature. One man demands I answer him as another moves in closer. I'm in the phone booth still and look around for a way out. In a split second, I realize my only avenue of escape will soon be cut off. I squeeze out of the booth and sprint down the block followed by a gang of who knows what. If they are fans, I'm not sure I want any. I don't slow until I get back to my hotel.

This is not the first time I have been accosted on the streets. Most people want a simple autograph, but always one or two jokers demand more. I try to explain about Bob, but no one listens.

At least inside my hotel, people are more courteous.

That evening, I return to my room to find a full three-foot high postal bag leaning against the bar. In the ultra clean, white-carpeted room, the scuffed old bag looks incongruent. Curious, I unclip the top and pull the string. The bag gets away from me and spills part of its contents onto the carpet.

"Oh my," I say aloud, grabbing the first of thousands of letters and postcards, all addressed to Bob or me.

"Fan mail!"

WHAT ABOUT ME?

Watching Stewart make a fool of himself on national TV makes me cringe. I watch in embarrassed horror as the ghost of a man tries, in his typically slow, inarticulate manner, to pull together even one normal sentence.

The stuttering bumbler I've known, simply, in one short second, vanishes. A new, extremely self-confident, highly articulate, cocky male sits in the same chair. He is a multiple personality, after all!

The new, deeper-voiced version, and he clearly introduces himself as Biker Bob, is lively. He jokes, banters, and sounds off about men. I don't like what he says, but he makes sense.

The new Stewart is more than articulate. He's quick with answers, and so fast on his feet, that he even flusters the immovable, unstoppable, Susan Olsen. He finally gets her off balance enough that she blows up. In all the years I've watched Susan Olsen, I have never seen her stumble. My Stewart, in a few short minutes has broken her into a rage.

Stewart stirs a feeling that I haven't experienced for a long time. He is sexy.

I sit in the office lounge with four of my co-workers, including the hunk that fixes our computer systems. My mouth hangs open for the entire ten-minute interview. When a commercial interrupts the intense interchange, people in the coffee break room normally flare up with conversation to overpower the intrusive commercials. They are silent.

Channeling Biker Bob

Only an insistent jingle about a dishwashing detergent permeates the air. By the time my mind catches up with what I want to say, the new, sexy, Stewart Chance is back.

This is the first time I have even considered that maybe Biker Bob has sexy validity.

He takes command of Susan Olsen for a second time, something my old Stewart could never do.

When the interview is over and it's time to go back to work, no one in the room moves or speaks. We all sit mesmerized until someone finally turns the set off.

As if a spell is broken, everyone automatically leaves the room without a word. I'm so stunned that I can't move or talk, but a strange feeling of pride bubbles to the surface. Strange, because I have not once in our entire marriage ever thought that Stewart has done anything that warrants my feeling anything but pity for him. I actually feel pride. Admittedly, I have a twisted pride, but I'm proud, nonetheless.

No one says a word to me all day. No one mentions that my husband has made a fool of himself, but twice, made a fool of the famous Susan Olsen. No one congratulates me, chides me, belittles me, or razzes me.

At night, after the kids are asleep, I turn on TV and see my bumbling husband on Daniel Leatherman. He transforms himself into the fun-loving, wild-eyed, unpredictable, sexy guy who meets Leatherman, nose to nose, in goofiness and intelligence. They are a perfect match and the crowd roars.

In the middle of the interview Stewart gets serious and speaks for five minutes while a stunned Leatherman listens.

I hope he calls after Leatherman, but he doesn't. In fact, the bastard doesn't call for another two weeks. I have seen him four times on different talk shows, mostly recorded on our VCR, but does he call? I'm finally giving up on him, when, out of the blue, he calls at a god-awful hour. He offers to fly me out to New York for the weekend, but we immediately get into a squabble. Before I can hang up on him, he says good-bye, and the line goes dead. I'm so angry, I pace the house half the night.

He asked me to join him in New York, and he actually said the word romantic. Until I remember the 'R' word, it still has not occurred to me that he wants me with him. Katherine says I chase Stewart away, but through everything, he still wants me. It's three in the morning before I call back and accept his invitation. For the first time during the last impossible year, we actually talk to one another without getting into an argument. My butterflies of love flutter, like when I was a teenager.

This brings us to the present moment. I'm sitting in first class next to a little Puerto Rican fellow on an uncomfortably hot plane. The pilot says we are tenth in line to take off from Sacramento. I'm excited about and, at the same moment, dreading my arrival in New York. I don't know what Stewart will be like. Has he changed much over the last months? Who will be waiting for me at the other end of this flight? Will he even like me? Will I like him? Hundreds of questions roll through my thoughts as the plane lumbers along at a snail's pace.

I have been thinking about these issues for a long time, but still have not come to any conclusions. The only thing for sure is I'm flying, at my husband's request, to New York for a romantic weekend. Most of me anticipates seeing him. That is all I need for the moment.

Will Stewart be meeting me at the other end, or will his other half be there. A secret part of me, though I barely admit it, wants to be swept away by the wildly sexy loose cannon called Biker Bob.

I halfheartedly listen to the stewardess as she goes through the motions of showing us how to fasten our seat belts and use the air bags. The little thickset Latin nervously introduces himself, not by his name first, but his rank.

"I'm Major Hiendez," he says.

Oh, someone save me. He's a military jerk.

"Renee Chance," I respond, smile and turn away searching for anything to occupy my attention. I'm not about to get stuck for the next four hours being talked at by this little man. I end the exchange and quickly snatch an in-flight magazine from my pouch.

Five minutes go by, and I think I'm home free, before I hear his irritatingly squeaky voice again. "Where are you going?" he asks with a thick Spanish accent.

I can't believe the little twerp is coming on to me. I'd tell him to get a life, but my entire upbringing is laced with good Christian ethics. I respond in a short, "New York to meet my husband." I give him a perfunctory smile and return to my magazine. The husband part usually slows them down.

I stare into my magazine, trying to find an article to catch my attention, when he says, "I'm going to Cooba."

There is a catch to his voice, a nervous twitch I haven't heard until he says the word Cuba. I can't help myself; his declaration is much more interesting than the article.

"Isn't Cuba off-limits to Americans?" I ask while continuing to gaze my magazine.

"Yes it is," he says. "I was raised in Cooba. I have not been home for thirty years."

I look up. I have to look. The dink is really going to try and get to Cuba. Now he has my interest.

"If Cuba is off-limits, how do you plan to get home?"

176

Channeling Biker Bob

His smile is at the same time disarming and worrisome. I don't know what to think. He says nothing, just continues to smile and looks at his copy of the magazine.

Because I'm next to the window, I watch the ground slip past, first over the majestic Sierras and Lake Tahoe, then out onto the upper desert of Nevada. We come upon the salt flats of Utah.

After the Rocky Mountains, the Great Plains leave me nothing to look at. I don't want to turn back for fear that the dork will want to continue his conversation. He's drilling a hole in the back of my head, ready to speak the moment I turn from my window.

In my boredom, I think more about Stewart, our kids, and my parents. My thoughts go back to a hot summer day five years ago when Mom and Dad flew in from Miami. We met them at the airport. By the time we got them home Mom had snapped at, ridiculed, and undermined Dad at least ten times.

"Charles, can't you do anything right?" she snipped at him when he missed a bag on the turnstile. Dad, in his undaunted manner, smiled and said nothing. As a teenager, I remember many times when Mom chop him to pieces and fed him to the dogs. She never gave him a break, but he never stuck up for himself, either. As a teen, I vowed never to have a relationship like theirs. Yet, a relationship like my parents is exactly what I have. I despise my dad for not sticking up for himself. I also despise Stewart for the same noncommittal behavior, but lately things have changed.

That day coming home from the airport, I watched my Mom relentlessly ride Dad and watched him take the beating like nothing happened. The last thing I want to turn into is a harpy, but I realize a old harpy bitch is exactly what I've become. I decide right here and now, while staring out the window, to make a change in my relationship.

More than five years of weekly therapy with Katherine, and nothing has shifted. I'm still a harpy old bitch. I still relentlessly ride Stewart. I never give the guy a break, and I have not been able to stop. I don't know why he stays with me. When he took off for Barstow, I was sure he had gone for good. When he hooked up with that bimbo, I already half expected that he had left forever. Something inside me said that I can't treat a man like that and get away with it.

A small part of me wouldn't mind having a piece of the hunky computer guy. I'm certain he's attracted to me, but as klutzy as Stewart is, as embarrassing as he acts at times, I still love him. He hasn't called for weeks. He said he was too busy, but I know why. Katherine says every time he calls, I give him a hard time. I try to be pleasant, but he says one wrong thing, and I start snipping at him. I can't help myself.

The trip to New York, our last chance rendezvous at the other end of the country, might just be that, our last chance. I'm determined to not let my angry bitch take over. I promise myself only nice words will come out of my mouth. I will keep my bile to myself.

Until the other day, Stewart was the last person on earth I wanted to have sex with. Now I don't know anymore what I want. I mean, I can't compete with that redheaded slut. I saw her in his hospital room; I must be ten years her senior. Compared to her, I look like an old battle-ax with wrinkles I can't cover any longer.

"Do's you fly to New Yorks many times?"

The dork sitting next to me interrupts my thoughts. I decide what better chance than now to practice being a nicer person. I turn and force a smile. "No, this is my first trip to New York."

Wow, I can be nice after all. I'm responding with pleasant conversation, though I want to murder him. I'm feeling proud of myself as I go back into my thoughts.

Katherine tells me keeping a pleasant attitude will be impossible until I get to the core of what--.

"I've only beens to New Yorks myself once before," he says.

I can do this, but how do I ask him to stop talking, without completely losing my composure and jumping down his throat?

"Is that so?" I say, thinking of a way to politely dump him.

"Went to a play on Broadway. Many years ago, with my wife, when she still lived."

I don't want to hear about your dead wife, my mind screams. I don't want to hear about your pathetic little life. Leave me alone, alone, alone. Don't you get it, you idiot?

He's looking expectant.

"Broadway you say?" My sugarcoated response will surely give him the message I don't want to talk.

I'm not able to get my message across. Am I crazy listening to forty-five minutes of Cooba's incessant rattling about his dead wife, his lost job, even his runaway cat. I'm trying not to listen, but some of his dribble gets in. I say yes or no occasionally. I'm right on the edge of exploding all over the sad little man, when a stroke of genius hits me. I excuse myself to go to the bathroom. I get up, walk five rows to the front of the plane, and stand by the locked door. I glance back and see the twerp looking around, then back at me. Oh no, he can't be waiting for my return. I scan the other seats in first class and sadly only one is empty, probably the person in the bathroom. I consider going back into coach to rid myself of that chatterbox, but this is the first time I have ever flown first class. I'm determined to enjoy the experience. The door opens and a woman steps out. With great disappointment, I watch her walk to the only empty seat. In the bathroom, I take my time. As long as no one else is waiting, I'm safe in here. I relieve myself then pull out my make-up bag to apply fresh lipstick. The quiet is a relief, I want to stay here for the rest of the flight.

***

I sit in my dressing room after doing nineteen different shows last month. Nineteen times, before Bob shows up, I have made an absolute ass out of myself. Each time, before he takes over, Bob has forced me to go it alone a little longer. I have to admit, I'm feeling more comfortable in front of the camera lately.

I have one last show, and my commitment to the network is over. One last spine-chilling on-camera event later this afternoon, and I'll be able to go home. My first thought should be about my wife and children, my family. Although I admit nothing, my first thought is toward a powder-blue machine.

Renee is arriving this afternoon, and I'm hoping to lay a foundation for a new relationship. Bob suggested she come out to New York, but I'm more than apprehensive about our reunion. How can we be in the same room without killing each other? Or more accurately, after the Melinda incident, how can we be in the same room without her killing me?

"Don't worry, Kid, you two will work things out," he said this morning just before my wake up call. "Like you faced the blaze in the house, face the woman's fire. "A woman can bring us down to our knees, or into our hearts. It's up to our warriors to know the difference. Go in with your warrior intent to resolve your conflicts, one issue at a time."

"We have accumulated so many issues in the last six months alone, I don't know where to begin."

"Start with Melinda. Renee will want to know your intentions."

"The biggest one first, huh?"

"Yes, the biggest one first."

I'm standing in the airport. The crowds file past as I search through the throng for Renee.

"Stewart," she yells as she runs over and gives me a hug. "I'm so glad to see you."

She hasn't given me a greeting like this since I remember.

After the initial shock, I carefully reach my gangly arms around her. I lean down as she stands on her tiptoes to reach up to me. Holding her close, and reeling in the pleasure of her wanting to hold me, I'm still confused about her intentions. Does she need solace, or is she just glad to see me? I hope for the latter.

"Stewart, I can't wait to tell you what happened," she says as she pulls me along the concourse. We are back in the limo, rolling down the freeway to Manhattan before I realize that she is talking about a little Cuban bothering her on the plane.

Renee talks during our entire trip across town. She rambles on about her plane experience, our kids, the house, and excitement of being in New York.

She talks to the driver, asking embarrassing tourist questions, like what building is that, where is Manhattan, can she see the Statue of Liberty, is this the street where they filmed "Prince of tides"? She is thrilled to be in the back seat of a network limousine, going first class. I experience a curious intensity about her I haven't seen in a long time.

The last time I saw her excited was when she got that job at Billing's Carpeteria after nine years of being a mom. Have five years gone by so quickly?

In the last four weeks, I have been wined and dined, driven around and walked under these walls of concrete and glass until they mean nothing. I've never found much interest in bustling cities in the first place. I like quiet country roads, mirror-smooth lakes, wide-open desert, and expansive ridges, where few people care to travel.

Renee's perspective gives new meaning to the word city. She ooh's and aah's at each turn. She points and prods me at every block, until we reach our hotel. Although we have less than first-class accommodations, Renee doesn't know the difference. To her, our room is first class, the best accommodations she has ever seen. I'm embarrassed that my wife of eighteen years has never stayed in a fancy hotel. I have never been able to afford even second-class lodging.

Renee bounces around our apartment sized hotel room, one room to another, looking out the windows at Manhattan, the East River, and the other skyscrapers. She runs into the bathroom, jabbering about its mirrors, then back out, snapping off compliments about the furniture. She looks out another window and yelps, all before I give our bellboy a five for his efforts.

Once he's gone, she skips over to the door and snaps the dead bolt, then deftly locks the security chain. She turns back toward me with a look I recognize, but have not seen in a long time. She puts her hand on her hip and says, "Let's discuss what's been happening to you. I want to know what you have been doing. Tell me everything."

Oh shit, I'm in for a long protracted battle. I remember asking her here for a romantic weekend, but if she wants to jump right into working out our differences, I guess I'm ready. Bob and I have talked about being in my warrior for love. He forced me to agree, when he said, "The only way to keep a woman's attention is by being ready to do battle with her."

I'm ready. I have been getting ready for three days. No, more like eight months, since Bob and I had our first conversation. Now that the moment is upon me, I freeze. I stand at the edge of the dining room table trying to get into my biker mode, trying to get into my warrior, but everything I have been planning flies out the window. Everything melts away like whipped cream over a hot slice of pie. My tenuous manhood pools at my feet, pouring out my fingertips onto the polished walnut table. My face drops, and I look at the floor.

"'But for right now," she says as she pulls out the barrette holding her glistening hair. She shakes her head and bellows of blue-blackness cascade over her shoulders. I glance up and see something close to her look of rage. One thing for sure, it's intense, but if not rage, what?

"Right now," she says. "I want you!"

Holy shamoly, what the hell have I gotten myself into?

She kicks off her shoes as she steps across the entry, tearing off her dress, pantyhose, underwear, and carelessly leaving them in her path. She runs at me, cat like, ready to rip me to shreds.

"What happened?" I ask after a long post-coital cuddling.

"What do you mean?"

"I mean, what made you act different? For ten years you haven't given me the time of day. What changed your mind?"

"I haven't changed my mind, Stewart Chance. I still think you are a bumbling jerk, only now, you're a sexy bumbling jerk. Since I saw you on Susan Olson, I've had an undeniable desire to have sex. Not just plain old sex, either. I've wanted wild, unbridled, copious amounts of the kind of sex we just had. As soon as I rest, I'm going to want more."

Oh no, she wants more? Not that I'm complaining, I'm just not used to sex lasting so long, or being this physically demanding, or so deliciously wild.

I'm glad she suggests resting first.

"But Renee!" I want to change the subject fast, before she attacks me again. "You've never been like this all the time we've been together. What made you change your mind?"

"What you said during the interview with Susan Olsen."

"What do you mean?"

"She asked stupid questions about our private lives. I remember her trying to trip you up into revealing our sex life. I was afraid she would trick you. You jumped out of your seat spouting off about privacy."

"Bob did that," I admit. "Bob came through me."

"Through you, or not, who cares. I know what I saw. I saw my husband standing up to that meddling talk show bitch. For the next ten minutes I watched you cut her to size, talk circles around her, and leave her speechless. That was sexy."

"Bob has been coming through me since the first day I slammed the door in Sheldon Wheeler's face."

"You know, Stewart, I still can't believe any biker spirit comes through you. Katherine says another part of you is surfacing. I mean, look at the sex we just had. Are you Biker Bob now?"

I shake my head. "But--"

"But nothing, your biker guy is you, a you who has been buried too long. Katherine says you probably have a Multiple Personality Disorder; it's more common than you think. This part of you scares me, but at the same time, it turns me on. The only thing I don't understand is, where did you get that silly men's movement stuff?"

I want to tell her it was Bob, but she isn't going to listen. As usual, once Renee's mind is set, little will budge her conviction.

She suddenly rolls on top of me and we leap into another hour-long sexual frenzy. Toward the end, because both of us are tired, things slow to a smoother pace. We find a rhythm that is intimate beyond belief. When we reach our final moments, we look at one another. Our hearts are connected.

When a last ripple of our lovemaking turns to exhaustion, she breaks into a long, slow sob.

"Renee, Honey, are you okay?"

Her sobs gain momentum, grow into a wailing. Her chest heaves as she is wracked with deep grief.

After a minute or two, her wailing subsides. Five more minutes go by, with me in deep anxiety about what happened.

Finally, she calms. With a great deal of sniffling and snorting, she says, "Oh Stewart, I love you." She breaks into another bout of tears, followed with sniffles.

"What happened?"

"I swear, Stewart," she says in a weepy voice. "What just happened is the best sex I have ever had. You were so present that you helped me reach a height I have never, ever, gotten to."

"If what we did was so good, how come you're crying?"

"I thought about our last eighteen years. How much we have missed makes me sad. I thought about the rest of the women on our planet and realize what they have been missing. I'm crying for them, too."

Crying for them? Why does she cry for them?

"I didn't hurt you, did I?"

"Oh no, Sweetheart. Oh no, what happened makes the life I have lived until today hurt."

Women are the strangest creatures I have ever met.

She cuddles up, crooning and stroking my body, kissing and talking softly for the better part of an hour until we fall asleep.

Chapter 11

EVERY DOG HAS HER DAY

After what I might describe as the best sex I've ever had, the wildest sex I've ever wanted to have, the closest, most intimate sex I may ever have, Stewart and I fall asleep until the phone jars me awake in the dark. Patters of light rain are tapping on the little concrete deck outside our room. The sound of the city, far below us, creeps into my waking consciousness between rings. As usual, Stewart grabs the phone.

"Yes?" I hear, as I try to return to sleep.

"Yes. . .yes." A minute goes by before he says another yes. A number of no's gets thrown in, and a resolute, acquiescent, final yes before he hangs up.

"Who was that?" I ask, but I'm not sure I want to know so late at night. The single syllable answers Stewart gave to the caller were odd, odd enough to want to know.

"Martin Vander," he says.

"What did he want at such a god-awful hour?"

"He wants you and I to go on Murry Podich tomorrow."

"I thought your tour was over."

"I canceled yesterday to meet you at the airport. Now they want both of us."

My sleepy mind slowly assimilates the request.

I sit up and turn on the light. "They want me on Podich?"

Nik C. Colyer

Stewart blinks and comes awake. "Vander thinks we would make a good story. I told him no, but he said to talk to you. He'll call back first thing in the morning."

"You don't want to go on Podich? Stewart, what's wrong with you? Murry Podich is a big talk show host."

"I already did his show," he says. "I've been on Susan Olsen, Leatherman, Leno, Jerry what's his name, and a myriad of other supposed biggies. I'm tired of television. I'm tired of spotlights, tired of talk-show hosts, but I'm mostly tired of Bob spouting all kinds of men's stuff, of which I know painfully little."

He gets up. As he walks into the bathroom he talks louder. "I'm getting two huge bags of fan mail every day from all over the world. People ask me questions I can't answer. I'm tired of Bob looking so good and me knowing nothing."

"Oh," I say. "I didn't know you felt that way. But Stewart, I haven't had my moment of glory yet. I haven't been on TV. Won't you go with me and give me my fifteen minutes of fame?"

***

"I'll let you know in the morning," I say so I can go back to sleep. I had been dreaming of Melinda, of her violent explosions culminating with her unique brand of sex. I had just gotten to the sex part when the phone rang. I'm ready to go back to my dream, the Melinda dream and what she has in mind for me. Renee's new approach to sex is a close second to Melinda. Renee pulls up fast on the inside lane.

I drift off, starting into disjointed thinking, memories mixed with dream fantasies. Soon I'm driving my Harley. The one left behind in an entirely different world. My world of numbers, invoices and managing people. I traded my old-world for a hectic, lights, camera, action, world.

I'm riding Blue, my one stabilizing factor, a bridge between two worlds. My bike is the single most calming talisman I have known since this whole mess began. I'm twisting the throttle, feeling the engine thumping below me. A smile crosses my face. A feeling, again of freedom, flying without wings, sailing without a ship. Tears of relief well up behind my sunglasses.

A Harley pulls in next to me close to the dividing line. I nudge my bike over, making room for Bob and his extremely long front end.

We ride side by side in darkness. Our two headlights are the only lights for miles. Finally, Bob signals me to pull over.

We drive under a massive willow tree and turn off our machines, unfurl our kickstands and step off our bikes in unison. We are a high-wire act, tandem riders, and tandem dismounts.

Channeling Biker Bob

Bob walks out into the middle of the two-lane road and stares up at a billion stars. There are no words between us, just gazing up at the spectacle.

After a third shooting star, he says, "do Podich with Renee."

"Shit, Bob, I'm tired of dealing with those talk show dicks."

"Podich is important for what I have to say and also important for Renee and you. The Podich appearance will solidify what has begun between the two of you."

"I had sex with my wife and she said it was the best she ever had. I don't remember doing anything different, but something happened. I'd like to repeat the experience, but I have no idea what I did."

"You focused on her alone".

"Focused? I don't get it."

"Be present, I mean really present. You were present with her the last night because the two of you had been apart for so long. It was easier to focus with her. You were able to think like her and move the way she wanted to move. It may have been the best sex she ever had, but with a little work you can repeat it."

"Come on Bob, that is not all I have to do. I must have done more than simply, be present."

"Being present is not that simple, Chance."

A large shooting star flashes across the sky. After it disappears, I say, "it can't be that hard."

"Try to keep your thoughts on a subject for one minute."

"Easy enough, what subject?"

"Pick an simple one, because it's not easy."

I smirk. "Okay, sex is an easy subject for me."

Bob reaches over to his wrist and pushes the light on his watch. "Start in ten seconds, nine, eight, seven." By the time he reaches zero, I have already thought of two things related to sex, but not exactly on the subject of sex. Fifteen seconds into his countdown, I slip again. My mind goes away from the great sex Melinda and I had when she punched out Nick. The thought is related, but not exactly on the subject. I drift seven more times in that single minute. I end saying the word sex, sex, sex for the remaining fifteen seconds, trying to keep my mind on the subject.

"Okay, I see what you mean."

"Keeping you're mind focused on one thing is a bitch, but you can succeed. Most of the eastern spiritual practices have a great method for keeping in focus. Get some books on meditation and get your ass in gear."

"You mean to say all I have to do is practice meditation and I'll become a good lover?"

"Well shit, Chance, of course not, but you'll have a good start. The rest comes from being more sensitive to your partner. Being more caring helps, too."

"Being sensitive. Isn't that a little mushy coming from a tough biker guy like yourself?"

"To a tough biker who isn't secure in his maleness, this stuff may be too mushy. Most bikers fit into that category. Hell, most men fit. Even you say the assholes in my group are children dressed in tough-guy garb. When you said that statement aloud, they wanted to tear you apart. Most tough guys are emotional children, bullies not secure enough in their own maleness to think that being sensitive is a strong trait. Nothing is more male, tougher, than a big old burley guy on his knees, close to the floor, playing with a newborn. I find nothing more male than a gnarly biker walking slow enough for a toddler, who holds his finger for support.

"Being tough is being strong enough in one's own sense of self to allow emotions, even to cry without embarrassment."

I think about Nick and his tearful displays.

"One percent of the population rides Harleys, Chance. One percent of Harley riders are men secure enough to show their emotions. They'll get on their knees and play with a newborn. They are confident enough to make love with a woman with more parts of their body than their dicks. You'll find a whole man is needed to make love with a woman; his entire being, not just ol' one eye."

I look out to the horizon and see dawn breaking. We could have been standing here five minutes or five hours, I can't tell.

"Nick gave me a card with a logo that said one percent of one percent. I also got one from a group of bikers around Barstow. Is that what the card means?"

"Was the card black with gold lettering?"

"Yes."

"They are a small group of riders. You will do well to hang with them. Not that they have any answers, but at least they're beginning to ask the right questions."

"I can't believe those guys are sensitive. They looked hard."

"Oh, I'm sure they are, but they are working toward being men, not insecure little boys dressed in tough-guy garb, but fully realized, well-rounded men."

We are looking at the stars again. The blackness of the sky, the faint glow of dawn.

"Okay, I'll go on Podich with Renee," I say. "I mean hell, what have I got to lose?"

"Chance, your mouth. Shit man, you're cussing like a sailor. I'm proud of you."

Channeling Biker Bob

As usual, without any warning, my thoughts are on Renee and being more present, then I'm lying beside her, feeling her slow rhythmic breathing.

Rain patters on our concrete deck and the metal lawn furniture. I look across our bed out the window and see dawn.

I'm ready to do Podich. I want to wake Renee and tell her, but this morning it's too calm to break the spell. I lie in bed for fifteen minutes before the phone rings. That pain-in-the-ass Vander is giving me his last wake-up call, finding out if I'm going to do one more goddamn show.

Renee stirs on the second ring, snorts, and rolls over.

The third ring begins and I pick up the phone.

"Good morning Mr. Chance. Are you awake?"

"Yes, now I am," I whisper, not wanting to wake Renee.

"Well, what about Podich?"

"Yes," I say and quietly hang the phone up.

"Was it Vander?" she asks in a sleepy voice.

"Uh huh."

"You going to go on with me?"

"Yup."

"Oh, Stewart." She turns toward me, pulls her body against mine and kisses me hungrily.

Two hours later, while ordering breakfast, we're sitting side by side, holding hands like high school sweethearts.

Vander comes in and sits across the table from us.

"Okay, we've got everything set up. At first we wanted you come out one at a time, but we decided that the two of you entering together would have more impact."

"How long in front of the camera?" I ask, chopping my sentence.

"Twenty minutes tops."

"Twenty minutes?" Renee asks. "Will we have twenty minutes of things to say?"

Vander's constant smile widens. "With Biker Bob, you will be lucky to get two words in edgewise."

Renee looks at me as Vander makes a quick exit.

"Is this true, Stewart. Will your other half upstage me?"

I want to say, "I don't know Renee, I'm hardly ever around," but she still thinks Bob is a split side of me.

"Keep Bob under wraps while I'm telling my story."

"Ump," I respond with a mouthful of eggs, strategically placed for the express purpose of not being able to give a clear answer.

"What is Murry Podich like? How is his set?" Her nervous questions roll on.

I keep stuffing food in my mouth. She keeps asking a staccato of one-sentence, half-thought-out, questions. From spending years with her, I know the questions need no answers. Her questions are to dispel nervous tension, to dissipate the rising anxiety of doing something wild and risky. The questions help.

We meet the limo in front of the hotel. During the entire journey to the studio, she asks more questions. When she finally runs out of questions, she answers her own, or tells a story. I have learned not to get in the way of these copious events. I look out at things she points out, without comment, of course. I lift my eyebrows at critical moments, with no comment. I do the appropriate listening thing all the way to the green room. Podich's set doesn't have separate dressing rooms.

A guy with his leopard sits on one end of the couch, Mel Gibson on the other. Once she sees Mel, Renee's chatter ceases.

"Look, Honey, Mel Gibson," she whispers in my ear. I look over, but don't comment.

Five minutes later, Mel is called, and he vanishes. A monitor is on, but silent, hanging from an upper corner of the room. We watch Mel go out, and shake hands with Maurey, then plug his latest movie.

"Oh no, Stewart, what am I going to do?"

Here is the first question I need to answer. I slip a response in before her next salvo. "Just be yourself."

"What are you going to do?"

"If only I knew."

The time of waiting is over. Renee and I are led down a familiar hall and to the curtain on stage left. We watch the show live. Mel is being kidded while he plays with the audience.

Soon, Renee and I are introduced. I grab her hand and we stroll out under the lights, all three cameras pointing at us.

Podich walks over to greet us and shakes our hands. The crowd claps wildly. Renee tightens.

We sit and Murry begins by asking Renee about home life and her work. Unexpectedly, Renee takes to being on stage like little ducks take to water. She has Podich and the audience giggling at all the right pauses. In less than five minutes, she has them eating out of her hand. When she reaches the part about me being a hero, the audience, me included, roars. Renee has a knack for timing.

Podich asks me a question about being a hero. I'm getting so sick of stupid questions. I'm glad this is the last show.

Podich starts into another question. Bob is coming; the tingle is at my fingertips. Quickly, the feeling sprints up my arms, into my chest, and mercifully into my head. I'm being pulled back, back into the safety of my void, the dark unconsciousness. I hear Bob talk. I hear his words coming out of my mouth, spoken through my larynx, but I feel nothing. Oh no, I'll be around. Although I hate being present, Bob has forced me a few times. I try to pull back, but Bob pushes on, holding me inside my own body with him.

"Stay with me," he says. "This one will be interesting."

I jump up, see the scene change, feel the shift in focus, and Bob is off and running.

"Who gives a shit about being a hero," he says. "Let's talk about the frustration of getting into an argument with the opposite sex and not being heard. I want to talk about fair fighting between the sexes."

Podich smiles, obviously ready for Bob.

***

Everything is going fine. I tell a funny story about work that makes the audience laugh. I have no idea I can be funny, but my goofy side comes to the forefront. I've always been a little playful at parties, but to think I can clown around in front of the nation and make everyone laugh!

Mr. Podich and I are having a great conversation about Stewart's silly little adventure. He turns to Stewart. The next thing I know, Stewart's eyes change to a wild gleam. On TV I've seen him look this way before, but never with such intensity. He jumps up like a jack-in-the-box, swings his arms, starts spewing forth wild allegations about women and about sex, and he wants to talk with Mr. Podich. Murry and I were having such a nice, friendly conversation. When Stewart starts cussing, he ruins everything. I have never seen so much energy coming from him, not even a sliver of such passion. He's acting crazy and yelling. His cussing repels me, and at the same time, attracts. A knot tightens and tingles in my stomach. The more he speaks, the tighter my knot, the more tingly things get.

Mr. Podich is ready for Stewart, like he knows what to expect. He shifts the focus to Stewart and asks one-sentence questions. Stewart spouts out one-minute dissertations about fighting fair, taking turns talking, and not interrupting while the other person talks. I don't understand where Stewart gets this stuff. Stewart, Mister Inarticulate, gives a five-minute speech on letting the other person talk as long as they need to, without interruptions, without interjections, without even lifting an eyebrow. I see the validity in his concept.

Podich feeds him another one liner about the difficulty of not interjecting, and Stewart stops, goes inside for the answer, then says, "Not interrupting is the one most important part of fair fighting. The agreement allows both people to be heard."

I hate Stewart when he swears, but cuss he does and continues to, until I can't stand it any longer. I finally say, "Stewart Chance, will you stop your swearing?"

He slowly turns away from Maurey, who has been holding his own. He faces me squarely. My knot doubles.

"I'm not Stewart Chance right now," he says. "I'm Biker Bob."

I give him my smirk, and point at the camera. "Just stop cussing, will you? We're on national TV."

His face contorts. His mouth forms a number of words, yet speaks none of them. His arms raise, hands and fingers outstretched like a Bible-thumping preacher, and he says, "I'll do what I fucking well please." He spins and continues with Murry.

I am furious. I'm beside myself. I want to get up, spin the jerk around and slug him in the nose. I want to kick him in his crotch. I can't believe I'm even thinking this, but I surprise myself when I mostly want to take him in the back room and have sex. Biker Bob, the gross split from Stewart, is a total jerk, but the way he carries himself, the way he takes charge, it's wildly arousing, uncompromisingly sexy.

I'm so angry that I can't say another word, even when Murry tries to include me in the conversation.

He senses my rage, leaves me alone and allows Stewart to run with the discussion until I can't stand his rudeness any longer. Damn it, this is my interview. He is supposed support me. This is my debut. I yell at his back, "Stewart Chance, get back in this chair and shut up for a minute."

He spins, gives me a wild-eyed look and says, "Why?"

"Because, because, I want to talk."

"Okay," he says calmly. He turns, struts back and sits.

***

I'm inside of my body watching the entire horrific episode between Bob and Renee. The two of them face off, and I'm helpless, unable to even lift one of my fingers to intervene. I scream at Bob in the background, trying to get him to back off and give my wife a little room, but he says, "This kind of stuff will bust that log jam in your relationship."

Renee's fifteen minutes of glory turns into a disaster. Her debut in front of the nation is, for lack of a better word, the shits.

I don't know what I'm going to do, how I'm going to make any of this up to her. After Bob's monologue about relationships, after his run-in with Renee, after we walk off stage, he relinquishes the body he has been borrowing and allows me back in the driver's seat. Heat irra-

Channeling Biker Bob

diates from her. I sense the tension, the gnawing, bone-crunching, rip-me-from-limb-to-limb rage. Bob created this disaster, and gives my body back, leaving me with the mess.

Renee doesn't say a word. She is not walking, but marching in front of me. I'm being pulled along in her wake of anger.

We're not going back to the Green Room. We're taking a different path over cables, past dusty props, under booms, and stored overhead lights. She leads me into and out of dormant sets. I follow her behind a wall at the far end of the building. Renee keeps turning first left, then right; weaving in and out until she has me backed into a dark unused corner. I'm ready for the tongue lashing of my life. I'm taken completely by surprise when she grabs me by my new Hawaiian hibiscus short-sleeve shirt and pulls it open, popping all seven buttons. She slips her hand down the front of my pants and takes hold of me. Not ready for such a surprise, I still spring to the occasion. She unbuttons my Levi's with her other hand and wriggles me free. She takes me like a wild animal would pounce on its prey, unbridled, uninhibited, knocking over dusty boxes. Our wild standing copulation in a corner of an unused set far exceeds the memory of Melinda.

***

We spend a day filled with sight seeing, eating in fancy restaurants, and strolling in the park. I'm exhausted from following my excited, want-to-get-as-much-fun-in-as-possible wife. Sleep has beset me, but only after Renee's final attack. While I'm asleep, Bob comes into our bedroom. I follow him into the living room.

"How did you know how she was going to react to the embarrassing way you treated her?" I'm assuming, and rightly so, that he is already aware of what took place after the interview.

He says, "though she probably will never admit it, Renee has been secretly wanting you to take command. She has been at the helm most of your relationship, and she's tired. What I did would have been debilitating to most people, but Renee has wanted a man for a long time. Last night, in bed, you pushed against her boundaries, allowing her to drop her hard-shelled guard. The show finished the job. Once her guard dropped, once that soft part of her became accessible, all she could do was want you.

"Your job is to keep her open, keep her communicating. Open all those old wounds from your eighteen years together and relive them, this time from your thirty-nine years of experience. Find out about being a man, what it takes to be with a woman, and mostly find out about yourself."

Geez, Bob, that's a lot to do. Where do I begin?"

191

"Tons of books are available on the subject. You could try an end-less list of seminars and workshops on men's issues. Put them to practical use. This kind of work takes years, but trust me, it is worth it. I'll be close by if you run aground, but I don't want you to lean on me. Go out and find your own way."

"How do I keep Renee interested once she finds out I'm not you?"

"You're doing great, kid. You've got a good start on things, just keep concentrating on getting your manhood back. She may be dis-appointed at first, and for now don't let on that I am anything other than a split part of your psyche. The mystery will be enough to keep her guessing. Trust me, she'll stick around in anticipation."

***

In the morning, Sunday morning, our last day in New York together, she wants to have sex. Last night's sex wasn't that great, and I'm afraid I won't measure up. For that reason, I say no.

"I swear, Stewart, you never said no to me before," she says with a sparkle in her eye. "Do you know how sexy it is for you to say no? I'm all tingly inside."

I want to get off of her saying-no-is-so-sexy subject, so I shift. "I'm going back to Barstow tomorrow. Will you fly to Barstow with me? I would love to take you for a ride on my Harley."

"I don't know, Stewart. I've got too much work at--"

"Screw work. I'm sure they'll spare one or two extra days for a hero and his wife. Come with me, come see my little house, come sleep with me, without the kids, just you and me."

She gets a glassy-eyed look. "Yes," she says. "Yes."

***

On Sunday morning he says no when I want sex. Ever since that moment, for the first time in years, I truly desire him. Not the shirt-ripping, wild-woman, I-can't-get-enough desire I felt yesterday, but a glowing, soft, gentle desire for my husband.

The limo drops us off at the airport. I can't believe I'm going back to that crappy little hellhole in the desert. I'm going to ride on the back of his Harley. I feel like a horny teenager, following my man to the ends of the earth for love. If it weren't happening to me, I would think we were sickening.

The flight across the continent to San Bernardino Airport is boring. By dusk, we are driving to Stewart's little house at the end of the lane. He unlocks his front door, gets me settled into the house, then goes around back.

Channeling Biker Bob

I'm much too tired to go for a ride, so he charges off for an hour by himself. Stewart has never gone anywhere by himself. He never could stand being without me. Taking off like he does is a relief, and even a little erotic. I guess I have sex on my brain.

The next morning, Stewart takes me out on his Motorcycle. At first I'm nervous, but once I realize that he isn't going to be a maniac and get us killed, I relax.

"This is kind of fun Stewart," I yell over his shoulder.

"Doesn't the wind feel good?"

"Yes, and I like that I can see everything all at once."

He nods, pulls up to a stop, then turns left onto a broken pavement back road. We drive up into the hills and stop overlooking a long valley.

Once we get off the bike, I lock my arm in his and walk with him to the top of a small ridge. "The Desert is beautiful from here."

"The desert is always beautiful," he says. "We just have to slow down enough to enjoy it."

We sit and I lay my head in his lap. After a long time of listening to the wind and watching the sun climb into the sky, I say, "Stewart."

"Yes."

"Can we just stay like this forever."

WHAT'S IN A YEAR

Twiggy and I ride out on a bluff overlooking Barstow. We park our bikes and step close to the crumbling ledge. A hundred feet below lay old dead cars, rusting refrigerators, yard trash, and an endless list other human discards. A rusting and bullet-riddled sign warns of a fine for dumping, but no one pays the warning much attention. The ground a hundred feet below is an EPA disaster, but the ledge is clean and our view of the desert has charm. Still buzzing from an hour of riding, we look out a hundred miles to the east onto flat, open country.

I break the silence. "A year has gone by since Bob and I completed that grueling month of talk shows."

"Really," Twiggy says. "Time gets away from me."

"I haven't told anyone, but for the first three months, two postal bags of letters came to my house every day."

"No kidding?"

"Even now, I get two or three dozen letters a day. Most of them are addressed to me, but Bob is who they are writing to."

"Come on, Stewart, take some credit. Remember you let those talk show dicks take pot shots at you."

"Yeah, I guess, but each letter has a story, and they always have a question. I don't have any answers for most of the questions. Bob has systematically answered each letter. When I wake every morning, I find a stack of letters, hand addressed in Bob's careful, draftsman's script.

Channeling Biker Bob

He answers every correspondence with a hand-written personal response."

"I didn't know anything about the letters," Twiggy says.

"I kept them secret, because I'm embarrassed."

"What do you mean?"

"Bob answers them and leaves the envelopes open for me to sign. It's like I'm impersonating him."

"Have you talked to him?"

"Yes. He doesn't mind. Truth be known, he prefers it, but I still don't feel right.

"A few months ago, I started reading the letters and Bob's responses. Each question is an issue I also want answered, if I could only be intelligent enough to think of the question. Many letters leave me in tears, because they are so close to the truth about our struggle to get through life with our honor intact."

Twiggy looks at me. "Honor has been stripped from us at every turn, by every situation."

We stand in contemplative silence.

"I've copied the letters. I'm keeping a file."

"What are you going to do with them?"

"Someday, I want to write Bob's story."

"Wow, man, that would be one powerful message. You know, you really are our point man."

"Thanks, but writing scares me. It's too big a project."

"I'd like to write a book of my own some day."

"Do you know how to write?"

"No, but I'm sure I could figure it out. I mean, how hard could it be?"

"What would you call your book?"

"I don't know, something about being more loving and less of an ass, like I used to be. Maybe I'd call it, 'The Lover'."

We stand, looking out for another minute. A breeze whistles through the scrub. A redtail hawk circles in a cloudless sky.

"Whatever happened to that redhead that saved you from the fire?"

"You mean Melinda?"

"Yeah, you heard from her lately?"

"She called last month and told me she had found some grizzled old codger in Northern California who knew something about anger and how it connected to her dad. She quit her job in L.A. and has been living closer to him in Cazadero, just west of Santa Rosa."

"They lovers?"

"No, he's helping her sort out her anger."

"No doubt she's a pistol," he says.

"Do I detect an interest?"

Twiggy's face reddens. "Guess now that I'm not so much of an ass-hole, I'm kind of interested in a woman who'd meet me head on."

"Well," I say, "she'll certainly do that."

We have another moment of silence while the wind whips my hair.

"How's your family," he asks.

"Renee and the kids are still in Sacramento. I don't think she'll ever move to the desert. She visits sometimes, but I usually go see them.

"We spent a blissful six months of a second honeymoon. Now my therapist says we're in the power struggle phase."

"Yeah, I know. You bring that shit to our men's group every week."

"That's why I like hanging out with men like yourself."

"Why?"

"Because you and the other men have helped me deal with my new relationship. Without all of you, I would still be a whimpering male, groveling at her toes, waiting for her to throw me a bone.

"These days Renee and I fuss and fight a lot, but I think we're going to make a success of our new marriage. I need you guys to help me stay in my warrior with her and not hide out. "

Twiggy says, "We need all of us, knowing every move, to help each other stay present, especially around our women."

"When Renee and I are together lately, I feel honest love emerging."

He smiles. "Ain't that what being with a woman is all about?"

"What's that?"

"They're willing to show us how to love."

Comments directed to: Bikerbob@ncws.com